AuthorHouse™
1663 Liberty Drive
Bloomington, IN 47403
www.authorhouse.com
Phone: 1 (800) 839-8640

Published by AuthorHouse 08/01/2018

ISBN: 978-1-5462-4725-8 (sc)
ISBN: 978-1-5462-4724-1 (e)

ONE O'CLOCK TEE

No, this title is not a typo.
The story is not about _tea_.
It's about people, including some old codgers
who have survived through thick and thin for lots of years.
They've made this possible primarily by their friendship
on a golf course, by their respect for each other, and
in large measure, by their personal grit.
The story involves an ex-professional golfer
whose wife died from cancer, leaving him with a little girl
who has grown up and now faces problems of her own.
It features one of the wealthiest women in the country,
a romance or two, an old, unsolved murder case,
a crucial golf match, and some zany antics
in small-town middle America.

———————

J. A. Mattox

P.S. My dad played golf regularly for about fifty years
with a number of lifelong friends such as you'll find in
"One O'Clock Tee."
Some of the stuff you'll read here actually happened.
More or less.

Jesse Porter's first good look at the course almost made him shudder. What a difference between this and Pebble Beach or Augusta National or Wingfoot! For that matter, what a difference between this and any other golf course he had ever played. This must have been the course about which someone coined the expression "cow pasture pool." From where he stood, near the dirt tees of a narrow, barren driving range, he could make out four greens. All were sere and patchy with bare spots of sand. The fairways cried for water. Far away he made out the figures of three golfers, all kids, he decided.

A hot, dry wind gently but relentlessly blew from the west.

He sighed and shrugged. "So what the hell?" he mused quietly. He pulled a wedge from his burnished black leather bag and picked four red-banded practice balls from the wire bucket he had purchased at the little building about a hundred yards off to his right. Glancing back over there, he noted that the pretty brunette attendant was watching him through the open doorway. No one else was near the shop. Not a very busy day.

He lined up the balls and leisurely swung the wedge. It had a pleasant heft. His shoulders were stiff following the all-day drive from Albuquerque the day before. He adjusted his glasses. Next, with one arm, he aligned the club head close to the first ball as he dug his spikes into the ground. Finally, he rhythmically slapped the balls into the air, one after the other.

In twenty minutes he had worked through his bag, hitting a five iron, a three iron, and two woods. His swing lengthened as he worked, increasingly demonstrating fluidity and grace. He was of medium height with wide, sloping shoulders and a slender waist, and his swing produced suprising power. Finally, after smashing the last ball into a high trajectory that faded slightly before hitting a low wall at the end of the range, he shrugged again. He no longer felt the tightness in his shoulders. A light sweat covered his face. He felt good.

After replacing yellow knit covers on the woods he had used, he slid them back into the bag and pulled out a towel. Then he draped the towel around his neck and seated himself on a rickety, unpainted bench behind the driving tees. He stretched out his arms along the top of the bench, thrust his legs out before him, and took several deep breaths. "Not bad," he said to himself. "Could be worse." Then he laughed. "It has been a lot worse."

After a few moments he got up and carried the bag and empty bucket to the shop.

As he approached, the young woman who had been watching walked away from the door and disappeared from view inside the building. Porter judged that her age was about the same as his daughter's. She was square-jawed and wore glasses. Earlier, when he paid for the practice balls, he had appreciated her manner and smile. She had introduced herself as Nancy Grimsby.

He propped his bag against a rusty iron rack outside and entered the shop. It was plain and worn, needing some paint here and there, but clean. Very little inventory was displayed. An old metal cooler for soft drinks and beer stood in a corner. "Hello again," he said. "Here's your bucket."

"Thank you," she said, displaying a pretty smile. She took the bucket from him and dropped it behind the counter. "You hit those balls very well."

He smiled back. "Better than some. Not as well as others."

"Better than anybody I've seen around here in a long time, I can tell you."

"Thanks." He looked around and then checked his watch. "Do you think there's any chance of catching someone who needs a partner today?"

"You never know. We seldom have many players during the week. More on weekends. There are a few out on the course. You might join someone after they finish nine." She added, "We have only nine holes here, you know. You have to go around twice for eighteen."

"Um. I know. Nine and nine make eighteen." He laughed lightly, and she laughed, somewhat embarrassed.

Porter stood awkwardly, undecided. He looked at his watch again. "Well, I may just launch off on my own."

"There'll be some old-timers who show up every day at one o'clock. You could join them, I'm pretty sure, but they aren't in your class."

"Old-timers? Listen, I'm no spring chicken, Nancy."

"Yeah? So who is? I mean, there's a bunch of elderly, retired gents who show up to play at one o'clock. I guess there are eight or ten, and every day two or three or four show up. Whoever is here by one o'clock plays. It's a standing date they have." She shook her head. "But like I said, they aren't in your class. You might not--"

The STARR
Golf Course
Clydeston, Kansas

Silvio's

HIGHWAY

HIGHWAY

ERODED CREEK

N

PARKING

CLUB HOUSE

PRACTICE GREEN

#1 330 YDS PAR 4

#2 420 YDS PAR 4

#9 525 YDS PAR 5

#8 150 YDS PAR 3

#3 190 YDS PAR 3

DITCH

GOLF CART STORAGE SHEDS

DRIVING RANGE

#5 530 YDS PAR 5

#4 425 YDS PAR 4

MARSH

POND

#7 290 YDS PAR 4

#6 415 YDS PAR 4

BRIDGE

ERODED HILLSIDE

OLD 12

UNPAVED ROAD

we may have a limited number of golf swings left in us, and we don't want to waste any of them without hitting a ball."

Porter chuckled. "I see."

Braun squinted at him. "Yeah, maybe. If you don't now, you will in a few years."

Lowman swung and popped his ball straight up. Immediately, he called, "Mulligan!"

"Of course," observed Braun wryly, "there are exceptions to what I said. There is one extra swing right there."

Lowman drove his second ball straight. It came to rest about twenty-five yards short of Wallis's ball. A crooked little ditch with a few inches of muddy water meandered across the fairway about one hundred fifty yards out. Neither of the first two men had reached it.

Slim Braun hit next, using a two iron instead of a wood. His shot bounced about fifty yards out on the hard ground and continued down the slight incline, stopping near Lowman's ball. As he stepped aside for Porter, he said, "Into each life some rain must fall. Some shots must be short and dreary."

Porter nodded. He didn't want to sound condescending, but he said, "Well, you're all down the middle." As he prepared to drive, he felt all eyes on him. The three old men would size him up quickly. He also felt a need to hit faster than he usually did. He forced himself not to rush. Smooth back, strong pivot and shift, firm left side, sure follow through. His ball flew out and climbed true and high, fading slightly, and landed about forty yards short of the green It was more than twice the distance of Wallis's drive.

"Jesus!" exclaimed Braun. "I haven't seen a ball hit like that...since I don't know when."

Lowman said, "When you get as old as us, Porter, you won't hit 'em that far 'cause you can't see that far, and you'll lose 'em!" He cackled at his joke.

Wallis swung his cart near Porter as he drove past. He said, "My hip would come unpinned if I swung that hard, Porter."

They walked down, toward the balls and the ditch. Braun had a motorized three-wheeled Kangaroo cart that carried his clubs, and he walked along behind it, holding it primarily for balance. Porter pulled a two-wheeler.

Strange, he thought, that he felt such a sense of relief over making a good drive. He had wanted to look good in front of these old men certainly, like a professional, which he had not done for a long time. More than that, he wanted to make a good *personal* impression on these strangers--wanted their respect. He sensed already that these men were open, honest, and they weren't envious that he was clearly a better golfer than they. He liked them, and he wanted them to like him.

As he walked and then waited for them to make their second shots, he got his first good opportunity to assess them individually. Lowman's plaid sports shirt and old trousers hung on him as though he had shrunk inside them. His pants cuffs were rolled up. His golf shoes appeared to be ordinary old wingtips with spikes that he probably had screwed into the soles himself. Wallis wore that old Cardinals cap, and his pants bore paint spots on them. In contrast to these two, Braun's garb looked like something out of a sporting catalog. His clothes were clean and stylish. They hung well on his thin frame. He wore a bright orange knit tee-shirt with a little horse designed on the pocket. His slacks were cream colored and sharply creased. On his head perched a knit beret with an orange yarn tassel.

Porter had never seen anyone play as rapidly as these fellows. They obviously enjoyed one another's company, yet they proceeded with minimal chitchat and no unnecessary delays. When they approached their balls, they already knew exactly what they intended to do. They scarcely looked ahead in the direction they were hitting. No practice swings. Hardly more than a waggle of the club head and they were into the back swing. As soon as the ball was in the air, they were on the move again.

Wallis was on the green in three. He surprised Porter with his smooth strokes, apparently, as Porter understood, with a hip replacement. "He looks like an athlete from days gone by," Porter said to Braun.

"Yep. Played third base in the Cardinal organization after the war. Vietnam, that is. Got to triple A. Boy! They had a lot of good third basemen in those days, y'know. Really tough competition."

Braun and Lowman were on in four. Porter hit a wedge for his second shot, leaving the ball close below the hole for an easy putt.

To his delight, Porter watched all three old timers rattle their putts into the cup from three to twelve feet. They putted as they had played their other shots, without delay. Clearly, they knew every undulation of the green.

As they walked on, Braun asked, "You don't mind walking?"

"No. I enjoy it. I run almost every morning."

"Run? How far?"

"Oh, usually five miles or so. I got to town late last night, so I slept in today. I noticed this golf course when I came off the turnpike last night. So I decided to come here this morning instead of running."

Braun squinted thoughtfully. "You're some kind of jock, aren't you? Hmm. *Jesse Porter.* I know that name, don't I? By golly, you were on the PGA tour a while back, weren't you? Was that you?"

Porter nodded and smiled. "It was a while back all right. And I'll be happy for you to call me Jesse if you choose to."

"No wonder you lambast that ball the way you do. You probably think we play awful."

"Oh no! I think you play just great. Don't worry about what I think anyhow. I'm out here for my pleasure, not to coach you. And let's just wait until we finish before you tell the other fellas, okay?"

"Sure thing, if that's what you want. Can I ask you what you're doing here in Clydeston...Jesse?"

"Sure. It's okay. My daughter lives here. She works for a pharmaceutical company here."

"Ah, that's Starr of the Prairie Pharmaceuticals. Biggest outfit in the county, other than oil maybe."

"That's what she told me. She's a technician in some sort of laboratory."

"You fly into Wichita, did you?"

"No. Drove in from Albuquerque."

"Well awright! Sure glad t'meet you, Jesse. Good to have you in town."

At that point, Braun approached his ball in the fairway. Unlike previous plays, however, he seemed uncertain what to do. He looked at Porter and theatrically touched his hand to his forehead. "Ah, two iron or not two iron. That is the question," he said.

Porter chuckled, "Are you asking me, Hamlet?"

"Well, yeah. What do you think?"

"Try your three wood."

"I don't hit woods very well. Usually I avoid them." He pulled out his three wood and examined it doubtfully. "But I'll give it a whip if you say so."

As Braun addressed the ball, Porter said, "Stick your butt out more, as if you were about to sit down. Stand with the ball farther ahead of you, almost even with your left heel. That's it. Now keep your head down and follow through hard and straight. You just concentrate on hitting it. I'll watch the ball for you."

Braun struck the ball and it sailed farther than his usual drives, hooking slightly, and landing at the edge of the green.

From across the fairway, Wallis hollered, with a touch of surprise in his reedy voice, "Hey, good shot, Slim!"

Braun yelled back, in a high voice, "Yeah. If I'd hit a two iron, I'd probably be on the green." Then he turned to Porter and winked. "Thanks, Jesse. You can come back again tomorrow."

***

When Patricia Porter Cameron returned home from work late Tuesday afternoon, she found her father in the kitchen. "Hi, Daddy!" She hurried to embrace him. "I love you! I'm so glad you're here! I'm sorry I had to leave for work this morning, and I didn't want to wake you. So I sneaked out. I've been eager all day to get home. Oh! You're wearing glasses."

"The better to see you!" He hugged her. "And you look great."

"I'll bet you're worn out from your long trip."

"I don't hold up as well as I used to, but I'm okay now. I fixed us a snack for supper. Hope that's okay."

She put her face close to his and he pecked her cheek. Peering at the stove, she said, "Oh, that looks good."

"They are my New Mexico specialty. Burritos made with spinach and mushrooms. Hope you like it. I picked up some stuff this morning. Also some chenin blanc to go with it."

"I'm so glad you got here safely. And I must say I don't usually dine this well."

"Had to come see how your new job and housing and so forth are working out, hon. Tell me all about it." He had already made a fatherly inspection of the premises. The kitchen appliances weren't new, but they were in good condition. Likewise, the furniture was moderately worn but clean. He recognized a few of Patricia's own things that she had brought with her to Clydeston.

"Oh, Daddy, I must tell you that my job is everything I had hoped for. And more! Our lab here is much different from college, of course, but I'm getting the hang of things. My boss is brilliant, and he keeps commending me. He's a little Greek man named Topakis. He's a friend of my college profs who recommended me, and that's how I got the job. I'll probably be taking more courses soon. There's a community college here, and Wichita State is only half an hour's drive from here."

"That all sounds terrific. I'm happy for you and proud of you."

"Right now I have an exciting assignment. Quality control is lending me to product development for a while. Among other things, we're responsible for preparing the medication that's used in clinical trials."

"That's research in people, right?"

"Yes. We have many interesting studies going on. There's one especially--" She stopped and laughed. "I'm really running on, aren't I? Well, there's just lots of stuff going on. Just pull my chain, and I gush like a broken faucet."

Porter laughed with his daughter. "You really have a lot of enthusiasm, Trish. It's wonderful to see. I'm happy for you."

"Well, what I really want to tell you is that I'm involved in things that are important. You know, things that can have an impact on people's lives. I may actually be able to make contributions to people's health."

"That's terrific. You deserve a break."

"And I can make a living. That's great, too. Good job. Great place to live. This is a company apartment complex. The company makes it affordable."

After a moment, he asked, "have you met any interesting fellows?"

"Daddy, please don't worry about that. When Johnny ran off with his little blonde friend, I was a basket case. You know that. But I have gotten over it. I suppose Johnny couldn't get over losing our baby at the time. I'll never forget the experience either, but I can handle my feelings now. I have pulled myself together. I now have a college degree and a great job. I'm okay."

He hugged her again.

"You and I have a lot in common," she said. I know it was tough for you when mom died and you gave up your golfing career. I didn't appreciate your problems when I was younger, but I do now."

"I'm awfully proud of you, Trish. I'm glad we have each other."

"I love you, too, Daddy."

He sat on the sofa and said, "Were you avoiding my question?"

She frowned. "What do you--Oh, well, I haven't been in town very long, you know."

He grinned. "What's the new guy's name?"

"Doyle Dugan." She sat on the other end of the sofa. If you can stay for a few days, I'll bring him around to meet you. He's a reporter. As such, he knows everybody in town and all kinds of stuff about them. You'll like him."

"I'm sure I will."

She changed the subject. "Did you look around town this morning? What do you think?"

"Well, I think I saw where you work. What a big place! Very impressive." He waved his hands. "I didn't try to go in though. I found a little grocery down the street a couple of blocks from here and I got those things for dinner. And I got in a round of golf this afternoon."

"Why am I not surprised? First time in town and you find the nearest golf course right away. Well, I want you to see where I work. How about coming over tomorrow morning and I can show you around. I'll write down the directions. It's easy."

"Okay, I'd like that. I saw the place today. I can find it. But will they let visitors roam around the place, with medicine being manufactured, and all that?"

"You won't *roam*, Daddy. Of course we have lots of security. But at least I can show you where I work. And there are P R people who conduct tours. I think you'll be surprised at how modern, scientific, and extensive it is, especially for a little ol' Kansas town like this."

"How many people are employed here?"

"Over two thousand right here. And there are separate offices for different things in Wichita and Kansas City, and I don't know where all.

And there's a national sales staff of six hundred or more. I don't know the exact numbers."

Porter raised an eyebrow. "Wow! I had no idea."

Largest employer in the county, by far. Among the largest in the state, I'm sure." She added, "Maybe you should think about getting a job here and living close to me." She grinned.

"What? Give up my new career as an auto salesman?"

"Car sales?" she exclaimed. "What happened to the restaurant?"

"Honey, the restaurant folded. I was reluctant to tell you until I learned how you're doing. But I'm okay, I'm now working for a fellow I've known for a while. He has a Buick dealership. That LeSabre I'm driving is a demonstrator. I'm okay."

"Oh, I'm so sorry to hear about the restaurant. When did that happen?"

He shrugged. "A couple of months ago. I didn't want to worry you with it. I only had a small investment. It was much worse for my friends who were the principal owners."

"Goodness.... Well, maybe you can think about staying here. Really! I can help you find a job."

He chuckled. "I'm not a scientist, honey. I doubt that I have any qualifications for a pharmaceutical company."

"It would be wonderful to have you close again." After a quiet moment, she said, "You didn't say anything about your golf today."

Porter smiled. "It was a little unusual, to say the least."

The next morning about ten-thirty, Porter pulled his LeSabre to a stop at the gatehouse for the Starr of the Prairie Pharmaceutical Company. The guard there directed him to the visitors parking area.

In the lobby of the sprawling red brick administration building, he identified himself and asked for his daughter. While he waited, the receptionist, who was a large, middle-aged woman with yellow hair and brown eyes, seemed full of friendly questions about the visit.

After a few minutes, Patricia appeared from a side door.

The receptionist handed him a visitor's badge and wished him a nice day. Then his daughter escorted him outside, through a neatly manicured courtyard and about a hundred yards down a paved road with tall, square red-brick buildings set back from the road by more lush green plots of grass.

Far across the tops of the brick buildings, Porter could see the steel skeleton of another huge building under construction. A crane was delivering steel beams to the top, where a multitude of workers swarmed about.

Sprinklers chattered all around Porter and his daughter, nurturing the lawns. He saw only three other persons out of doors. These three wore white lab smocks. They walked slowly, faces turned toward one another, apparently wrapped in an intense conversation. He imagined that the buildings on these grounds must be filled with highly educated persons dedicated to the company's success, growth, and, very likely, huge profits.

"Everything looks extremely well tended," he commented. The best golf courses in the country don't look neater."

"We're in the health industry," Patricia said. "Have to keep it immaculate." She turned toward another building. "We'll go through here, Dad, to my space." She led him into a welcome air-conditioned hallway inside. She pointed out her desk and various small rooms containing endless instruments, files, and notebooks used in testing the company's products before, during, and after manufacture. All the employees Porter saw here seemed wholly occupied with their work. A couple of them glanced at Patricia as they passed by.

He noted the intensity and enthusiasm in Patricia's voice as she explained things to him. When he had been with her several months earlier, as she left Albuquerque to come to Clydeston, she had been filled with anxiety. He felt great relief to find her so fulfilled with her work now. "You've really found your niche, haven't you, Trish," he said. It wasn't a question.

'Yes. I appreciate the fact that I can make my way now, in a professional setting, on my own." She grew more serious and added, "You know, when Johnny left me, I was truly scared for a long time that I wouldn't be able to make a decent living for myself."

"I know how that is. It's scary."

"I couldn't have made it without you."

A man in a white smock came from a room where five other men and women sat around a conference table. When he noticed Patricia, she motioned to him. "Doctor Topakis, I want you to meet my father, Jesse Porter. Dad, this is my boss, Doctor Topakis."

The men shook hands. Doctor Topakis said, "Hello. You just caught me between meetings. Seems like all I do sometimes is attend meetings. Well. So you're visiting Pat, eh? We're really pleased to have her with us, Mister Porter. She's catching onto our systems rapidly." He smiled at Patricia as though to confirm what he had said.

"That's good to hear."

Patricia said, "Maybe this would be a good time to ask for a raise."

In mock seriousness, Doctor Topakis frowned and said, "Don't push your luck, kid!" Then, laughing, he turned to Porter and went on. "Your name is not uncommon, sir. I'd say...it sounds familiar.... Porter ....*Porter*."

Patricia beamed. "He used to be a professional golfer. You may have seen him play on TV."

"Oh yes. That's probably it. I'm a big sports fan. Used to be anyway. Nowadays I just have to settle for a little tennis now and then. Are you still on the tour, sir?"

Porter shrugged. He was getting used to being a *forgotten* player. "I haven't played professionally for quite some time," he said softly.

With a touch of pride, Doctor Topakis said, "You might be interested to know that our company provided the municipal golf course here in Clydeston."

"Really?" said Patricia. "I didn't know that."

"Someone told me that just yesterday," Porter replied.

"Well, that was some time ago. And these days it's actually not in very good shape, I understand. It's a little course on the north side of town. Just a couple of miles from here. The country club is open to the public and it's in much better condition, so that's where most people play."

"I've seen the municipal course. In fact, I played there yesterday."

Patricia said, "Daddy told me he met some funny old men there."

"Unusual maybe," Porter corrected. "Not funny."

"As I said, I understand that the land for that course was donated to the town many years ago by Clarence Starr," Doctor Topakis said. "He founded this company, you know. He gave Clydestown a ninety-nine year lease. And paid for the original construction. It had eighteen holes in the beginning. But I guess it got a little rundown and the city couldn't make it pay after the country club opened. So, some years ago, they converted it from eighteen to nine holes. Unfortunately, I don't find time for golf any more except for special occasions like the annual fund raiser and entertaining guests. Then it's always at the club." He laughed as he added, "Never break a hundred myself."

"I see, said Porter. He nodded. "Interesting."

They fell silent for a moment. Then Doctor Topakis said, "Well, listen, if you'll excuse me, I need to rush on to the next meeting." He checked his watch again. "Really nice to meet you, Mister Porter. Enjoyed chatting with you. Pat can show you around this place, I'm sure." He quickly shook hands with Porter. "Hope you enjoy your stay in Clydeston." He nodded, turned away, and briskly strode down a nearby hallway.

Patricia said, "Next door there's an exhibit hall you might like to see. It shows lots of the work I'm involved in." She opened a side door, and Porter followed her out.

The door opened upon a covered walkway to the next building about thirty feet away. Already the late morning temperature was climbing, and the humidity smacked them as they stepped out.

Contributing to the moisture in the air were lawn sprinklers. One sprayed water directly onto the walkway. Patricia paused, timing the arcing water until it passed momentarily. Laughing, she sprinted to the doorway ahead. Then she turned back and called to her dad who was waiting for the spray to pass again. "I made it, Dad! You can do it. Don't get wet!"

He laughed and dashed in turn as the sprinkler passed again. Patricia held the door for him, and he continued through ahead of her. Inside, he immediately realized that some sort of special activity was in progress. Floodlights brightened the place and a group of about ten people turned to him, wholly surprised by his abrupt entrance.

He tried to stop quickly. His shoe soles were wet, however, from the passageway outside, and when he reached the tile floor inside, his feet flew from under him. He fell like a load of lumber, sprawling and sliding. His momentum propelled him into the knot people, and he collided hard with a woman, knocking her to the floor. His glasses flew off.

Everyone yelled. Overwhelmed with embarrassment, Porter tried to help the woman to her feet. At the same time, three other men tried to early in the day when it's not so hot, but chooses the camaraderie, I guess. Dehydration is the big concern this time of year. We keep thermoses of water on the carts. Slim carries one of those little squeeze bottles that cyclists use."

"He told me he has cardiovascular problems."

""Ha. His heart is as good as anybody's. He just doesn't like to think about the cancer." Doctor Jensen pointed ahead toward the pastor. "Glenn over there claims golfing keeps his weight down. What he really needs to do is reduce his caloric intake."

Porter nodded. "Most of us do."

"You appear to be in excellent condition."

"I run several times a week. Four or five days usually."

"Good for you." Doctor Jensen continued, "Abe Lowman is a wiry little fellow. He's probably not a pound overweight. He has always been that way. Hard as a five iron."

"What sort of work does he do?"

"Oh he's retired, of course. All of our gang are retired--except me. Glenn is a part-time pastor. Abe worked for many years at S O P."

"S O P?"

"Yep. That's what we call Starr of the Prairie. It's a pharmaceutical concern. Our only truly major industry, outside of oil and agriculture."

"I know the place. I just hadn't heard it referred to as S O P. As a matter of fact, I visited there this morning. My daughter works there. She's a laboratory technician."

"Ah, I see. Then she's the reason for your visit to Clydeston?"

"Right." Porter added, "I met the owner this morning, too." With the thought of his visit, however, Porter envisioned the beautiful Larona Starr and then, almost simultaneously, his incredibly clumsy and embarrassing exhibition at the lab.

Doctor Jensen smiled broadly. "The owner—that would be the inimitable Larona Starr. Beautiful redhead with lots of jewelry."

Porter agreed. "And a very, very confident attitude. Gorgeous woman. Really stunning."

"That's Larona all right. She's a legend around here. In fact, she has a national reputation. There aren't many women in the country who own and run such large companies. Inherited it, lock, stock, and barrel, from her husband, Clarence Starr. It's his name. *Starr* with two R's.

"He started it from nothing, back in the sixties. His father had been a pharmacist in Dodge City back in the days when anybody could make and sell anything they wanted. The boy, Clarence, sold his dad's stuff out of their automobile trunk. He peddled their products to almost every state in the country, I'm told. He had a gift of gab, and he practically established the company single-handedly. When the war expanded in Vietnam, he got government contracts, and the business blossomed. His brother helped. They were both excused from the draft. I never heard how that happened or how he wound up in Clydeston."

"Wait a minute. The Starr brothers must have been older than--Mrs. Starr can't be more than forty. How--"

They had reached the second green and Slim Braun was about to putt. Doctor Jensen shushed Porter. Braun stroked a putt that dropped in after a curved trajectory of nearly twenty feet. Everyone howled with delight, and Slim cried, "Out of the sweat that covers me, cold as ice from head to toe, I thank whatever gods may be, when my ball curls into the hole." Then he bowed.

Doctor Jensen explained to Porter, "Slim used to be an English teacher. Sometimes he gets carried away."

Porter laughed, "I like it. But tell me--"

Glenn sidled near. "I understand that you are a golf professional."

"Oh, I was for a few years," Porter said. "But my wife died of cancer. Years ago. It really tore me up," he sighed. "I spent a lot of time taking care of my daughter then. She had lots of problems due to her mom's death. And she got married to a worthless young kid. They had a baby that died at birth and the jerk of a husband ran off. So I had to concentrate on my daughter. I simply didn't have time for golf. And when I tried again... the young bucks playing then said they were sorry but beat me anyway. Everything just fizzled. Finally, I gave it up."

"Oh, I'm so sorry, Jesse. I didn't mean to pry."

The other golfers turned away after hearing his story and proceeded to the next tee. Doctor Jensen found himself alone again with Porter, so he picked up his own story. "I was telling you about Clarence Starr. You can see that he had a lot more insight into things than most of us. In the

"She must have her hands full," offered Slim. "Can't be easy running a giant business like she does. I've met a lot of those people who work over there, and most of them give her high marks. You know it could have gone down the drain when Clarence died."

Porter asked, "What do you mean, Slim?"

Before Braun could continue, Nancy said, "Sorry, fellas. That's it for now. We're going to a party this evening in Wichita, and I hafta go home and try to make myself beautiful."

"That shore won't take long," said Abe as she collected their empty bottles.

"**I learned** something about your company's history today, honey," Porter said to Patricia.

"What's that?" She was clearing the dinner table, and he was helping.

"I met a Doctor Jensen at the golf course along with some of those fellows I told you about yesterday, and he told me some stuff, some of it curious."

"Yes, but I bet it wasn't as curious as your meeting with Larona Starr this morning," she teased.

"Okay. Have your fun. But I tripped. Slipped."

"I know it, and so do half the workers at S O P. Bonnie, one of my lab associates, was talking about it this afternoon."

"Well, at least your Doc Topakis seemed like an understanding guy. He's certainly not going to punish you for my screw-up."

She nodded.

"Anyhow, you must admit I made an impression."

She changed the subject. "I don't know the Doctor Jensen you mentioned."

"He's a local fellow. General practitioner. I have the impression he is a longtime pillar of the community. He's badly paralyzed in the legs but plays anyhow."

She said, "You'll soon know more people here than I do."

Porter started to ask something but hesitated. He cleared his throat.

Yes?" Patricia asked.

"Trish, what would you think if I'd hang around for a couple of weeks?"

Her face lighted up. "Oh, would you? I'd love to have you stay. You can stay all summer--as long as you wish!"

"Well, I don't know about all summer. I'm not sure how long I can leave my job. I'll call Dave tomorrow--in Albuquerque--and see what he says."

"This is wonderful. You can play lots of golf and take things easy for a while. You could also play at the country club, I'm pretty sure. Wouldn't you rather play with better golfers?'

"I drove by the country club course. It looks fine, and I'm sure it offers all the amenities.... But I must say that I really enjoy playing with this group of old guys. I'm not really sure why. Probably because I don't feel that I must compete. I...I lost that need to compete a long time ago. A bunch of real golfers crushed and squeezed that right out of me. And these local guys have an unbelieveable cameraderie and a certain spirit that attracts me."

Patricia frowned. "I've never heard you say anything like that before."

He held up his hand and went on. "This one o'clock gang have very clear and different priorities. They just play up to their abilities because they love the game and each other. They have what you might call a commitment to life."

"*A commitment to...* My, we have become philosophical!"

"Yeah." He laughed. He felt a great relief in having asked to prolong his visit. "Anyhow, I think I'd like to stay a while. If that's okay."

"**Wow! It's** hot today!" Slim Braun seethed. "Only mad dogs, Englishmen, and old golfers go out in the midday sun. Oh my god! Look at that!"

He pointed at Abe Lowman, who had just appeared from the parking lot, and then doubled over with laughter. Immediately Wallis, and Porter joined Braun's outburst.

Lowman pranced and grinned as he approached. He pirouetted stiffly to show off the outfit he wore--a beige tuxedo replete with frilled shirt and brown bow tie. The suit was much too large for him, and the pants cuffs had been rolled up to expose his skinny ankles, white sweat sox, and old golf shoes.

"What the hell are you supposed to be?" demanded Wallis.

"You like it?" Lowman asked happily. "I found it at a garage sale this morning. I thought I should get it so I can look as sharp as Slim always does."

"But it's a tuxedo, of all things," said Glenn.

"I know that. But you couldn't beat the price, Lowman explained. "It only cost four dollars!"

Wallis exploded with laughter. "Four dollars!"

"Yeah, and when I put it on, I found fifty cents in the pocket."

When the laughter subsided, Lowman pulled off the jacket. "I guess I'll play without this. It'll be a hunnerd before we get around. Mebbe I won't go the whole nine today."

"That college boy I played with yesterday damned near passed out with the heat," Wallis said.

"Hey, Ray, how much did you take him for?"

"Twenty bucks and greens fee."

Porter gently inquired, "I thought that you all don't gamble."

Wallis eyed him narrowly. "The one o'clock gang don't. But that yahoo insisted on givin' me a stroke a hole. What's a guy to do?" He shrugged and grinned. "Surprised his ass a little."

"Gambling's a sin!" declared Glenn.

Lowman winked at Wallis and elbowed him. "Hell, Cal, it ain't really a gamble when you bet against someone who slices the ball as much as that young man did."

The Reverend eyed Lowman's expressionless face for a moment and spoke in a tone somewhat firmer than usual. "Are you making fun of the way I play?"

"Oh no. Come on, Cal. No offense intended. We know you play that--that *style*--intentionally."

Glenn seemed to accept that. "Well then, all right. I do allow for *maximum fade,* actually." His momentary pique quickly dissipated in the overwhelming geniality of his nature.

The players proceeded in much the same manner as Porter had observed previously. They moved as quickly as they could and struck their balls without delay. There was little conversation other than an occasional jab at one another's shortcomings, especially Lowman's elegant new garb, or comments on the searing heat.

Wallis suggested to Braun that in view of the heat, he--Braun--should ride in a cart instead of walking. Braun declared, "Ah, but I love to walk around this beautiful place. I know not what course others may take, but as for me, give me a golf course or give me death."

"You're crazy!" said Wallis. "You'll probably get both, very shortly."

There were no more than half a dozen other golfers on the course. In the late afternoon, after the peak temperature, more players would show up.

When the group reached the fifth green, they noted how little traffic passed on the nearby highway. Indeed the course seemed isolated and calm, a world unto itself.

Glenn waited his turn to putt. He faced a modest challenge of about four feet, straight in. As he addressed the putt and prepared to stroke the ball, suddenly, from an outdoor speaker above the drive-in diner across the road blared a western band and a wailing, nasal country singer. Glenn stiffened at the sound.

> *There was jist the two of us*
> *She knowed it from the first*
> *An' she never made no fuss*
> *When I ast t' do the worst.*

Glenn stiffened as the sound reached him. Instead of putting or stepping away, he remained hunched over the ball.

> *Lord, that woman made me trust*
> *Made me unnderstan' what love was*
> *Until she come, I knowed only lust*
> *'Til heaven smiled, on the two of us.*

Still Glenn remained frozen at address.

> *There was jist the two of us*
> *Till heaven frowned and made me cry*

perhaps. When my wife died, I was awfully depressed for a long time until I began running regularly."

She raised one eyebrow slightly at the mention of his wife but declined to probe further.

He said, "You are the one who really looks fit. You're about the best--" He cut himself off. "I'm sorry. I'm blabbering again. You must understand that I'm never as outspoken to strange women as I have been to you. I just--" He grinned. "Good gosh, Larona, you must be aware that you are a truly stunning woman. I have to say that. I'm sure I'm not the only man whose breath you've stolen away." He shook his head. "There, I've said it!"

"Thank you, sir. Do you think I should be offended by hearing that? I enjoy it, of course. I work hard to earn comments like that. Is it terribly immodest of me to appreciate them?"

He shook his head and changed the subject. "Are you sure you weren't hurt when we fell?"

"I'm all right.

"I think most women would have shrieked at least. Many would have cried."

"I never cry."

Porter sighed and sat back from the table. He couldn't trust himself to carry on a simple conversation with this woman. He knew he was totally in her power. Finally he asked, "Why did you want to see me today?"

"I recall meeting you at the plant several days ago, of course," she said with a smile, "but I didn't really know who you are until yesterday."

"And who am I?"

"Pastor Calvin Glenn called me yesterday afternoon and told me about you."

Puzzled, Porter said, "Yes, I know Pastor Glenn. But why would he--"

"Among other things, Pastor Glenn helps operate Harrison House. That's a home here in Clydeston for orphans and other children who need special help. Abused children. Youngsters with serious problems of all sorts..."

The server brought over Cokes and some sort of biscuits for Deacon.

She continued. "Every year we conduct a fund-raiser event for Harrison

House. Pastor Glenn and I are co-chairpersons. The last two years our fund-raiser has been a golf tournament."

Now Porter could see it coming. The old tightness began to knot his stomach.

The pastor informed me that you used to be a professional golfer. His idea is to invite you to play "with people who will contribute to the event. There are many who will pay large sums, I'm sure, just to have you accompany them for a few minutes. We get large numbers of influential contributors out of Kansas City, Wichita, Topeka, Salina, everywhere. Some from out of state."

He said, "That's not really something I...."

"You could give them a free lesson or something. Watch them hit their little white balls and tell them how to improve whatever it is they do. You must have many anecdotes from your professional days." She stopped to sip her drink and her eyes shone across the top of her glass.

He frowned uneasily. "Larona, it's just that I.... When will this event be? I don't know how long I'll be in town."

She reached both hands out and held his. "It's weekend after next... two weeks. I'd regard it as a great personal favor to me."

At her touch, he felt like a schoolboy. Emotions stirred in him that he had not experienced for years. He patted her hands in turn and nodded. "I guess I could do that."

"Oh wonderful! There won't be much for you to do. It should be lots of fun. And it's such a worthy cause." She added, "And I'll be in your debt, Mister!"

Porter nodded again. "Okay." Already he felt he had made a mistake. His stomach was really churning now.

"I have to leave tonight for Dallas," Larona said. "We're having a series of sales meetings there and in Atlanta and out in L. A. I'll be gone for about a week But perhaps we could meet this afternoon briefly at the country club before I go. We could discuss it with Walter Edwards. He's the general manager at the club. And I can probably get a few others on the committee to come, to meet you. We can work out exactly what your role will be. And we can get your name and photo into our advertising plans. And so forth."

He said, "I need to caution you that my name no longer carries much weight, if it ever did. You're very likely overestimating my drawing power."

actually think I'm a tremendous klutz." Very seriously he added, "I don't understand. Do you just want a clown around for laughs?"

"No, Jess. It should be obvious that I have a very high regard for you."

"And I for you, Larona. But I've never met anyone like you. You surprise me over and over."

"I knew the moment we met--when you came crashing into my life-- that I had never met anyone like you, either."

"You have so much prestige, it's daunting."

"What do you mean?"

"Everybody kow-tows to you like you're a queen. And this company you run, to me it's overwhelming. It's like a--like I don't know what. Everything about you hits me like a tsunami!"

She laughed. "A tsunami!"

"Yeah. You and S O P together seem to run everything in sight. I hardly know what to think about you."

"Really? Am I that bad?"

"Hell no, Lorana! That's the trouble. I think you're that wonderful! You are extremely special. You just overpower me. I'm scared of how I... how I feel about you."

"I've never met anyone like you either."

They rode on in silence until they reached the S O P administration building. He parked at the front entryway.

She said, "I have to leave town in an hour. I'll be on the road at least four days. You know that. Dallas, Atlanta, Washington. And when I get back...."

"I'll miss you, Larona."

She touched her fingertips to her lips and then gently blew him a kiss. Her eyes seemed to flash like lightning. "I'll be thinking about you, Tsunami Man."

The next day brought no relief from high temperatures. Clouds boiled up in late morning, perhaps promising rain.

Porter thought constantly about Larona Starr and the captivating smile that sometimes danced at the corners of her mouth. He was amazed by the excitement he felt about her, the kind of high emotion he had thought lost to him forever after Cathy died. He dared not speak about his feelings, especially to Patricia, for she clearly expressed coolness on that subject.

Despite the possibility of rain, he arrived at the municipal golf course about a quarter till one. Slim Braun was there and ready. When Wallis and Lowman came, they were ready to tee off within minutes. Porter supposed that Pastor Glenn might be busy with preparations for the fund-raising event. "I think you guys once mentioned somebody named Harry?" Porter said. "Does he ever show up anymore?"

Braun said, "Haven't seen Harry for a while. His wife is ill, extremely ill."

Porter knew how that situation went: it simply tore your guts out. He sympatized with the unknown Harry.

Before they got ten yards down the fairway, another golfer hailed them. They stopped and waited for him. He was another old fellow. His face was deep red, as though sunburned, and his bright blue eyes shone like little flares. He hurriedly drove a bouncing ball down the fairway past them. While they waited for him to catch up, Slim Braun told Porter that the newcomer was Jack Karns and that he had come to Clydeston years ago. He had been an accountant with Starr of the Prairie Pharmaceuticals until his retirement.

As they continued to play number one, Braun passed along more information to Porter. He said Karns still worked part-time, mainly on tax returns for his friends, including this crew of golfers.

And then another new man caught up, so Braun introduced him to Porter, too. It seems Tom Tipton was a real estate broker who maintained an office on North Vine Street in Clydeston. His hollow cheeks accented his large nose. He shook hands with Porter despite paroxysms of coughing.

Lowman cried out, "Holy cow! Now look who's coming!"

Once more, everybody looked back up toward the first tee and saw Doctor Jensen speeding down to them in his golf cart. "Wait for me," he called out.

When the cart reached them, Lowman stepped close and said, "Hey, Doc, don't you know this is Tuesday, not Wednesday?"

"A couple of patients cancelled their appointments, and I had just enough time to catch you guys," he explained.

"This is a big group today," observed Porter.

"Um," grunted the doctor. "About the most I've ever seen at one time. Surprising that we'd get so many on a day when it looks like rain."

Porter said, "There are seven of us. Do you want to split into two groups? Or what?"

"Nah, just get moving," said Wallis. It's one-thirty already. Let's play golf or we're all gonna get wet. Just go from here. We don't need to go back and start over."

"Someone can ride with me in the cart."

"Thanks, Doc. I will," said Tipton.

Karns put up his hand. "Wait. Before we do anything. I want you all to know that today is my birthday. So I get to hit first!"

"How old are you, Jack?" asked Doctor Jensen.

"Seventy-one, replied the CPA proudly.

Wallis "scoffed, "Haw!"

"I knew it was your birthday," Lowman said. "I brought you a dozen of these little orange-filled chocolates, shaped like golf balls." He held one out for Karns to see. "They're really good."

"Hey! Thank you, Abe"

"I tasted one," said Lowman, "just to be sure they were good enough fer you! And they sure were, but they were meltin' so fast, I had t'eat 'em!" He popped the last one into his mouth. "That one was gettin' soft, too!"

All seven men, including Karns, laughed, but they let him have honors as requested. Then the others shot, and they moved onto the parched course.

They played quietly. With so many in the group, they moved more slowly than usual, taking care not to pass in front of a player about to hit away, demonstrating greater consideration than usual. Joking and needling were forgotten.

Tipton's coughing was the most common sound. After the second hole, he picked up his ball and rode the electric cart to the next green. There he dropped the ball, chipped, and putted. Then he rode again to the next green. He simply hadn't the strength to make full swings.

Thus they worked their way, essentially alone, a little knot of persevering humanity, proceeding back and forth across the hot, dry ground, the skies growing ever darker and more ominous.

They teed off on number eight, a modest par three with a tee shot needing to carry about eighty-five yards across the edge of a large, brackish pond. For some, such as Doctor Jensen, who could not count on driving the ball in the air for that distance, and Tipton, who was too weak, a land route around the right side provided a surer path to the hole one hundred fifty yards away.

Ray Wallis was one who could safely risk a shot straight across the pond to the green. On this occasion, however, he felt a rising wind in his face. This caused him to force his swing in the pursuit of more power, and he produced an enormous duck hook. The ball circled hard left, across the water and into a marshy area of reeds and cut tree branches, far left of the green. "Dammit," he muttered, and he hit a second ball just right and short of the green.

As the other men chipped on, Wallis swung his dilapidated old buggy around in the direction his first ball had taken.

Abe Lowman, who was riding with him, warned, "You can't find your ball in there, Ray. The cattails are too thick. Hell, it's too soft fer this cart."

"I think it's dry enough," Wallis snapped. "You can see the marsh is dried out. Dammit, that was a practically new Spaulding."

"That's jist a dry crust on top of mud," cautioned Lowman.

At the edge of the marsh, Wallis stopped, careful not to get mired down. Both men got out and slowly stalked along the rim of the pond, clubs in hand, beating the weeds aside, searching for a glimpse of the ball.

Suddenly Wallis cried out. "Jesus Christ! Abe, look there!"

He pointed with the handle of his club in one hand, and he motioned vigorously with the other. "Abe, look there! Hey!" he yelled as loudly as he could in his raspy voice to the other golfers on the green about thirty yards away. "Hey! Come here! Hey, come look over here!"

"What is it?" Lowman asked. He peered where Wallis still pointed. "I don't see…. Holy shit! What is that? How can that be?" His voice trailed off and his face whitened. He sat down on the spot and stared.

The other golfers came as quickly as possible. Porter reached Wallis and Lowman. Looking at the shaken man, he said, "Are you all right, Abe?"

Wallis grabbed Porter's shoulder and impatiently spun him toward the marsh. "He's okay, Jesse! Look out there! Look right there," he insisted.

Porter studied the clump of reeds, cattails, and tangled tree limbs a few yards out into the pond. The water which usually stood in the marshy edge of the pond had evaporated in the recent hot weather, exposing more limbs and debris.

There, thrust up between branches of a rotting tree, he saw what had so alarmed Wallis. "Damn!" he whispered.

"What is it? What do they see?" asked the other golfers as they arrived at the spot.

Wallis continued to point his club. "Look there! It's a *hand! There's a body out there!*" Lowman grabbed at Doctor Jensen's arm. "How can that be, Doc?"

"It just...doesn't seem possible," said Jensen.

"Call the cops," Wallis said. "We have t'call the cops."

As the group of men stood staring intently at the ghoulish hand and arm in the tangle of branches, they scarcely noticed the first drops of rain that fell from the lowering sky.

Porter called the police on his cell phone. Then he called the clubhouse and reported the event to an astonished Nancy who promised to direct the police if they came her way.

Within minutes, the rain was falling in windswept sheets. The sky was very dark, and the downpour was furious. Lightning crashed nearby, followed almost immediately by a clap of thunder. The golfers recognized the threat of lightning, but they remained huddled together in their carts. They shared raincoats as best they could by pulling them over their shoulders. The rain drove with such force that the cart roofs offered little shelter. Everyone watched the sky with great concern.

A police car raced across the course toward them, lights flashing and siren screaming. The golfers watched in frustration as the vehicle suddenly slid to a stop at the ditch that crossed beneath the eighth tee. Then the car circled back toward the fairway where it could cross, swung up by number four green and at last sped over to where the golfers waited.

When it stopped, its red, blue, amber, and white lights continued to rotate and flash. A big, blond cop jumped out into the rain. He was bareheaded and wore no slicker. He was immediately drenched by rain. "What's this about a body?" he demanded.

Doctor Jensen said, "Hello, Gabe. It's right over there." He pointed and the officer peered through the rain.

"I saw it first," Wallis announced proudly. He stepped forward. "I'm the one who found it."

"Yeah," the policeman replied perfunctorily. Without hesitation, he strode toward the bog. Although the crusty surface appeared solid, his first step off the bank took him up to his knees. He swore and pulled off his equipment belt and holster. Handing them up to Porter, he said, "Watch this stuff for me." Then he turned and energetically struggled toward the fallen tree and limbs where the arm and hand eerily beckoned.

By the time the officer had gotten halfway to his objective, a blue and white Bronco II pulled up. The young man who jumped out wore an olive drab slicker with a rain hat pulled down over his face. He carried a large camera wrapped in plastic. "Hey, guys," he called out. "I heard you found a body out here."

"Who are you?" Tipton asked.

"Doyle Dugan, from **The Times**."

Porter whirled quickly to look at the man when he announced his name. In the floppy rain hat, Dugan's face was mostly obscured.

"A reporter?" said Lowman. "You didn't waste no time."

Wallis said, "I saw the body first. I found it."

Dugan looked at him briefly, then shouldered past him and Porter, forcing them to step aside. At the edge of the pond Dugan yelled at the policeman. "Hey, Gabe! What are you doing out there?"

The officer shouted something unintelligible without looking around. He was spending all his efforts maintaining his balance in waist deep water and muck.

Lightning flashed, followed almost instantly by a booming clap of thunder.

"That's too close!" The policeman yelled. "I'll probably get electrocuted out here, dammit!" But he struggled on and in another moment, he reached his objective. Rain hit his face so hard that he had to peer closely to determine what was before him.

"Oh hell!" he bellowed, and he suddenly took the visible hand and arm in both his hands and pulled, hard.

The arm jerked out of the water, free, and the golfers stared at the sight.

like. We're going to a movie. I'll be home late. See you in the morning. Maybe."

She stomped out and slammed the door behind her, leaving him bewildered by her outburst.

Next morning, Porter ventured warily into the living room. No one there. In the kitchen he found a note from Patricia. Apparently she had written it the night before, after he had gone to bed. In her note she apologized for her attitude. She said she had shared her problem with her friend, Joyce, who had advised her, above all else, not to alienate her father. The last part read: "Please don't leave. I love you. See you after work."

"Whew," he said aloud. "That's good. I'll try to think of something nice to say about this Dugan guy. And most of all, it appears I need to thank this Joyce person, too."

The rain stopped and the sun was again at full force by eleven. Porter decided he would skip the one o'clock outing, but he wanted to know whether the incident at the pond had any adverse effects on his friends, so he headed the LeSabre toward the old course.

He found Nancy Grimsby on hand as usual, but no golfers had shown up. She greeted him with a smile. "I didn't expect anyone to play today."

He straddled a stool at the small bar. "Not much else to do right now. My daughter works, so I'm alone all day. I was going to go over to the country club and check that place out for that fund-raiser thing, but I decided to wait and see how the weather is."

"I heard that you are going to play."

"How about fixing me a hamburger please."

She turned to the stove. As the flames popped up, she said, "There have been tornado warnings around Emporia. That's up northeast of us."

"Really? I've never been around tornados."

"Don't be concerned. They shouldn't be a problem for us here. We haven't had any here for many years. Wichita has had a few over the years. Mostly they go across Oklahoma and Iowa and other states. We just got a bad reputation in Kansas from the *Wizard of Oz*." She laughed.

After a moment she went on. "That was some--uh--what would you call it? Some *adventure* you guys had yesterday, wasn't it?"

He nodded. "It was pretty exciting for a few minutes. We thought Ray had really found a dead body. But it turned out to be something discarded or stolen from a department store or something like that. It might have been thrown into the pond by kids. A prank. Who knows how long ago?"

"It'll all be in the newspaper this afternoon, you know."

"Think so?"

"Certainly. That's the most excitement I can recall around here in many a moon. I wouldn't be surprised if it's on TV tonight."

"Sure, Story of the year. Of the decade. They'll probably make a TV series."

They both laughed and she turned around to check on the hamburger.

Porter said, "Say, that reporter who showed up--Doyle Dugan--do you know him?"

"Not personally. Mostly I've seen his name through **The Times.** Why do you ask?"

"Just curious. Over at the pond yesterday he sounded pretty arrogant and disrespectful to some of the guys. Just my opinion. I hope he doesn't write a story that way. I wouldn't like to see our friends insulted in print."

"I'm certainly not an editor, but as far as I can see, his writing is usually fairly straightforward. I don't pay much attention to how people write. Except many letters to the editors are usually pretty silly. I've never paid much attention to Dugan. Sometimes he reports on town council meetings and he likes to pick on councilmen. But that's his job, I guess. He's been at the newspaper for a year or two, I think. Before that, I wouldn't know. Might have worked at S O P. Almost everybody in town has."

They fell silent for a moment. Then Nancy served the hamburger, and Porter asked for coffee.

"You lived here long, Nancy?"

"I grew up in Clydeston. Been here all my life so far. Same for my husband Josh. I don't think you've met him yet."

"Does he work here on the golf course?"

"Oh no, not here. This is strictly a one-person operation. He does some repairs and greens work though, when he can. We both supervise the fellows who maintain the course. Mostly they are boys from the community college. It's close by, you know. And cheap labor," she added with a laugh. "You've played here. You know by now what a low-budget operation it is."

After pausing, she went on. "Josh is employed full-time in maintenance on the production lines at S O P. He also does what auto and construction jobs he can find." She shook her head. "He seems to work all the time. Our daughter Jennifer is in high school. She's an *A* student and wants to go to med school. We save every penny we can scrape up. But I don't know if we'll ever be able to afford it unless she gets a big scholarship."

She seemed to cloud up.

Porter looked away. Staring out the window by the front door, he said, "Yesterday's storm was a real doozey. I bet the runoff will fill the pond over there. The fairways needed it, too."

She nodded.

After a moment, he said, "I guess you've known these old fellas in the one-o'clock gang for some time. I don't wish to pry, but what can you tell me about some of them?"

She smiled again with pleasure at the thought of her friends. They're terrific old guys. You know that. Always very gentlemanly around me. They would do anything for me, I think. I don't know what to tell you. They mostly have pretty ordinary lives as far as I know.

"Tell me about Doctor Jensen."

"Doc? I've known him all my life. He is the nicest man in the world. He was our family doctor when I was a little girl. He was in practice when doctors still made house calls." Her expression hardened. "His daughter was my age. Jennifer. I named my daughter after her. We went all through school together. She died years ago." Nancy sighed heavily. "An auto accident. Then Missus Jensen died...only a few months later."

The memory of Porter's own wife's death suddenly surged up bringing unexpected pain. "Damn, that would be...." He shook his head. "Two deaths like that--That would be too much for many of us to take."

"Yes." Nancy's voice filled with emotion. "Abe Lowman's son was in the same accident." She laid a white plastic knife and fork in front of Porter.

He said, "Jensen and Lowman seem like especially close friends. You'd think that if their kids had a fatal accident, it might have driven them apart."

"Oh, they didn't hit *each other*. They were in the same car...." Her voice choked off.

"What is it, Nancy?" he asked gently.

"Well...it's kind of.... I haven't thought about it for a long time. You see, Doc's daughter, Jennifer, and Abe Lowman's son, Jaimie, were sweethearts all through high school. I was close to both of them. After graduation, Jaimie went off to Afganhanistan. I think he was gone about two years. When he came home, he went to work for S O P. They offered to put him into a special sales program where he had to travel all over the country, training in hospitals or something like that. Well, anyhow, they decided they couldn't settle down right away, and they decided to put marriage off for a while.

"Then when he came back to Clydeston to stay, he got into a fight with some strangers one night and was beaten up. He had major head injuries." Nancy shuddered at the recollection and caught her breath. "Doc had the best doctors in the country looking after Jamie. Finally they said they could do no more than keep him alive. He was going to be...a...*vegetable*... for the rest of his life. Jennie was beside herself, of course. Then one night in the middle of winter, she sneaked Jaimie out of the hospital and took him in her car and she crashed it into an underpass and...they both died."

Nancy was crying.

"That's a terrible story," Porter said softly. He swore and shook his head. "Did anybody know who those strangers were who beat up the young man? Or why?"

"I don't think so. Some itinerant drunks, everybody said." She added, "There was lots of talk, but nobody seemed to know anything for certain."

She put the hamburger on the counter in front of Porter, but he just stared at it. "I guess I lost my appetite," he said. "So--the loss of those kids actually drew Doc Jensen and Abe together rather than wedging them apart, huh?"

"Yes, they've been very close as far as I know. Supportive of each other. They don't socialize much, I suppose. Except for golf. But after Doc's wife died, he has been alone all these years except for his medical practice and his golfing buddies."

"How about Abe? How did it affect him?"

"I don't know how he took it personally. I mean, I'm sure he felt a terrible loss. But he's always been sort of private, y'know. He jokes a lot, but he's not very open about personal things. When those guys were young, society had a different code for men in my opinion. They didn't talk about their emotions, like today. They just swallowed everything unpleasant and made the best of things."

Porter nodded.

"I was closer to Jenny than to Jaimie," Nancy went on. "Abe has another son somewhere. Abe and his wife live alone here now though, I believe. I guess they don't have much. They just get along day to day, I suppose. He's always complaining about finances."

"He retired from S O P, didn't he?"

"Yes, but he didn't make much there. I mean, I don't know exactly what his job there was like, but he's not an educated man. He may never have finished high school. I really don't know. Quite a different background from Doc Jensen's, for sure. They probably wouldn't be close friends except for the loss of their kids, like you said." She added, "And their golf, of course."

"Abe's a very amiable guy," said Porter. "He has a tough sense of humor. In fact, that whole bunch seem like very honest, pleasant fellows."

"My goodness, I've talked a lot. I hope you don't think I'm always rattling on like this."

"Not at all. In fact, I asked you."

"I can tell you one more thing, for sure. They like you," she declared.

He chuckled. "Why do you think so?"

"Oh, just little remarks I've heard. Nothing in particular. If they didn't like you, they'd let you know. They talk about your golfing ability, of course. They've never played with anyone as good as you."

"I wouldn't know...." He reached for the hamburger and spread some mustard on it.

"How long were you on the tour? Why did you give it up?"

Porter shifted uneasily on the stool. Pointing to a cabinet behind Nancy, he asked, "Is that pie fresh?"

"Uh huh. It's lemon. Like a piece?"

He nodded.

Nancy stood before him, waiting. Clearly, she hoped for an answer to her question.

So Porter said, "Well, I had a couple of good years on the tour, and I thought it would last for a long time. But it didn't. My wife had been a tremendous booster for me. Her name was Cathy. We had a baby girl, Patricia, and and everything was wonderful for a while. Then we learned that Cathy had cancer. Things really went to hell after that. She got worse and worse...." He turned toward the window.

"I'm so sorry," Nancy said. "I didn't mean to pry."

"It's all right." Porter cleared his throat. "Cathy died after seven long years and a lot of surgery and pain. I became severely depressed. I couldn't take time to play golf. Also I had my little girl Trish to take care of. I ran out of money with the medical bills. I took a variety of jobs. We got along okay, I guess, but I simply couldn't compete at golf. It was no longer important. Cathy had been my great support. Without her cheering me on, I had no confidence.

"Of course, in spite of all that, I actually tried for a while though. Then I hurt my shoulder and didn't let it recover properly. That really finished me. I never was able to get my swing back to normal. There's still a hitch at the top of my backswing."

"Your swing looks awfully good," she offered.

"But it never got back to where it needed to be. You can't play at the top of the pyramid if you're not one hundred percent. Only one or two bad strokes and you're out of the competition. When I tried to come back, those guys climbed all over me, like sharks in a fish pond."

"That's too bad" Nancy said with obvious sincerity.

He said, "Now may I have that pie?"

She turned to the counter just as the phone rang. She answered it and then grinned. "Why, yes, he's here." She couldn't resist a gleeful little clucking as she handed it to him. Silently, he mouthed the words: *Who is it?*

Nancy grinned and shook her head.

"Hello. This is Jesse Porter."

His reaction was similar to Nancy's. But in addition to surprise, he felt an unexpected surge of pleasure at the sound of the voice on the phone. "Why...uh...gee! It's great to hear from you, Larona! Where are you?"

Patricia worked late, so Porter left a note for her. It said only that he was having dinner with Miz Starr, to discuss a fund-raising event. So *"don't wait dinner."*

The Starr house was located in the development where he had bumped

"Anyhow, on a trip to Santa Fe, he bought some hand-made jewelry from a man from Cochiti. They got into conversations about what Clarence was doing, and the man told him he was a Zuni medicine man. He had married a Cochiti woman, you see, so he was living at Cochiti. Anyhow, this fellow said he made a wonderful cough syrup that he would make for Clarence to sell. It turns out that this fellow used a certain kind of cactus that he dug up on those big cattle ranches south of Santa Fe. Then he ground the cactus to a pulp and extracted a liquid that he used as a cough syrup.

"So Clarence made a deal with him. And that was the beginning of Clarence's good fortune and put him on the road to wealth and to what we see today as Starr of the Prairie Pharmaceuticals." Larona smiled.

"That sounds like a fairy tale" Porter said. "Did that stuff really work?"

"Oh yes! But that's another story that I won't bore you with right now. What *I* want to hear is *your* story about what happened at the golf course yesterday."

"Okay," Porter said, "but if there really is more to that story, I want to hear it. I find it hard to believe that a cough syrup made all these big buildings that you have today. I was told that they came from government contracts."

"Tell me about the golf course and storm and bodies," she demanded.

"Okay," he laughed. "I guess the newspaper's out, and everybody has read it by now. Wallis and Lowman saw what they thought was a body in the pond on the eighth hole. We called the police and a cop named Gabe something-or-other waded in and found that it was a store mannequin." He laughed. "It was serious for a few minutes--until we found out it wasn't a human body. That's about all--except that we got very wet."

Larona shuddered. "Ugh! I can just imagine. I'm glad it wasn't real. Wouldn't that have been ghastly!"

"Tell me about your trip, will you? I thought you weren't going to come back for a few days. How is the guy who had the heart attack?"

"He will survive, they said. Thank heaven. But he could not possibly return to the meeting."

"Couldn't go on without him?"

"Oh no. It had been his idea in the first place," she explained. "So when he could not participate, the rest of the group--mostly lawyers--couldn't decide who should take charge."

"What was it about?"

"Oh, some companies want to get the Food and Drug Administration to back off their current stance on TV advertising," she said. "I don't think you and I want to go into the details now, do you? The sales meetings went on without me. Our regional managers run that sort of thing, actually. Sales meetings."

"Okay. So you just came home, huh?"

"Exactly. Much better than listening to a bunch of lawyers who never agree on anything."

"You travel a lot, don't you?"

She smiled and nodded.

He said, "This margarita is very good."

"I'm glad you like it." Larona's eyes were locked on Porter as if she were studying every move, anticipating the next move, reading his mind.

"You said on the phone that we could talk about the golf fund-raiser. I'm not certain I should have agreed so quickly to participate. Maybe we--"

"Oh tush. Not to worry," she said, dismissing his concern. "I have dinner planned for us. We can talk about the golf thing then if you wish."

"Dinner?"

"You aren't in a rush, are you? Gertrude has left for the day, by the way. Doors are locked. Deacon is outside, guarding the yard and gates. We can take our time--get acquainted. I've really looked forward to this, Jess."

"Sounds fine, Larona. I'd really like--" He stopped short and faced her, very seriously. "Dammit, Larona, I want you to understand how much I've been taken by you. I don't want to spoil our relationship. But I've only known you a few days and--"

"I've known you for only those same few days, too, Jess."

"Look, I'm trying to say that whatever happens, I want to be your friend. I'm very *fond* of you. But...you're such an important person in this town. I hear your name everywhere I go. But it's always in the context of your company. I need to know more about the *real* Larona Starr."

"Ah, but the company and I are inseparable, Jess. It's really all I know."

"I'm sure there's a lot more to you than that."

"Oh my! You're pushing me into areas that I never talk about, Jess."

She rose and fetched the pitcher of margaritas. Refilling his glass, she said, "Well, okay, Mister Tsunami, you asked for it.

"Clarence Starr founded his little pharmaceutical company just about the same time I was born. He spent most of his life and undivided attention to its development. My dad went to work with him when I was only a child. The company took off during the Vietnam war years. He also personally sold goods out of the trunk of his car, in every state in the nation," she smiled and added, "except Hawaii, I guess."

"He didn't have to do military service during the Vietnam years?"

"No. He had flat feet," she laughed. "Actually, he was excused by young Doctor Jensen, who happened to be on the draft board at that time."

Suddenly she added, *"Omigod!* I'm going to tell you something else that only one other person in Kansas knows!"

Porter raised his hand. "Look, you don't have to--"

"Oh yes! Don't you see? I want to tell you everything!" Suddenly she crowded over to the end of the sofa and, holding his face in both hands, she kissed him hard and passionately.

The embrace lasted for a long time before Porter pulled her hands away. "Wow," he whispered. "What brought that--"

"I'm going to tell you things I've never told anyone else. Things that some people may think to themselves but have never truly known."

"Look Larona, I don't--You don't need to--The margaritas--"

"Be quiet, Mister Porter. Chalk it up to the margarita if you wish." She smiled and pulled back a few inches from him. *"This is it: Clarence Starr was a homosexual.* Doc Jensen knew it, and he believed Clarence could never tolerate being in the army. He feared for the young man's safety, so he declared him ineligible for duty. How about that?"

Porter shook his head. "I don't know what to say."

"You don't have to say anything, but I have to add this. Over the years I have come to accept that my father and Clarence were very close. *Very...very close!* That's why Clarence Starr took such good care of me and mother when Daddy died. But I've never discussed it with anyone. Not even mother."

Porter nodded. "Doctor Jensen mentioned that Clarence Starr helped you and your mother. But that's all he told me."

"Actually, Clarence put me through college. And he actually married me so I could inherit the company when *he* died!"

"Wow! There's a lot I don't know about you, Lady!"

"I may as well explain it all to you. When Clarence learned that he was dying, he tried to get his brother Ron Starr to take it over. But Ron didn't want it. So Clarence said if I would marry him, he would leave the company to me. Can you imagine that! That's what actually happened. Ron agreed to stay on as President for a couple of years while I tried to learn everything." She added with a smile, "Big retirement package for Ron!"

"Wow! What a challenge that was for you!"

"Challenge, certainly. *But what an opportunity!* And I didn't really have much choice. How could I tell Clarence I didn't want his company after all he had done for mom and me? And we had a really great steering committee. And Ron could do everything under the sun. I could have made a mess of it, but I got the hang of it. We've done all right. I've been lucky."

"I would have to say it has been a lot more than luck, Larona. I can't imagine how you've come so far. For one thing," he added, "you must have been besieged by men who saw an opportunity--"

"Oh, of course there were some. But I've been too busy, and most of the men in my life were afraid of me anyhow. Over the years, there have been two fellows that I thought I could care for, but I learned before we got to the altar that they only wanted control of S O P."

She took a deep breath. "You cannot imagine what a relief it is to get all that off my chest!"

He cleared his throat and raised his hand as thought taking an oath. "I swear to you that I don't want control of Starr of the Prairie Pharmaceuticals. That's not--"

She laughed and squeezed his raised hand. "Oh, Jess, I know that. I just want to know that you are okay with these revelations. It's pretty scary stuff."

"Indeed it is." He exhaled and said, "I want you to know that I think you are the most wonderful person I know. I want you for myself and I don't want to lose you because someone else thinks he or she can dictate life styles for everybody else. Actually," he added, "I feel greatly honored--really--that you were willing to share all this with me, and I promise I won't breathe a word of it to anyone."

As an afterthought, he asked, "Have you ever told anyone else?"

She laughed. "Are you kidding? In this town?"

"Whew! This was a real blockbuster, lady! I had some expectations when I came over this evening, but nothing like this!" He held her hand and said, "Well, you'll probably sic Deaon onto me, but there is one more little thing...." He paused.

"What is it?"

"I just...want to know, but you don't have to tell me...."

"Yes?"

"I've been wondering how...how old you are."

"Oh, Jesse! You can't ask a woman that! That's--I am more afraid to tell you that than what I've already told you! You'll stomp away from here."

He said, "I'm forty-nine. You must be ten years younger than that."

"Oh...." She held a fist up to her mouth, not wanting to answer him. At last she said, "I'm *a bit* older than you think, Jess. I'm *fifty-three*. There! I've said it."

He raised his eyes and studied the ceiling for a moment. Then he exhaled and looked at her again. Softly, he asked, "What month is your birthday?"

"October."

"Oh well then," he nodded. "We're okay, sweetheart. My birthday is in February. So the difference is really less than three-and-a-half years. No more than a blink of the eye! I just hope you like old guys."

Before he could speak further, she leaped off the couch. "There's enough margarita left for one more round."

He took off his glasses and hugged her tightly. "Be my girl."

"Don't you want dinner now?"

"Later, darling girl."

"Oh my, I think the Tsunami Man has arrived at last. And it's about time!"

Night had fallen by the time Porter woke up. The sky was cloudy and dark, so there was little light illuminating the bedroom. It took him a few seconds for him to realize that Larona's head was on his chest.

He moved his legs slightly and put one arm across her shoulder.

"Oh, you finally woke up, Jess?" she asked in a soft whisper.

He shifted his body so that he could lie with his head on one elbow. "Hey, I'm awake. What's your name again, Lady?"

She struck his shoulder playfully. "Oh you! Is this how you're going to be? Poking fun at me after all I've done for you!"

She cuddled closer and he kissed her. "My god, you are wonderful!" he said. "Have you slept?"

"A little. Not much. I've been waiting for you."

"Aha! Well, here I am, ready and--"

"That's nice, but there's something I want to know."

He sat up and plumped the pillow behind him. He kissed her again. "I just don't really know much about you. I want to know you, Jess."

"My story is hardly worth pursuing. Much less spectacular than yours."

"Oh, Jess, I don't agree. Don't you realize that from the moment I first saw you in the exhibit room with Patricia--"

"You mean ever since I went into my act as a stumble bum?"

"Oh, forget that," she laughed. "But yes, even then--instantly--I wanted to know more about you. I want to know *all* about you."

"Well, I guess I owe you that. So okay." He exhaled and gathered his thoughts. "First let me say that I want very much to be with you as much as possible. I really enjoy your company--and I don't mean your pharmaceutical company. I simply don't know how to tell you how I feel. I'm afraid to say some of the things I'd really like to say."

"Are there any women in your life?"

"Only my daughter."

"You said your wife...."

He shook his head. "That was Cathy. She died twenty-two years ago. Cancer. Apparently it started with Trish's birth. And Cathy, well, it ate her up for seven years before...before the end."

"Oh, I'm sorry, Jess. I'm very sorry. I know how devastating that is because my dad suffered...I'm truly sorry."

He sighed. "It was a long time ago."

"Patricia was just a youngster then."

"Yes, she never knew a mother who was healthy enough to play with her or to care for her or teach her womanly things."

"You brought her up alone?"

"Pretty much, yes, I did, basically, along with a parade of baby sitters and nursery schools and such." Porter took a long breath before continuing. "Cathy had some surgery shortly after the cancer was first diagnosed, and she had more. For seven years, surgeons kept hacking away at her, saying they thought they had got it all. Then they'd find more.

"All that time, I spent caring for her and for Trish. I had made pretty good money on the tour--at least, it was good for those days--nothing like today's purses. Anyhow, it had come easily, and I assumed it would get bigger and always be there.

"I never won a major, but I had a few top tens in pretty big tournaments. But everything I made went quickly for Cathy's surgeries, hospitals, doctors, therapy. We had a little insurance, but not enough. I laid off the game too long--most of the time while Cathy was fighting for her life.

"Then when she died, I went into deep depression and when I tried to go back to golf, I just couldn't find the timing. Those guys ate my lunch. They beat me badly, destroyed my confidence. I just don't know how to play with confidence any more. Cathy had been my great supporter. She was like a coach and manager and a whole cheering section. Without her...." His voice tailed off. Then he went on. "Besides all that, I needed to be with Trish, of course. So my professional career was finished. The technical term for it is 'flushed down the toilet.'" He laughed sarcastically.

"One day, when I looked around, I realized everything was gone. I've had lots of different jobs, sales mostly, just trying to keep things together, trying to find enough to give Trish what she needed. I've had several jobs cooking. I really enjoy that."

"Cooking?"

"Yes. I got a job as a short order cook and even did a brief tour as chef in one pretty good restaurant. About a year ago, I found a partner and we opened a restaurant in Albuquerque. But it was the wrong time, and we didn't have enough capital. We closed a couple of months ago, and I've been trying to sell Buicks since then."

Larona studied him for a moment. Then she said, "You tell me all this very matter-of-factly. You don't appear to be depressed now."

"No, the depression was about Cathy. It was there though, and it was tough, but I learned to deal with it some time ago. Now I just operate on a simpler, lower level. Now, as many have learned to say, I just take it one day at a time."

Porter realized that Larona had edged nearer and was resting her head on his shoulder. He didn't know when it had happened. He gently put a hand into her silky hair and stroked her head. It seemed wonderfully right and natural. "Do you think there's any more margarita?"

"I'll get it."

"No. On second thought, don't move," he whispered. He put his hand on her shoulder and drew her closer. I've had enough to drink." Somehow he knew that despite the briefness of their acquaintance, there were-- miraculously--no walls between them.

She said softly, "Remember, I'm not a young woman, Jess."

"Hell, it's okay. Remember, I'm an old man."

"I feel like a girl."

"You make me feel like springtime."

She closed her eyes and he kissed her.

She opened her eyes and smiled. "That was nice."

He said, "I thought about you all the time you were gone these last days. Every minute since we met jogging the other day, I feared I'd never see you again."

"Would you believe I cut my trip short just so I could get back to see you again?"

It was nearly eleven a.m. when Porter walked into Patricia's apartment house. He was surprised to find her still at home, standing, facing him, with hands on her hips. He recognized it as the defiant pose she had adopted as a little girl whenever she was ready for an argument or a fight.

"Morning, Trish," he said casually. "Why aren't you at work?"

"Why aren't I at work? Why haven't you been home all night? Where have you been? Why didn't you let me know? I called the police! I thought you'd had an accident!"

"Really? I'm sorry. I left you a note."

"Your note didn't say anything about staying out all night!" She had not moved from her confrontational pose.

"I am truly sorry I didn't think to call you. Doesn't this strike you as a little funny? Overblown? I'm okay."

"I do not think it's funny. I worried. Where have you been?"

"I don't know whether I should tell you, honey."

"What? Why shouldn't you? What does that mean?"

He took a deep breath. "Okay. If you insist. What would you think if I tell you I spent the evening with Larona Starr?"

"What?" Patricia was astounded. "The *evening? You mean all night?"* She collapsed into a chair. *"Omigod!* I just cannot believe this!"

"Trish, I don't know what else to tell you. But you asked. You must understand that I'm a mature adult."

"It doesn't sound very *mature* to me!

"Well, I must say I feel twenty years younger today. It was the most wonderful night I can remember since--for a long, long time." He grinned and gestured aimlessly.

"I simply don't--*cannot*--believe what I'm hearing."

"Don't begrudge me this, Trish."

"Are you going to tell me next that you're in love?" she scoffed.

"Last night I was," Porter said. "This morning I still am!" He sat down on the couch across from her. "I don't know what comes next, but--"

Patricia jumped to her feet. "You just cannot be serious. That woman is not a nice woman."

"You shouldn't say--"

"She's using you. That's what she's doing. *Using you!* She wants to be sure you'll play in that golf thing that you told me about. That's all she wants: just a darned golf stooge!"

He laughed. "People don't make love just to entice someone to play golf, hon. Don't be silly."

"Did you say 'make love'? Oh! Laronna Starr would do that," Patricia insisted. "Her sense of values in highly distorted."

"Why do you say a thing like that?"

"I've heard it from a lot of people since I came to this town. It's unbalanced, erratic behavior! No one knows what she'll do next. I know it for sure now because she gave me a raise yesterday."

"What?" he frowned. "Well, that's good, isn't it? I don't follow. What's wrong with getting a raise?"

"I don't deserve it. That's what's wrong. It's a thirty percent increase, effective immediately. *Thirty percent!* When no one else in the department got anything! I'm the only one. Doctor Topakis confirmed it for me. And the word got out. It's actually embarrassing. No change in responsibility. No reason. Apparently she just flew in from somewhere and the first thing she did was notify Payroll to execute this raise."

Porter stood up. "Well, I think perhaps it has something to do with me. Maybe. But it's a reach for this to make you think she's not--"

Patricia cut him off again. "Doctor Topakis said it was dictated directly by Missus Starr. That woman knows nothing about my work. I'm not sure she even knows I'm your daughter. And she can get you to do anything she wants by using me."

"If that were the case, I think she would have mentioned it to me. But she did not."

"Oh my gosh, golly, and gee whiz, Dad," she said. "Don't you think, just maybe, she knew I'd tell you? Good grief, how naive can you be!"

They fell silent for a moment. Then Patricia said, "Her office called me yesterday at work to see if I knew where you were. I suggested the golf course. I thought they were just following up on this fund-raiser thing. I thought that was nice. I didn't realize she wanted to seduce you."

"Com'on, Trish. Don't talk like this."

"Daddy, I've heard stories about Larona Starr ever since I came to Clydeston. They say she beds men all over the country. I've *been* skeptical until now. I knew she was arrogant and liked to throw her weight around. Now I know she's an out-and-out whore!"

Angrily, Porter fired back, "Wait a minute! Don't say things like that!"

They glared at each other, and he said, "It's not true. You're trying to make something out of...out of something you don't understand."

"Doyle Dugan told me she's--"

"*Doyle Dugan!*" Porter flared. "Listen, I'm not too impressed by that young man either. Talk about arrogance--He strikes me as pretty arrogant himself."

"You don't know him. You haven't even met him."

"I met him on the golf course, day before yesterday. And he was downright rude and disrespectful I know that firsthand."

"You don't really know him."

"Well, maybe you don't really know Larona Starr either," he countered.

"It's not the same."

"Then why haven't you brought him around for me to meet? Are you embarrassed by him?"

"Embarrassed?" She clenched her fists. "How dare you? I don't have--"

"Time out!" Porter raised both hands and spoke softly. "Hold on a minute. I'm sorry, Trish. We're both in disagreement here, and I don't want to make it any worse. I'll just pack up and get out of here."

He turned toward the hall and the bedroom where he was keeping his things.

"What will you do?" she asked. "You mean to leave town?"

He stopped. Without looking back at her, he said, "Not yet. I'll stay somewhere else. I'll find a motel. We'll both be more comfortable. But I'm not going to leave town until Larona and I.... Well, we'll see."

"Oh, I'm sorry, Daddy," Patricia said. She began to cry. "Don't leave. I don't want you to go. I'm sorry."

He came back to her and hugged her. "I don't want to go, Trish. And I certainly do not wish to hurt you. I love you."

"You know I love you, too, Daddy. I just don't want you to be used by that woman."

"She won't do anything I don't want. I'll be all right."

"I don't like her."

"I'm aware of that," he said, and they both laughed.

Patricia daubed at her eyes with the back of her hand.

"Promise that you won't make some rash decision to quit your job. We'll work this out, Trish."

"I have to go to work," she said. I'm very late. It's a heck of a thing to be half a day late the first day after getting a big raise." They laughed again together, and she wiped her eyes with a kitchen napkin.

"You can tell them you were celebrating."

"Sure. Sure. It'll be all right. I'll just explain to everybody that I didn't know my father would be such a problem after I grew up." She hugged him and asked, "Will you be home this evening?"

His phone jingled. He picked it up to answer, but first he called out to Trish, who was going out the door, "I really don't know. We'll talk some more."

Before he could say *hello*, the caller was already talking excitedly: "Hey, Jess! You there? It's Dave! Jess, you there?"

Porter recocognized the voice of the owner of the Buick agency where he worked in Albuquerque. "I'm here, Dave. What's up? I've been intending to--"

"Okay! Just listen up, will you?"

"Sure, go ahead."

"A Robert Garcia came in early this morning. Early. Do you know him?"

"Never heard of him. Who is he?"

"Damn! You never heard of him? Well, he shore knows you! Come on, Jess. What are you up to?"

"Wait a minute, Dave. I don't know what you're talking about. What did this guy accuse me of?

"He didn't accuse you of nothing. Okay? Just listen a minute. Early this morning this guy--nice lookin' dude, well dressed, about our age, he walks in and asks to see the manager or owner of the dealership. Says he wants to place an order to lease some Buicks. You hear that, Jess? *'Some Buicks,'* like more than one. So I asked him what he needs. He says he wants two-year leases *for forty-five Verano sedans and six LaCrosses.* Then he says *'soonest.'* Forty-five and six. That's fifty-one cars, Jess!

"I says, 'Soonest?' He says, 'Right away. As soon as possible please.' I had been standing but I had to sit down. I said, 'Where do you want these cars delivered, Mister Garcia? Here?' So he pulls out a stack of documents about eight inches deep, sorted through them, and gave me a list of names and addresses for the delivery of fifty-one automobiles. Now get this, the addresses were for Southern California, across Arizona and New Mexico, including two in Albuquerque, and into western Texas. ASAP! *Soonest.*

"Now, Jess, do you know what this is about?"

"No, Dave. I told you, I--"

"Well, Jess, as I said, *He knows you.*"

"I don't understand, Dave. Who does he represent?"

"I have his card. Here. It says he's the Southwest US Regional Sales Manager of Starr of the Prairie Pharmaceutical Company! You ever heard of that?"

"Oh my goodness!" Porter laughed.

"You know him or not? Why are you laughing? And where in the hell is Clydeston, Kansas?

"Starr of the Prairie is one of the biggest companies in Kansas, Dave. That's where I am now. Not far from Wichita. You know where Wichita is, don't you?"

"Jess, what's so funny? This is the biggest single order we've ever had. How did you do this? What's going on?"

"Let me explain--"

"I've already called half a dozen of the phone numbers Garcia gave me. I called Buick home office and Wilbur Thompson--you know, our local attorney. He's been checking it all out ever since Garcia left. It's all legit! Buick national center is aware of the order. They endorse it! What I want to know is how in the hell did you pull off this deal! You are a genius! I was about ready to fire you if you didn't come back with our LeSabre. Now I don't care how long you stay in--where is it?--Clydeston. Where in the hell is that? What are you doing out there with a pharmaceutical company anyway? Taking Voodoo medicine or something?"

Porter shook his head and sat down. "I'm sure it's all legit, Dave, although this is the first I've heard of it. I can explain. Give me a moment. You see, there's a lady here who owns Starr of the Prairie Pharmaceuticals. It's one of the biggest companies in the state and she is probably about the wealthiest woman in the country, for all I know.

"This automobile deal is different, but it's probably just her way of doing a favor, sort of."

"Ordinary people don't work that way."

"They might if they could, Dave. Listen, I'll bet anything that this is a legitimate deal. I think you should proceed as soon as possible. *Soonest.*"

"Do you know this woman? What do you think of her?"

"I think she is wonderful."

"What? *Wonderful?* You sound like you may be in deep trouble, Jess."

"I'll talk with her, Dave. Meanwhile, implement the order. That's my advice."

"Well, okay, but you need to know that if this deal blows up, it'll be your ass!"

Porter laughed. "You're exactly right, Dave. I couldn't have said it better!"

As soon as Dave hung up, Porter phoned S O P and asked for Larona Starr. He was told that she had just returned to the office after being out of town for several days and she would be tied up in meetings all day and was not taking calls. Her secretary promised that she would inform Ms Starr that he had called. "ASAP" she said.

"Soonest," he echoed.

The heavy rainstorm had blown away and left Clydeston skies crystal clear and calm. By the time Porter reached the golf course, the daily cumulus clouds had begun to build again far away on the western horizon. His mind was awhirl, first with the memories of the romantic night before and second, the torment instilled by his argument with Patricia, and not least, third, what Lorona had done as a special business deal for him.

Yet his golfing instincts were so strong that these personal concerns did not keep him from noting that the parched ground had soaked up much of the welcome rain. Only bare spots and low places appeared muddy.

Slim Braun and Jack Karns were in the clubhouse when he entered.

Nancy cheerfully hailed Porter. "How did things go with Missus Starr, Jesse?"

Her question startled him. Then he realized she was only referring to the phone call and invitation he had received here the day before. He shrugged.

"Okay."

"What's that?" asked Karns. What about Missus Starr?"

"Oh, she called Jesse here yesterday, Jack," replied Nancy with mock seriousness. "Seemed most urgent. Certainly must have been a critical matter because it's the first time she ever acknowledged the existence of this golf course as far as I know."

"What are you up to with *her*?" asked Braun.

"Nothing special," Porter assured him. He tried to think of a satisfactory lie, but ideas eluded him. Then he said "Something about a golf exhibition. She wants me to help in a fund-raiser."

From outside they heard Ray Wallis shouting angrily. The three men went out, and Nancy watched from the doorway. She shook her head, recognizing Wallis' problem.

He and Lowman were fussing with great animation over Ray's dilapidated golf cart. "The battery's down again," said the little man.

Wallis swore. "It's not the battery. It's the damned wheel here. The grease has froze up in this wet weather."

"Froze up?" said Braun incredulously. "It's been nearly one hundred degrees for a week."

"Well then, I suppose you won't wanta ride when I get it goin', will you?" Wallis challenged.

Braun withdrew rather than get involved in an argument. "Thanks for the invitation, Ray, but I'll walk as usual."

"I'll ride," Lowman said. "You'll need me along to push when the battery farts its last fart."

Wallis muttered something under his breath. He looked at his watch. "Com'on. Let's play golf. It's after one o'clock."

Karns said, "Ray, why'nt you think about getting a new buggy?"

"You must think I'm rich or somethin'," Wallis replied.

Lowman said, "Well, you're a darned sight richer'n some of us."

"Not Jack Karns," said Wallis to no one in particular. "He's loaded." Then he teed off with an angry stroke and topped the ball. It rolled down the middle of the fairway, creating a mini-rooster tail of water as it passed through a water-filled depression. He stood with hands on hips and glared at the ball. Finally he turned to his fellow golfers and burst out laughing. "This may not be my best day."

"At least you didn't lose the ball," Lowman observed dryly.

Porter and Karns shared a golf cart. As they rode, Karns said, "Ray's an ol' sweetheart, ain't he? He just cannot stay angered long."

"His cart has seen better days," Porter noted.

"Yeh. Ain't we all? I think he doesn't want to invest in a new cart that might last longer than he will."

"He could afford one though?"

"I'm pretty sure he can. I guess Abe might not. I guess that's why he doesn't already own one."

"Um," Porter nodded.

"Yeh. Guess I shouldn't talk about people's finances. What I know of

Abe is just hearsay anyhow. He has a son who has been having a tough time, trying to get a new business started. Some kind of retail thing. I'm not sure what. I understand that Abe has strapped himself trying to help the boy. *The boy! Ha!* Hell, he must be forty or older."

"I see. You're an accountant, aren't you, Jack?"

"Yeh. Spent a lot of years with S O P. I started just shortly before Clarence died. Say," he grinned, "what was this stuff Nancy was saying about you and Larona?"

"Nothing," said Porter quickly. Again he was jolted by the idea that someone might already know of his night with Larona. "Larona--Missus Starr--heard I'm a golfer, and she just asked if I would help do some fundraising thing at a golf exhibition she's in charge of. I think Glenn put her onto me. Told her I used to be a pro."

They stopped for Porter to hit his ball, and Braun walked over. Karns spoke loudly. "That may not be all Larona will be wanting from you, Jess." He winked.

Braun said, "Hey, Jack, is Jesse getting it on with Larona? Heck, he's only been in town a few days."

Karns laughed. "He's still young enough. Not like us, Slim. Hey, Jess, we used to tell a guy to smile if he got any last night. Now we say smile if you got any last year or so!"

"Got any what?" Braun asked innocently.

Porter tried to retain his composure, but he burst out laughing as he swung his wedge, and he knocked his ball into a bunker.

"Hey! Look, Slim. He's grinning. Does that prove it?"

Porter just laughed and shook his head as if they were crazy.

Braun said, "Do your joys with age diminish? When mine fail me, I'll complain. Browning."

"When yours fail you? Hah!" jeered Karns. "Yours failed you decades ago. The only joy you get anymore is maybe a good shit!"

On the fifth tee the golfers had to wait for the foursome ahead of them. Although there were five old-timers, they played much faster than the foursome ahead. The old men hit their balls down the middle and were seldom in trouble. The players ahead, on the other hand, frequently spent time searching the rough for misdirected hots. The old-timers stroked quickly upon reaching their lies whereas the players in the foursome ahead always spent half a minute, at least, determining wind direction and heft of club. Seemingly unaware of the players following, the front players refused to wave the others through.

On the sixth tee, therefore, the one o'clock gang chose to bypass the slower group. Instead of playing down six fairway, they aimed left and played back along the fifth, toward the eighth hole, which had no players approaching it.

As they neared the pond on their right, Karns reminded Wallis of their earlier adventure on eight. "Hey, Ray, there's where you found your dummy."

"Yeah," Wallis said and steered his cart toward the pond. "That reminds me."

"Reminds you of what? Where are you goin'?" asked Lowman. "Your ball's up ahead."

Wallis continued straight toward the pond. "I never found my Spaulding. Remember, that's what we were doin', lookin' for my ball, when we saw that thing. Mebbe I can find the damned ball now."

"The ground's too soft now, Ray," warned Lowman. "The water's deeper! Damn! Don't drive in there. You'll git stuck! Somebody else prob'ly found your ball by now anyway.

"I won't git stuck."

The other golfers watched in dismay as Wallis' cart slowly sank up to its floorboard in the marshy ground.

Wallis tromped on the foot pedal, but the the cart's wheels merely spun. They rotated ever slower, and after a few short moments, they stopped altogether.

"The damned battery's dead again," said Lowman. "I tried t'tell you."

"Yeah, you're always tellin' me something. Why don't you get a cart of your own, you're so smart?"

"You know damn well I can't afford one," said Lowman. "Where would I git the money? Even a used one costs a couple thousand dollars. Now, you gonna git us outta here?"

"Jist like this," said Wallis. He stepped out of the cart and sank to his ankles in muck. The water was two or three inches higher. Slowly he struggled to firmer land. Karns held out the handle of an iron for Wallis to grab and steady himself.

After a minute, Lowman reluctantly followed. The two men looked at each other for a long time. The shoes of both men were covered with mud. Their pants were wet halfway to their knees. Finally Wallis said, "I'm shore sorry."

Restraining his anger, Lowman said, "Okay. I accept your apology."

"Damn!" said Wallis. "I don't mean I'm sorry about you. I mean I'm still sorry I didn't find my ball."

After the day's abbreviated golfing, Porter phoned Larona again and left a message that he would be at the front entry to S O P when she finished for the day. He took a sandwich with him and waited in his Buick until a quarter till seven. As soon as he saw her, he jumped out and held the door for her. Many employees were still streaming by. Porter sensed that when some of them smiled, they believed they understood his relationship with her. He thought perhaps some of them actually understood it better than he did.

She beamed. "My gosh, I missed you today, Jess."

"I missed you, too."

"I longed for you. It was very difficult to concentrate on things I needed to do."

He got in behind the steering wheel. "I've missed you, too." He grasped the steering wheel with both hands, until his knuckles whitened. "It just came to me. You see how this is, don't you? I want to take you in my arms and kiss you. But I realize our relationship must be kept quiet."

She had leaned toward him. Now she sat back, puzzled. "Why do you think that, Jess? I expected a warmer greeting."

"I'm sorry. I was eager to see you, too, and I was full of excitement until a few seconds ago. But it's obvious, suddenly. Don't you see? All these people are watching us and wondering. You're the owner of one of the most prestigious businesses in the Midwest. I'm nobody. You have huge responsibilities. We've only just met. How can these people expect--What do they expect--How can I possibly be right for them? For us?"

"I don't know what to say, Jess. I thought that night--"

"Oh wow! Last night was wonderful! But I don't know how to proceed.

What comes next? I don't expect us to go on like this. Sneaking around. Making denials to people. I don't want you to think I was looking for a one-night stand."

"What's wrong? Tell me, what triggered this?"

"I'm trying to. But it is just now beginning to crystalize, when I saw all these people who work for you, depend on you...." Then he spat it out. "I want to know why you made that big deal, leasing cars from the Albuquerque Buick Center where I work. From your employees' point of view it's like you're putting me, a complete stranger with no experience in your field, ahead of hundreds of your people, who are busting their butts every day--" He shook his head. "That bothers me a lot. I thought you are a more caring person. Is your life just about wealth? Can you just explain that to me, Larona? Please."

An undertone of anger became evident as Larona Starr replied. "Okay, Jess. You have concerns. Don't you think I have concerns, too? Do you think I am taking advantage of you somehow? Do you think I play little games like this often? Perhaps a new boyfriend every three months, just for entertainment, eh? When my husband died, men came out of the woodwork, pursuing me. But they were only after my money, the corporation, some lofty position. A couple were even my own top executives, and I had to fire them. I got a reputation a long time ago for being insensitive when all I was doing was fending off chauvanistic jerks. And, oh yes! I got a reputation for sleeping around. I know that, all right. That's because there are so many people envious of my situation that they make up reasons to pull me down below their own level. The sex stories are not true. They are lies. And I am awfully tired of them." She wiped a tear from her eye.

"Larona, I--"

"Hear me out," she ordered in her executive voice. "You said we must talk, and I agree."

He agreed. "Go ahead."

"For many long years I've avoided giving myself to any man. Not only not giving them sex. I mean not giving them a full time partnership in my life. Then, the first time I saw you, I just knew, somehow, I don't know why, that there might be good chemistry between us. God, you are attractive to me! Most men our age are paunchy and run down. Your eyes blaze and I just want to touch you when you're near. I love your voice. The way you move. Your humor. I've been starved for years for someone who did not approach me for my money or just a quick roll in the hay." Finally, she smiled and added, "Also, now I can say I truly admire your...*stamina.*"

"You are a piece of work, Larona!" He chuckled. "I don't know *men* who would be as frank as you. I want to tell you I--uh, care deeply about you--for you. I certainly didn't want to have an unfriendly confrontation with you now. That's the very last thing I wanted. It just happened."

He took a deep breath and added, "I just don't see how I can fit into your life."

She studied him for a moment and said, "There's something else, isn't there?

"I'm reluctant to say it." He took her hand in his. "It's my daughter. Trish. She has...uh...serious reservations about you. About us, that is."

"Is it the pay raise?" Larona asked. "Was that wrong somehow?"

"She thinks you're trying to buy me for the golf affair." He laughed weakly. "She's really wound up about you."

"Oh no. It was not about the golf appearance. I suppose I was really just trying to buy your goodwill. Along with hers. I've been accused of that before. I simply thought it might help."

"It was a little heavy-handed, I'm afraid."

"I see. Well, I don't think I should take it back how."

"No," Porter agreed. "The important thing is that we got this out in the open." Hesitantly, he added, "And I just got news about the Buicks you ordered from the Albuquerque dealership where I work."

"Oh! I suppose you think that was out of line, too!"

"It's a big deal, Larona--"

"No, Jess, it's not a big deal!" she replied firmly. "You don't seem to understand that we have over seven hundred sales people all across the country. They *all* get company cars every few years. It's a primary perk for them.

"We lease those cars, and we replace them regularly. We have several people here in Clydeston who do nothing but maintain our automobile fleet. The cars I asked to be replaced today were all nearly ready to be replaced or I wouldn't have ordered it. I just thought it would be nice if <u>you</u> got something out of it instead of dealers I don't even know."

"What happens to all those cars being replaced?" he asked, already greatly relieved by her explanation.

"Our people have an opportunity to buy them and keep them if they wish--at a very good price. Or we sell some to dealers. And the rest are just returned to Buick under the existing lease agreement."

"Oh," he said. "I see. I didn't realize--"

She slapped his knee. "And you'll get a nice commission from your boss, I expect."

They had not moved from the parking space at the curb. Employees continued to pass as they left at the end of their workday. "You were right, Jess," Larona said. A lot of those folks will think we're having a hellacious conversation here, won't they?

"I think we have had a monumental conversation."

"Do you have any other questions, Jess?"

He shook his head and edged away from the parking spot. "No. Not now. I'll be happy to take things as they come. Just please don't overdo it."

"Good," Larona said. "Your place or mine?"

"I just told you about Trish's attitude."

"Okay. Mine."

By Wednesday the stormy weather had moved out of the region altogether. The day appeared ideal for golf. A slight southwestern breeze smelled clean and fresh, and it was not strong enough to influence the flight of golf balls. The ditches which crossed the golf course carried modest amounts of water. Here and there, the walls of ditches, softened and undercut by rain, had caved in. Many parts of the fairway grass had regained a new green life and already needed mowing.

Ray Wallis' golf cart had been extricated from the mud at the edge of the pond by Nancy Grimsby's husband Josh.

Reluctantly, Wallis had purchased a new battery and paid a couple of teenagers to scrub the cart. Now he rode in it proudly, as if it were new, although it clearly would benefit from at least a dozen touches of paint, refurbishing to seats, wheels, and other parts.

Pastor Glenn joined Porter in the latter's rented buggy as the one-o'clock gang teed off. "The Lord has given us another beautiful day," he observed.

Porter agreed. His spirits had not been higher for many years. He was full of thoughts of the beauty and companionship of Larona Starr. "Yes, I think this is the prettiest day we've had since I came to Clydeston." He felt as though he had been on a honeymoon. Since Saturday, Larona and he had been apart for only a few hours each day. During those periods, she had dealt with business affairs in her office. He had spent his free time golfing and resting.

His relations with Patricia had been polite but rather quiet. Very limited conversation.

"Not so humid," noted the pastor. "Actually."

"Um. The whole gang seems to have turned out today, too."

"I'm sure we consistently have the most golfers on Wednesdays. That's when Doctor Jensen plays, of course, and he has always been a kind of-- what? A kind of organizer of the group. The prime mover actually."

Whenever Glenn hit a wood or long iron, Porter bit his tongue to keep from offering advice to help eliminate the inevitable great roundhouse slice which ensued. He tried to think of a way to coach the pastor without appearing to do so, but he feared he might offend the old gentleman.

While they all stood around and putted on the second hole, Doctor Jensen spoke to Porter. "I understand that you will be the premiere attraction at this year's Harrison House fund-raiser."

"Thought I might help, yes."

"Oh, by the way, Jess," chimed in Glenn, "I intended to thank you. It's wonderful for you to agree to help us."

"I understand that it was your idea," replied Porter.

"Well, actually it *was* I who told Missus Starr about your golfing prowess."

The doctor said, "I heard it was her idea for you to play."

"She extended the invitation. But--" Porter, pretending to be angry, said, "Glenn here suggested it to her, I believe." He turned to the pastor and shook his fist. "And I'll get even with you for that, ol' buddy!"

Tom Tipton said, "Word around town is that you and she--" He broke off in a paroxysm of coughing. He reached into his cart and picked up a pack of S O P cough drops.

Porter said, "It seems to me that a number of persons have been trying to make a connection between Larona Starr and me. She merely asked--"

Lowman cut in. "Sounds like you're the one who connected."

Porter felt some resentment, but he restrained showing it, as much as possible, and replied flatly, "It that a problem for anyone?"

"In our small community, Jess," explained Pastor Glenn, "some persons feel a need to watch--very carefully, actually--every little thing that the town's leading lady does. It may affect many, many people."

"Leading lady?"

"Most eligible wealthy widow," interjected Braun.

Glenn went on..."Well, yes, actually, I mean, she is actually Clydeston's most significant employer. And whatever influences her, of course, influences just about--"

"Com'on, guys!" Porter laughed. "What are you trying to do? Upset my game? Let me putt."

Jack Karns said, "There are games, y'know, and then there are *games*. You can putt a ball into a hole or put other things into y'know...other things." He guffawed and several others laughed weakly. Glenn turned away.

Wallis spoke up. "You guys make your jokes if you wanta, but I'll tell you when my Ruby was dyin', that Larona Starr came and visited and held her hand a lot. Personally. I appreciated that more than I can say. She didn't hafta do it. I was retired long before that. I'd do about anything fer that lady."

The golfers looked at each other with some embarrassment and much surprise. Wallis didn't often offer such long statements about personal thoughts and feelings.

On the fourth hole, Porter boomed a tremendous drive. Several of the old men shook their heads in disbelief as they marvelled at the sight. When they left the tee and started down the fairway, Pastor Glenn said, "You must not be upset by these fellows' remarks and jesting."

"I'm not, Porter replied. "It's okay. As a matter of fact, I enjoy it most of the time." He added, "Did you see my drive? I could not have hit that if I were upset, believe me."

They climbed into the buggy, and after a quiet moment, Glenn said, "Well, you know, actually, I was just wondering...." He looked around, not wanting to be overheard.

"Yes?"

"I..uh...was wondering if you have any tips actually...that is, tips that might help me hit my ball like you do." He squinted as though suffering a slight pain. "Less slice, you know."

"Well, let's see...." Porter took his time answering, for he saw the need for tact. "You're really very consistent with your shot, Cal."

"Yes, but it's a consistent *slice*. Actually, I'd receive more respect from these men if I hit the ball straighter."

Porter nodded. "Okay. Let's try this, Cal. When you drive on the next hole, do three things. First, be sure your grip is tight, so the club won't turn in your hands. Second, don't swing so hard. You swing with so much force that you pull your right foot clear off the ground and the clubhead moves *across* the ball, imparting a side-spin which causes the slice. Swing easier so you keep both feet on the ground. Better balance that way, too."

"Aha! Yes, I see that. Actually, that sounds very good. What else?"

The other thing is to try for a more vertical swing. Your swing is pretty flat, you know."

"You mean try to go up and down rather than around?"

"Yes, that's right. Shorten that back swing a bit, and you can control it better. Now, listen, I don't believe we want the others to think I'm coaching you...."

"Oh, right, Jess. I'll just try it on my own, actually, like it's my idea. Next hole: both feet on the ground; vertical, easy swing."

"That's it. And remember the firm grip. When you line up your shot, don't allow for a slice because you're going to eliminate that."

"Right. I'll aim straight. I've got it, I think." He laughed. "Actually, it sounds easy, you know."

After Porter, Wallis, and Loman drove off the fifth tee, Glenn stepped up and addressed his ball. Immediately, several of the gang noted a difference in his stance. Tipton started to say something, but Porter raised his hand, gently shushing him and the others.

The pastor swung easily with a more vertical arc. Both feet stayed down. The ball flew out almost straight. "Lord be praised!" he exclaimed.

"Lord, my behind," said Karns. "Looks more like Jess Porter's work than the Almighty's, if you ask me."

Porter shrugged innocently. "Who? Me?"

"Karns said, "Can I ride in your cart and get some help?"

When Pastor Glenn's turn came up on number six, he stepped up with great confidence. He swung, hard, in his old roundhouse manner, and his right foot left the ground. His ball rocketed out, high, and turned abruptly in a huge slice. Trusting that he had found the secret for a straight drive, he had not allowed for the old slice, so this time the ball circled far beyond the fairway.

All the golfers watched the flight of the ball as though fascinated that one could be so far off course, as though they were viewing some sort of comet which might never again be visible in their lifetimes. They all saw the ball strike a large rock far away at the bend of a ditch and bounce high and even farther to the right.

"Damn," coughed Tipton, "I've never seen anything...." His voice wheezed to silence.

"That musta gone clear to hell," Karns chided.

"Doctor Jensen noted, "That's over by old number twelve."

Abe Lowman mused, "I haven't been over there since...since they converted from eighteen holes to nine."

Braun said, "Prob'ly nobody else has either."

Pastor Glenn seemed to melt from his usual ebullient, outgoing personality. Quietly, he struck a second ball, topping it weakly down the middle about eighty yards. He turned to the cart and climbed in. When Porter joined him, he meekly asked, "Jesse, would you mind driving around that ravine and up the hill? I believe I can find that ball." Raising his voice so the others could hear, he added, "I don't think it actually went as far as some people seem to think it did!"

"Sure, Cal." Porter swung the cart in the direction of the errant drive.

Lowman called out after them, "Come on. Cal! "You'll never find that ball!"

Porter waved, "You guys go on. We'll just take a quick look around." He drove across the creek and up the incline of an old fairway deep in weeds. He stopped at the top of the rise where he could make out vestiges of an overgrown green and a sand bunker. They stepped out of the cart, and together the two men started carefully down over some large rocks where they thought Glenn's ball might have ended its journey.

"I'm sorry to waste your time, Jess," said pastor Glenn. I just got so pumped up by that one good drive on five that I actually lost my concentration, I guess. Actually, I hit this last shot just the way I always have."

"It's okay, Cal. It's hard to try something new and to be consistent. Needs practice." He was trying to ease Glenn's disappointment. He knew there was almost no chance of finding the ball, but he could give the pastor some moral support by searching for a few minutes.

They scrambled over the rocks and surveyed the area. On the hillside the recent hard rains had caused a heavy runoff, and large gullies had appeared. Pastor Glenn said, "I don't suppose we can find it. It's actually very muddy. The ball might even be buried."

Something caught Porter's eye and seized his mind like an electric shock. He moved to get a better view. Then he whispered, "Sweet Jesus!"

Almost instantly, Glenn swung around and said, "Jess, you really should not use the Lord's name in--"

Porter cut him off sharply. "Look, he said and pointed.

Only about ten yards away, from under a slab of mud, protruded, unmistakably, a human skeleton hand.

Porter realized immediately that this was not the hand of a department store mannequin.

"Sweet Jesus!" swore the stunned preacher.

The other golfers responded immediately to Porter's shouts, and all but Tipton and Braun proceeded to the place where he stood and Pastor Glenn knelt. Glenn had already uttered a brief prayer, but he remained kneeling because the strength had run out of his rotund body like juice from a plump peach.

Only one hand and wrist of the skeleton were visible. Apparently the body had lain under a collapsed earthen embankment for a long, long time. The recent heavy rains and runoff had eroded the ground over the hand, clearly exposing it and the wrist.

At the point where the hand showed, near the base of a hill below old number twelve green, the ground leveled out. Wallis and Lowman circled the high ground and drove up a slighter incline to the site, followed by Doctor Jensen and Jack Karns. Slim Braun, who was walking, and Tom Tipton, who tried to avoid exerting himself, waited on number six fairway, in Tipton's cart, about a hundred yards away.

Pastor Glenn now sat on the ground with his back to the exposed hand. Porter stood beside him, his arms folded, and stared in disbelief.

Wallis and Lowman arrived first. "What is it?" Ray called. "Is Glenn hurt?"

"No. He's okay. But you'll never believe this," Porter replied solemnly.

Lowman swore when he saw the hand. "I don't believe it. Damn, damn, and double damn!"

Wallis walked up close to the hand. "You found a real one this time, looks like," he said casually, then knelt for a closer inspection. "This is incredible! That's two in a week. What the heck is going on out here?"

When Wallis reached out to touch the long fingers, Porter cautioned him. "Better wait, Ray. This one looks real. The police won't want anything disturbed."

"Oh. Yeah. Of course. I wonder if there's a whole body to go with this hand. We'll prob'ly wind up lookin' like jerks again." The old-timer struggled to his feet and addressed Doctor Jensen, who had just pulled alongside.

"How long has it been there, Doc?"

The physician just shook his head. "Hard to say. When the body's fully uncovered, the lab people can tell us."

Wallis said, "I thought you could tell that kinda thing."

"Well, on TV they can, but all I can see is the remains of a hand, Ray, and it's nothing more than bone. It'll require tests to determine anything."

Karns said, "I wonder who it could be."

Doctor Jensen said, "Maybe the police can tell us." He pulled out his cell phone. "I'll call them."

Lowman said, "You gonna call the cops? Let's jist cover it up. We looked like dummies when Ray found that dummy."

"*When Ray found it?*" Wallis objected. "You were right there with me! I wasn't the only one thought it was a body!"

Porter said, "There's no doubt is there, Nate, that this is a human hand?"

Doctor Jensen shook his head. "It's real. No doubt."

"Well then, we have to call the police. Go ahead, Nate. I'll call Nancy and tell her what's going on. And someone needs to stay here until they come."

"I'll stay," Doctor Jensen said, and he began to call in his report.

"Me too," said Lowman.

"I'll stay, too," volunteered Pastor Glenn.

Wallis said, "Well, not me. The last time this happened, I was a laughing stock. This time I'm gonna finish my round. I'm not gonna miss another day of golf and look like a jackass jist 'cause *you guys* found a body. See you later."

Gabe Morrison, the same policeman who had waded into the muddy pond and dragged out the mannequin, arrived only a few minutes after receiving Doctor Jensen's call. This time his Chief came with him. They drove up close to the golf carts and the knot of men who awaited them. Slim Braun had joined the group while Tipton and Wallis went on.

The Police Chief surveyed them as he got out of the black and white. He spoke first to Nancy Grimsby, who had rushed over after receiving Porter's message. The Chief said, "You shouldn't be here, Nancy. No need for you to see this." He spoke as if he did not expect an answer.

"I think I should be," she said.

"Um. Okay." The Chief faced Porter. "I don't believe I've met you, mister."

Morrison said, "This is Jesse Porter, Gene. Remember, he's the golf pro I told you about."

Porter stuck out his hand and read the name tag on the Chief's shirt pocket. *Chief E. Still.* "Glad to meet you, Chief Still."

The officer grasped Porter's hand and pumped it firmly. "Oh yeah. I remember yesterday we had a missing person inquiry from your daughter."

Porter shrugged and laughed lightly. "That was a simple misunderstanding." He decided Still was about his own age. The Chief's hair was graying and full under his cap, which was tipped back on his head. His features were small and even. Strength of character and confidence showed in the way he carried himself. His gray eyes seemed to assess Porter's personality as well as his physical appearance.

"I've heard interesting things about you, Porter."

Jesse wondered if that was a reference to Larona. He said nothing.

Still nodded to Lowman and Karns. When he saw Pastor Glenn, he asked, "You okay, Reverend? You look kind of pale."

"Actually, I'm fine," replied Glenn

Still looked around. "How come you guys were up here? Nobody uses this hole anymore, do they?

Glenn said, "Actually, I--"

Porter jumped in, "I was trying to show these fellows a trick shot. I screwed up and hit it wrong. It was a brand new ball, and I thought maybe I could find it. I guess it's lost, though. No matter."

Chief Still eyed him warily. "Must be a heckofa trick."

"I'll practice and maybe show you sometime."

Still turned to Doctor Jensen. "What can you tell me, Doc?"

"Not much. We didn't want to uncover the body before you arrived."

Gabe Morrison said, "Mebbe there ain't a body under there. Mebbe the hand is all there is. Or mebbe it's another dummy." He laughed but nobody joined him.

Still said, "Get your shovel, Gabe, and call an ambulance. That'll be the best way to transport the remains. Tell them there's no rush."

To the others he said, "Stay back, fellas--and Nancy. We'll have to search the area for clues. I don't expect any though. This gent has been here for a long time, I expect."

"Can you tell it's a man?" asked Braun.

"No. I just assumed it." Still turned to Doctor Jensen. "Can you tell, Doc?"

"Not yet."

Before much dirt had been removed, Doyle Dugan drove up. He started taking photographs as he climbed out of his Bronco. "You old guys are really something, you know that? Two bodies in a week! How come nobody else around her finds bodies, Chief? That's your job, isn't it?"

Chief Still replied curtly, "Stay back there by your vehicle, Dugan. Out of the way."

Dugan kept approaching, ignoring the Chief's admonition. "Next week, you guys will probably find an extra-terrestrial or something. Who discovered this one, anyway?"

Chief Still tugged his cap down over his forehead and stepped in front of Dugan. "Okay, Dugan, since you don't seem to understand when I tell you to back up, I'm going to give you a scoop. These golfers here were down below, trying to hit trick shots, and when they finished, they came up here to pick up their balls. That's when they found the body. And that's when they called me. That's all there is to it. Now step back out of my way."

Dugan shrugged and stepped back.

Pastor Glenn caught Porter's eye and started to speak, but Porter shook his head and Glenn said nothing.

Two more black and whites had just arrived, and their occupants set up a perimeter for all others, including Dugan, to stay behind.

Chief Still carefully uncovered one whole arm. He motioned for Doctor Jensen to stand beside him and watch closely. The bones appeared to be intact. Remnants of shirt material fell away at a touch. Additional rotted fabric appeared. Soon it became evident that the body had been wrapped from knees to armpits in a rug.

"Looks like a man's wristwatch," Chief Still muttered as he carefully brushed mud and dirt from an encrusted wrist band. "It's an I D bracelet. Looks like turquoise and silver--so tarnished it's hard to...." Without removing the bracelet from the wrist, he turned it to look at the underside. "There's a name."

"What is it? What's the name?" cried Dugan.

"Shut up, Dugan. I'm not sure. It's really tarnished. Oh, it's initials." He added, "Looks like J P G. And more. L and S maybe."

Porter suggested, "Might be the initials of an Indian designer. We see lots of bracelets like that in New Mexico."

Doctor Jensen said, "The arm bones look pretty large for a woman. I'm guessing it's a man."

The Chief grunted and stood up. "This may be a lot more sensitive than I thought at first. Gabe, put up some more tape. I want good security for the site. Keep everyone out. I'm gonna call in the state police. They have specialists who can proceed with this matter much better than we can." He strode to the black and white and called his office on the radio.

Dugan followed quickly and photographed Still in the seat of his car as the Chief made his call.

"Aren't you going to dig him out? What's the name on the bracelet?"

"Still reached over and pulled the car door closed. Then, after he had finished with his radio call, he squinted at the reporter. "How did you get out here so fast, Dugan?"

"I happened to be at the hospital when Gabe called there."

"Yeah? Just my luck! Would you know where those hospital people are? They oughta be here by now."

"They were coming right after me. There," Dugan said, "Pointing at an approaching ambulance. They're coming up the hill."

"We won't be needing them other than to transport you to the hospital if you don't quit interrupting me and my people. We're not going to need any more help until the state police show up. Why don't you just shove off?"

Dugan frowned. "You keep changing the subject. A minute ago you used the word *'sensitive,'* Chief Still. What did you mean by that?"

"Just shove off, Dugan." The Chief got out of his car and walked toward the site where Gabe Morrison was erecting sturdier posts connected with yellow plastic tape brearing the words POLICE INVESTIGATION--KEEP OUT.

To the golfers he said, "There's nothing more for you fellows to see or do here. You might as well go on about your business. If we have questions for you, I know how to find you."

Dugan circled the Chief until he stood face to face with him. "Why did you say this matter might be sensitive?" he repeated. "The public has a right to know. What if I write that you refuse to cooperate with the press?"

The Chief almost smiled. "If you do that, I might have to shake your hand, and you might not be able to type for six weeks."

"Very funny."

The Chief stepped toward him, and Dugan spun away and rushed to his car. There he immediately started reciting what he had seen into a small handheld microphone. After a few moments, he revved up his Bronco and raced back toward the road he had come up.

Abe Loman said, "What did he mean, Chief?"

Still exhaled wearily. "I just don't want to give that two-bit Dugan anything. But--Do any of you guys remember about fifteen or twenty years back, a guy with initials L and S, like are on that bracelet, he suddenly disappeared? No one had a clue about him. Does that ring a bell?"

"I remember something like that," Doctor Jensen said. "But I don't recall any rumors about murder."

"Well," Still said, "I'm trusting you guys to keep quiet about this for a few days, but unless I miss my guess, that fellow over there didn't crawl under that hillside by himself."

For dinner, Porter prepared a guacamole spread to add to hamburgers. He chopped two avocados and some onion, mashed them, and added lime juice to maintain the avacado's color. Often he had made guacomole for Patricia when she was a youngster, and he knew it had been a favorite. It occurred to him that someday he should make some for Larona, too. He decided he would surprise her with it someday.

Porter was the one who was surprised, however. When Patricia came home from work, he noted that Doyle Dugan parked behind her in the driveway and followed her through the front door.

"Hi, Daddy," she said happily. "You know Doyle, don't you?"

"Sure. Hello again." Porter shook the younger man's hand. It was like holding an empty glove.

"Doyle just told me about the body you found," exclaimed Patricia. "Good grief! That must have been gruesome!"

"Yes, it was a new experience for me, for sure."

Dugan said, "It's getting to be an old experience, I'd say. You and those old geezers found that mannequin a week ago, and now you--"

Porter bristled at the expression but said calmly, "You shouldn't refer to those fellows that way. They are fine men."

"Fine men?" Dugan cackled derisively. "Except maybe for Doc Jensen they don't contribute anything to the community. They dress like it was Halloween. Their golf is so--"

Patricia cut in. "Oh he didn't mean that, Dad." She frowned silently at Dugan as though warning him to be quiet.

"I'm sure he didn't," said Porter. "You need to understand, Dugan, that they are honest, good guys. They've worked hard all their lives, contributing to the community, and I resent the degrading labels you stuck on them just because they've survived a lot of years." His voice hardened as he added, "And what's more, they are friends of mine."

"Sorry about that, said Dugan indifferently. "Uh, I've been intending to come over and meet you, Jess. Trish tells me lots about you. Now, after today's adventure, I can't wait any longer. I'd like to know--"

"Is this going to be an interview for your paper?"

"Well, I'd like to get to know you, and now, since you used to be a sort of minor celebrity, and today I guess we need to get some more information about finding the body, so, yeah," he grinned, "I guess we can call it a interview. Okay? Is that a problem?"

"I've been wanting to meet you, too, for a couple of days. You're Trish's friend, and I had hoped you'd show up as a friend rather than a reporter."

Dugan made a face and waved the pen he was holding. "Huh? What's going on here? You got something against me?"

Porter said, "I'd like to like you because you're my daughter's friend, but frankly, Dugan, I think you have a poor attitude. I think you should show people more respect. I also noticed that the Police Chief doesn't seem to like you, for some reason."

Patricia put her hand on Dugan's shoulder as though to hold him in check. "Come on, fellas, I don't want you to get off on the wrong foot." She tried to change the subject. "Is that guacamole I see in the kitchen, Dad?"

"Yes," Porter said icily. He turned away and sat down. "If I overreacted, I apologize."

Chief Still is just a hard-ass," Dugan complained.

"Listen, Dugan, you know as much as I do about that body. Probably more. I just prefer not to see my name in the news relating to someone's murder, for crying out loud. What do you know about the victim anyhow? Sanford? If that's who it is."

"Sanford! Is that who Still told you it is? What's the first name?" Dugan almost shouted. "I knew that old cop was holding back on me."

"That's all I heard. One of the guys. I don't know who said what. I shouldn't have mentioned it."

"That's okay, Jess. The Chief probably hasn't confirmed it was Sanford yet, but you can bet it was. Still isn't the kind of guy who would use a name if he had any doubt about it." The young man frowned. "Sometimes the Chief acts like a jerk, but he's very cautious, I'll admit. Wonder why he told you?"

Patricia asked, "Who is Sanford?"

"Must have been a real bastard," said Dugan. "He was before my time in Clydeston. I haven't had an opportunity to research him yet, of course, but I've heard people at the newspaper mention his name. They say he was into drugs, gambling, anything to make a buck. Built a nightclub. Got involved in a real estate development that folded and hurt a lot of people around here, financially, I mean. And nobody knows where his start-up money for all those ventures came from."

"Do you think he was really murdered?" asked Patricia.

"Must have been," Dugan nodded. "I just caught a glimpse today before Chief Still chased me off. Looked like he was wrapped in a rug. It was dirty and faded, you know, but it looked like an Indian or Mexican design. He just disappeared one night and nobody seemed to know anything at all. Folks at my paper said Mexicans probably did it."

"Mexicans?" she echoed.

"Drug smugglers maybe." Dugan shrugged. "Shouldn't take long to confirm the ID. There may be military records. Dental records and such. A day or two at most. But the I D bracelet is enough for me now. It'll make a good story."

"Will you be the one to write it?" Porter asked.

"Yeah. Probably. Already did today's. But it's real brief because there wasn't much time. Just an announcement like. Have a lot more info for tomorrow. What you told me really helps. That's what readers like. Maybe some of your old golf buddies could help, you think?"

Porter ignored the question, and the two men sat quietly for a minute.

Satisfied that they would not come to blows right away, Patricia went to the kitchen to finish dinner preparations.

"You all ready for next week's big golf affair, Jess?" Dugan asked. "I understand you will be the main attraction."

"The Harrison House fund-raiser? Yes. I need to practice at the Country Club though. I hope to be ready."

"I guess you know, word has it you and Larona Starr have become quite an item."

Porter stiffened as he felt resentment of the reporter rising again. "An item? What is that supposed to mean?"

Dugan shrugged. "Well, apparently you're seeing her every day. She got you into the Harrison House thing." He grinned. "You know how people talk. She has some reputation. Would you care to offer comments, Jess?"

"Some people like to talk about things that are none of their business."

Dugan gestured aimlessly and leaned back in the big recliner. "Ah, Jess, everything is the business of newsmen. Especially in a small town." He grinned as though enjoying a private joke. "You know, word also has it that Larona and Lenny Sanford were an item those ages ago. Before the old man died, maybe. Not sure about that. Old Clarence--he was so much older than Larona that she very likely had to look around for some younger action." With a laugh, he challenged Porter. "What do you think of that?"

"What I think--" Porter choked off his reply. He rose slowly and stepped to the archway where could see Patricia in the kitchen. "I made enough dinner for two, Trish."

"Yes, Dad, I saw that. I'm just adding--"

"You and Mister Jerk can have it. I'm going out."

Earlier in the day--before the excitement at the golf course, Porter had called Larona and said he'd be in touch later. Now he wanted to talk with her and ask about Dugan's accusations regarding Lenny Sanford. But he knew he should cool off first.

Driving down Central Avenue, he approached the midsection of Clydeston. At a stoplight, he noted that the city library was on a corner across the street. He decided he might well spend a few minutes there. Perhaps he could learn something about all the questions rattling around in his head.

He pulled into the parking lot adjacent to the big stone building. On the front door a sign indicated that the library would be open for another two hours.

Inside, a pert young librarian greeted him. She wore large horn-rimmed glasses and a wide smile. Per his inquiry, she led him to an alcove near the back of the main floor. There she showed him a wall of shelves that contained cartons of microfische of *The Clydeston Times* going back many years. She turned on a boxy gray machine into which she inserted a plastic sheet from one of the cartons. A magnified image of the sheet appeared on a large screen in front of Porter. When she was satisfied that he understood how to work it, she left him and returned to the front counter.

Porter looked at the cartons. He realized that he didn't know where to start. He remembered that Nancy Grimsby said Lowman's son had returned from Iraq before the end of hostilities. Also he had the impression that Clarence Starr died in the nineteen nineties or very soon after. Maybe he could find something that would help cue him closer to the dates he needed. Arbitrarily, he plucked out a packet dated March, 1968. As he put a sheet into the machine, he thought he might as well search for a small needle in a large barn full of hay. Nevertheless, he would look for a few minutes.

The viewing screen on the machine displayed the front page of *The Clydeston Times* for March 1, 1968. After scanning the headlines for a few seconds, he twirled the dial at the side of the machine. The images on the screen blurred by until he stopped to look at another front page.

This is dark ages stuff, he thought. *All about Vietnam. Why couldn't they have this material indexed and computerized? Probably no one did that for little one-horse newspapers. Who would ever look it up other than some dummy who is infatuated with a millionairess, some dummy who cannot get along with his wonderful daughter, some dummy who is broke and tired....*

He kept turning the dial and pausing occasionally to scan headlines. They were dusty and smelled musty.

As might be expected, he found almost daily references to Starr of the Prairie Pharmaceutical Company. They were mostly brief articles about personnel promotions or stories of general interest to the community or announcements of honors accorded to Clarence Starr by medical and pharmaceutical organizations. He identified Clarence Starr in photographs that accompanied the stories. Starr had been a tall and distinguished gentleman with a small white moustache. He gave the impression of being very friendly. There was nothing about Larona.

Then he began to find stories announcing the development of a new residential addition called Walnut Acres. Tom Tipton's name and the name of his company, Tip Top Realty, appeared frequently. He was president of the corporation promoting the development. There were many advertisements for prospective home buyers. From the descriptions, Porter recognized that Walnut Acres was the area that now encircled the Country Club golf course. Interesting coincidence, he thought.

He found three long interviews with Tipton and detailed plans for the development. Only once did the name of Leonard Sanford appear. But there it was. Tipton was referred to as a "partner."

Then the big headline came up. Tip Top realty was insolvent, unable to pay construction costs. Receivership loomed.

Porter pushed his chair back from the machine. He removed his glasses and blinked to rest his eyes from half an hour's squinting. He told himself he had been lucky to find anything at all with this mode of research, and he decided he would do better to pursue this subject with Tipton himself, if Tipton would discuss it.

Of course, what he really had wanted to find was something pertaining to Larona. *No*, he told himself, he had *not* wanted to find anything about her, and that was what had happened. But he had only scratched the surface. It would take many hours to pore through all these sheets of data. He wasn't patient enough to undertake that right now. Maybe later.

He replaced the carton he had been using last and turned off the machine. Once outside, on the front steps, he punched Larona's number on his cell phone.

After a moment, she spoke. "Hello, Jess."

The sound of her voice electrified him. God, he thought, how could he get along without this woman? "Hi, Sweetheart! I told you I'd call. When would be a good time to come over?"

"Oh, Jess," she said. Then she lowered her voice as though someone else might be present. "Jess, dearest, something has come up. It's business."

"You're tied up, then?"

"For a while. You see, we license a product from a Swedish company, and some of their people have arrived unexpectedly. So we have to meet with them this evening. They may be here through the weekend. We'll have meetings--"

"I'm sorry if I interrupted you."

"Im sorry, too, but I mean because I'm tied up." She lowered her voice again. "Why don't you come over to the house? You can be there when I finish later. We're going to my office after dinner. I'll surely be home by midnight."

He was sorely tempted. He was also rankled by the feeling that he was sneaking around with her. "Maybe we should skip it tonight."

"You know I'd like to see you."

"You'll be tired, Sweetheart. I'll be in touch."

He wanted to mention finding the body, wanted to mention Sanford's name, wanted to hear her reaction. But he knew he must be able to discuss the matter at length, not in a hurried phone conversation. It needed to be face to face. Also, he feared to ask because he could not stand the thought of possible negative things he might learn.

"I'll miss you, dear," she said. "Good night" She hung up.

He'd miss her, too, he thought. Then he wondered if she really had a business meeting. *Swedes?* Could there really be *Swedes* dropping in unannouced? He had never met a Swede face to face! Then he wondered if she could have already heard about Sanford's body being found. She couldn't be connected with that! Maybe she was so upset about it that she made up the excuse of being busy.

"Damn me!" he said aloud, "for even thinking such things! Damn!"

A teenage girl coming up the library steps gaped in surprise at his outburst but said nothing and passed him quickly.

"It's one o'clock. Let's play golf," said Ray Wallis.

Abe Lowman teed up without a word and prepared to hit away.

Jack Karns said, "Looks like Cal's not gonna make it today."

Porter nodded. "He was pretty shaken up when we found that body. He may not want to come out here again for a few days." He added, "Does anybody know if Tom Tipton will be here today?"

Nobody responded.

After teeing off, the golfers started down the fairway in two carts and with Slim Braun escorting his three-wheeler. Whenever they stopped for a shot, they talked. On the greens, they paired off and talked. There was much more conversation today than usual. Their comments dwelt on the corpse they had found. It seemed to be drawing out personal memories and feelings never before deemed suitable for open discussion with these taciturn men.

Karns said, "The Pastor is a good man, of course, but he's a little effeminate sometimes, you know. I'm not surprised he was so queasy about the remains."

Braun offered mild support for Pastor Glenn. "Listen, that was enough shock to upset anyone. You don't expect to find a damned skeleton on the golf course of all places!"

"It didn't make Jess sick, "Wallis observed. He looked at Porter.

Jesse shrugged. He did not wish to be drawn into the middle of an argument.

"I wonder," said Lowman, "'if Glenn was upset fer some other reason."

"What do you mean?" asked Karns.

"Well, we all know that body was Lenny Sanford, don't we?"

"Chief Still hasn't said for sure."

"You can bet it was Sanford," Lowman insisted.

"So what if it was?" asked Braun. "What's that got to do with Glenn?"

"I seem to remember he was preaching in Clydeston in the days when Sanford disappeared. And then he left town shortly afterward. He got some holey-moley call from God. To go to another church," he said.

"You think Cal Glenn is guilty of something like murder?" Braun chortled, "Com'on, Abe. Be serious!"

"Well, that might explain why he buckled like he did, wouldn't it?"

Karns said, "Hell, Abe, if he knew that skeleton was there, he never would have gone over to that area looking for a golf ball, would he? Doesn't make sense. Do you know if Cal ever had trouble with Sanford?"

"Not fer sure, but lots of folks in Clydeston had run-ins with the guy. He was a no-good bastard, and he had that nightclub that a lot of people didn't like. He was into lots of scams that most people don't know nothin' about."

Braun nodded. "That's right. The big problem back then was over that Walnut Acres Addition. Hell, I lost money on a lot that we tried to buy. Lots of other people did, too."

Wallis chimed in. "That's right all right."

Porter asked, "What was Sanford's part in that?"

"It was his brainchild as I understand it," Braun explained. "He got some folks together--monied people--and promoted it. He claimed he had money himself, but he didn't. Except what he collected from dummies like me. The project went belly up. Then Sanford disappeared. Nobody ever seemed to know exactly what happened to him."

"Until now," Karns added.

Wallis said, "Tom was in on that deal. In fact, it was promoted through his real estate company. I'll bet he knows things that were never told."

They all fell silent for a moment, and Porter asked, "Tom Tipton?" He was reluctant to say that he had spent time in the library already, studying Tipton's part in the project. He didn't know why his curiosity had been aroused. There was a vague uncertainty gnawing at him, and it transcended the mere identity of the skeleton he had found.

Karns said, "Yeah, he had the biggest real estate business in town. He was the principal agent for the development--the front man. When it flopped, he lost everything he had."

"He lost his ass, all right," agreed Wallis. "He hasn't been the same since--all these years!"

"But Tipton wasn't accused of anything crooked, was he?" asked Porter.

Braun said, "Nah, just bad judgment for hooking up with a rat like Sanford. Basically, people figured Tom was honest. You have to give him credit, too, because he didn't cut and run. He stayed in Clydeston and kept slugging it out ever since. He tried to pay off lots of us suckers out of his own pocket."

"Remember when we found the body?" Lowman asked. "Tom didn't even come over t'look. Mebbe he wasn't surprised it was there."

"Oh hell, Abe! He has emphysema! It would have been a great exertion for him to climb around there. I don't think he's physically capable of doing it," said Karns.

"Well, mebbe," muttered Lowman.

Wallis said, "Remember, we don't really know for sure it's Sanford's body."

Lowman scoffed. "I'll bet it is! What's more, I'll bet his money is buried around there somewhere, too."

Braun laughed. "The old story about drug money? Com'on, Abe! You're getting carried away with all this stuff!"

"Com'on, Abe! Com'on, Abe! Is that all you guys can say?" The little man defended himself with increasing heat in his voice. "Don't laugh at me, Slim! Everybody has said it, for years, that Sanford ran off with dough from both the real estate deal and proceeds from his night club. There's too much strong opinion to ignore, man! Where there's smoke, there's fire, baby! It has t'be at least partly on fact."

"Wait a minute," Karns interrupted. "I can tell you something about that."

"What?" Lowman said. "What do you know?"

"Well.... Maybe I shouldn't have said that." Karns hesitated. "Y'know, I'm an accountant. Used to be anyhow. I had a moonlighting job for Sanford at the club." His voice dropped with this statement. "I've always kept this quiet, but...I did some bookkeeping for him."

Wallis responded with astonishment. "You're kidding! You mean you actually worked for Sanford?"

"Yeah."

"Man alive!" Wallis laughed. "I didn't know that! Ol' Clarence Starr would have trussed you up by the short hairs if he had known it!"

"Well, there wasn't much chance of that. Clarence had already died before I ever worked there. And I worked there only a very short time. But I want you guys to know that I saw a lot of Sanford's books and they were square. There wasn't any pile of dough for him to take."

"Hell, Jack," said Lowman. "If he had hot money, he wouldn't put it on the table where you could find it!"

"Listen, I'm a damned good accountant! *Was* anyhow. I could--"

Porter tried to intervene and cool the exchange. "What's this business about Clarence Starr? What was his relationship with Sanford?"

"Oh, all this happened years ago, Jess. You probably don't know what we're talking about," explained Wallis. "Sanford showed up and built a nightclub between Clydeston and Wichita. Called it The Pretty Kitty. It was a wild place, they tell me. I was there only once. Illegal booze, of course, and there was talk about drugs and illegal gambling. There could have been whores or anything, for all I know.

"Now, Ol' Clarence Starr was a heaven-bound teetotaler, and he tried every which way to keep Sanford from building that club. But he didn't have much success, and he was dying. He and Sanford only overlapped for a couple of years, and, boy! Clarence truly hated that man!"

"That's not all," offered Braun. "There was some talk about Sanford and Larona Starr."

At the mention of her name, Porter tensed but tried to show no emotion.

"There's nothing to that," said Karns. "Hell, she was probably fifteen years older than Sanford. Mebbe more."

Braun shrugged. "Not that much, I'd say. You never know about people. Did you see that turquoise bracelet on the skeleton's bony wrist? Remember, 'there are more things in heaven and earth, Horatio, than are dreamt of in your philosophy.'" Karns squinted at Braun. "What's that supposed to mean? What are you talking about?

"Nothing maybe, but Larona Starr wears--"

Porter interrupted. "Lots of western people wear Indian jewelry."

"Sure. But Sanford was from New Jersey originally. I doubt you see lots of people from New Jersey--men especially--wearing Indian jewelry."

"I guess we won't ever know fer certain," said Wallis.

Karns offered, "Almost everybody in Clydeston had a bone to pick with Sanford. He stared hard at Lowman.

Abe said, "Why are you lookin' at me like that?"

Karns raised his eyebrows but said nothing.

"I see." Lowman said, "I know what you're thinkin'. You think I had as good a reason as anyone for doin' in that sonofabitch." He poked his three iron hard into the ground and swore. "Well, you're right about one thing. I hated that bastard! All these years, I thought he had escaped. But now I can say I'm glad the bastard is dead!" Lowman spoke with a fury which surprised Porter. The little man had never given evidence before that he was so filled with hatred.

"Look, Abe," Karns said, softly now, "I didn't mean--"

Lowman cut him off. "That's all right, Jack. I'll probably hear the same thing from other folks when they find out Sanford has been in the ground out here all these years."

He turned to Porter. "Jess, these guys know what Sanford did to me.

At least, part of it. But you don't, so I'll just tell you what Jack was talking about."

Porter raised his hands as though to defend himself against the heat in Lowman's scorching words. "You don't have to tell me anything, Abe."

"That's all right." He took a deep breath and readied himself to tell his story. Then it poured out in a cathartic deluge. "My son James was in the army in Iraq. I had two sons. James was the only one who had to go to Iraq. He came home in ninety-two. He had gotten a leg wound and a purple heart, so they sent him home. At the time we thought that was lucky. But mebbe he'd have been better off if he had stayed over there and hid in the sand, the way things turned out.

"You see, shortly after he came home, this guy Sanford showed up. Jamie had known him in Iraq. We accepted Sanford like a son at first 'cause he and Jamie were close, closer than my two sons were to each other.

"Well, Jamie got a job with S O P. They wanted to train him in some specialty sales, and they sent him away to take some special courses in Texas. So he was gone a lot.

"That turned out to be a bad deal, 'cause while Jamie was gone, Sanford was supposed to watch out for Jamie's girl friend. Her name was Jenny. Before long, Jenny was more Sanford's girl than Jamie's.

"You heard how Sanford had been involved in this real estate deal in Clydeston and how he started up this damned nightclub. I'm sure it was all financed by drug money and that he had connections back east--God knows where. He was probably dealin' before he left Iraq. Mebbe even before he went there. Who knows?

"Anyhow, Jamie finally had a bellyful of his so-called friend, and they had it out. Jamie whipped Sandford's ass one night. Then two days later, a gang of guys--strangers--they beat up Jamie--nearly killed him."

Lowman choked as he went on, and his face clouded with his hatred. "They left him paralyzed. He could hardly talk. He was like a vegetable." Lowman shook his head in frustration, anger, and sorrow. He clubbed his three iron hard on the ground and twisted it.

Wallis put a hand on his shoulder, but the little man shook it off.

"He was all broke--The doctors said he couldn't never get no better. Never. And nobody could find the bastards who did it to him. I knew Sanford was responsible, but the cops couldn't prove it. Tears ran down

Lowman's leathery face, but he didn't wipe them. He just gripped his golf club, clenching and unclenching his hands.

After a moment, he continued. "About a month after the beating--one night--Jenny came t'the hospital and took Jamie out. Hell, he was a total invalid. Nobody knows how she got him out of the hospital, but she did it. She took him out and put him in her car. Then she drove out of town. North. She smashed the car into the concrete wall of the turnpike overpass three miles out of town. They hit that wall at a hunnerd miles an hour."

"Damn," Porter muttered softly.

"She put Jamie out of his misery, at least. And she went with him." The group remained silent. They had no heart for further conversation or golf after Lowman's story.

The little man seemed even smaller and older than before he had spilled out the tale. At last he said, "I can't play no more. I'm goin' back in."

Wallis said, "Me neither. Com'on. I'll take you, Abe."

As those two rode back toward the pro shack, Karns said, "I wouldn't blame Abe if he had killed the sonofabitch."

"He didn't," Braun said simply. He was with Doc Jensen the last evening Sanford was seen."

"How do you know that?" asked Porter.

"Oh, it was one of the very first things that came out when Sanford's disappearance was investigated. Hell, Abe was a natural suspect because of the beating his son had received. I remember all the talk that went on at the time, that's all. You see, Jamie got beat up, then Jamie and the girl died, then Sanford disappeared. All within a few weeks. Bing, bing, bing." It was like everybody knew what happened, but nobody saw anything. Nobody could prove anything."

They all fell silent for a moment. Then Karns asked, "Do you guys want to go on?"

"Not really," Braun said. "It's too hot anyway."

Porter shook his head. "Climb onto the seat, Slim. No need for you to walk back."

Braun loaded his little cart on the back and then crowded onto the seat with the other two men.

"Abe has another son, right?" Porter asked.

"Yeah," Karns said. "Robert. He lives in Wichita."

"If you're thinking he had anything to do with Sanford's death," said Braun, "you can be sure he was checked out at the time. He had at least a dozen people swear he was working at the time Sanford was last seen. Iron-clad alibi. He has a fast food franchise in Wichita."

"I see."

"Abe said that Robert is in pretty deep financial trouble with that operation," Karns added. "Abe tries to help, but he's not in a position to do much. He worries about that boy a lot."

"That must be pretty miserable for him," said Porter. "Sometimes you don't know how small your own problems are compared with those of someone else."

Braun said, "'Rather makes us bear those ills we have than fly to others we know not of.'"

Porter wasn't in the mood for Braun's quotations, but he managed a polite chuckle. "I know that one, Slim, and I believe you're a little out of context."

"You're right," acknowledged Braun. He tried to lighten the subject. "Did you ever think, Jess, that ol' Hamlet was probably too indecisive to play golf? He wasn't like you."

Porter went back to Patricia's place, showered, shaved, and dressed. He put on a white sports shirt and a lightweight blue jacket. For a long time he stood before the mirror, thinking about the image he saw there. He wanted to look sharp for Larona this evening. He seldom wore a tie, and he wondered if he should. What would she like? Pleasing her was important to him, but he was concerned that he might be bending to her every whim. She was a powerful woman, used to having her way with all sorts of people. Was she merely infatuated with him? Was she using him somehow, merely to satisfy some personal desire, as Trish suspected? Was she so taken by art and fashion of the Southwest that he even wondered if she might merely consider him a novelty from New Mexico? How could they be sure of developing a long-lasting, solid relationship in which they could share their feelings equally?

He sighed. The guy in the mirror wasn't going to tell him anything he didn't already know. Deciding against a tie, he chose a large turquoise bola. He knew she would like that. He pulled off the jacket. Too warm this afternoon. He would take it with him though. This evening, when he saw Larona again, he could wear it if they went out.

He prepared a pot of coffee in the kitchen. While he waited for it, his mind turned to the questions surrounding the dead fellow, Sanford.

Clydeston must have been really hopping when Sanford was operating here. Lots of new construction. Starr of the Prairie Pharmaceuticals must have been booming, and the Walnut Acres project was going on. Strange how most of the people Porter had met here--several at least--seemed to have had some involvement with Sanford. It might be interesting to try to untangle some of those old relationships. Sort out what really happened. If he were a detective, it would be a natural challenge, he thought. Of course, it had all been explored back at the time of Sanford's disappearance. Carefully explored by professionals. Not much left for an inexperienced amatueur and over-the-hill golfer to uncover at this late date.

There was one area he did want to investigate, however. Slim Braun had gotten Porter's attention when he said there had been talk about Sanford and Lanora Starr. That nettled him, disturbed him. Right now, that was more important than who did the fellow in.

The coffee smelled great and tasted almost as good as it smelled. Between sips, Porter picked up his phone and found Braun's number. Slim answered right away, and Porter told him he'd like to have him help prepare for the golf exhibition the next week. Slim agreed without hesitation. "Country club, tomorrow. See you there. Ten o'clock."

Then he called Larona at her office. She suggested that he come there and then, when she finished, they could go on to dinner.

Hearing her voice gave him a greater lift than did the coffee.

He wrote a note for Patricia, picked up the blue jacket, and left.

It was a few minutes before five when Porter arrived at S O P. Earlier than yesterday's meeting. But already, swarms of employees were emptying out of the buildings as he entered a parking area.

He thought he had put his concerns of the previous day to rest. But now, once again, he felt conspicuous, wondering if, surely by today, they all must recognize him as Larona's lover.

A greeter met him inside the front entrance and immediately led him to an elevator and then up to Larona's suite of offices on the third floor. There, a secretary named Betty Lou met him, seated him, and hurried to Larona's office to announce his presence.

Within seconds, Larona emerged from one of three glass-fronted rooms on the right. She greeted him with both hands extended before her and he held them tightly. She wore a fitted business suit, but it failed to diminish her femininity. He wanted to kiss her but refrained, thinking of the office protocol, her position, and the general nature of their relationship. All these things precluded such activity. He simply said, "Hi."

Larona said "Hi" and gave him a devastating smile.

He grinned and looked toward Betty Lou. She, too, was smiling, almost laughing, and she turned away to busy herself with some papers.

"I'm still tied up, Jess," Larona said. "It'll be just a few more minutes. I have a couple of FDA inspectors in my office with some of our manufacturing people. When you called, I thought I'd be free by now. Sorry. You won't mind waiting here, will you? You've met Betty Lou, haven't you? She can help if you need anything." She then turned away and hustled back to her office and closed the door.

"Won't you have a seat, Mister Porter?" Betty Lou offered. Her blue eyes danced as though she understood everything that was going on.

Porter picked up a magazine and impatiently thumbed through it. After a few minutes, he stood up and moved across the room to Betty Lou's desk.

She looked up. "Yes?"

"I thought perhaps you might answer a few questions for me. If you're not too busy?"

"I'll be happy to, if I can," she responded.

"Well, for one thing, I wonder how long you've known Missus Starr."

"Oh, a long time. I started to work here just a few weeks after she did."

"Wow! That must have been--do you mean you've been working with her all this time, like, not in some other department?"

Betty Lou smiled. "That's right." She held up one hand with her fingers crossed.

"I would like to know--I simply do not know how this company got so big so fast. How did it happen?"

"Many people ask that," Betty Lou replied. "Indeed our growth has been sensational."

Porter waited for her to go on.

She said, "I've always thought of it like this. First, Clarence's father, Edward Starr, was a genius in my opinion. Nothing would ever have happened without him. It all started nearly a hundred years ago. Edward ran his little pharmacy in Dodge City. That's where Clarence grew up. Father had homemade remedies for everything, and son sold them, starting at an early age. As soon as he could drive, he sold pharmaceuticals far and wide. He could sell anything to anybody. There was an old expression. They said he could talk a hound dog off a meat wagon." She laughed. "We don't see many meat wagons these days.

"Second, when U S Representative Farnsworth's wife--a person of vast wealth and a heavy smoker--when she ran out of the Starr's cough medicine, she and her husband invited, or perhaps *demanded*, that the Starrs come to Clydeston and re-invent that cough medicine. They brought Edward Starr here, gave him a ton of money and the necessary buildings and the educated helpers he needed to do the job." He synthesized the active ingredient that had made the cactus-version so effective.

"Clarence came along of course.

"Third, Representative Farnsworth managed to get everything Edward Starr created into U S government facilities. Big wartime contracts. Every base. Every P X. Every ship. Every hospital. Every agency. Every embassy. Most likely, into the White House even. You name it! That really secured the foundation that got S O P started.

"Fourth, Larona Starr came on board! With her natural charm and imagination she ran the marketing and advertising departments like nobody else ever did before or after."

"Ah!" Porter interjected. "That's what I want to hear about."

Betty Lou looked at her watch. "She'll likely be here any minute, I'll just give you a quick example."

"This is fabulous. I really appreciate it."

"It's fun for me, too," she said, "to recall these things.

"Okay" she continued. "I guess you have heard of *Koff-Off*, our first significant product. It came from a cactus plant and an Indian medicine man."

"Yes. That's what the old lady, Missus Farnsworth, wanted, right?"

"Right. Well, what Larona Starr did was simple. She made up slogans for it. Like *Koff-Off for Kids*. Simple. *But extremely memorable!*

"Then she found half-a-dozen terrific young artists who painted wonderful, beautiful western scenes--mountains, forests, lakes, *et cetera*. She hired them to paint pictures and include little children as herders for flocks of young goats. Indian children with young antelopes."

"I don't understand."

"Ah, baby goats and antelopes are *kids*"

Porter frowned. Okay, so--" He brightened. "You had a slogan *KOFF-OFF for KIDS*. Is that it?"

"Exactly."

"But--so what?"

"Just think about this: Almost every school in this nation has a nurse's office...."

He nodded. "So?"

"Well, nowadays, on the walls of most of those offices, hangs one or more wonderful reproductions of paintings of children--kids and animals--*kids*. And a high percentage of pediatricians have them, too. They love those beautiful, *free* pictures of kids and *kids*. Terrific reminders."

"Got it! All these nurses and doctors like the pictures, so they recommend *KOFF-OFF for KIDS*. Is that ethical?"

"Nobody forces them to make recommendations. And our sales people really love this program because nurses and doctors welcome them. Gives each side a chance to get acquainted with the other side. Everybody's happy."

He shook his head. "I'm not sure I fully understand. But it it works?"

"Oh it works!" Betty Lou laughed.

"Thanks, Betty Lou. I appreciate your explanations. Oh, I also wanted to ask about that photo over there." He pointed across the hallway. "Is that a photo of Clarence Starr?"

She stepped around her desk and stood beside him. "Yes. If you're really interested, we have an extensive display of company photos in the boardroom."

Porter said, "Sure. Why not?"

Betty Lou led him a few yards down the hall and opened a door into a large, dark, walnut-panelled room. She flipped on lights. A long oval table filled the center of the floor, surrounded by fourteen heavy chairs with green fabric and large brass studs. There were no windows.

"There," she said, pointing to a side wall, which was covered with many photos in neat, black frames.

But Porter was looking at the far end of the room, at a very large oil painting of the comany's founder.

"Very impressive portrait. Handsome old fellow, wasn't he?"

"Yes," Betty Lou agreed. "Mister Starr. Clarence. But he had a larger nose than the portrait shows. It flatters him, I think."

Porter laughed. She said, "Really, he did. Most old men seem to have large noses, you know. That's because in old age, the fat in the face disappears. The skin sags, so cheekbones appear relatively more prominent. You can notice it in women, too."

At a loss for words, Porter chuckled and said, "If you say so. I had never thought about it."

"I learned it from a portrait painter who said he always made allowances for that." She smiled. "You may wait here for Missus Starr if you wish. I'll tell her where you are."

"Thank you very, very much. I think I will."

She started to leave but paused. "You're a good friend of hers, aren't you, Mister Porter?"

"I like to think so, yes."

"Good. I've been with her for all these years, and I know she needs friends. Most people don't really understand her. She's so wrapped up in business matters that she doesn't have many true--that is, *reliable* friends. I like your looks, Mister Porter. You act like an independent sort.... Well, I hope that you...." Her voice trailed off. "I talk too much sometimes."

"Not at all, Betty Lou. I'm very pleased to know that you are Larona's good friend, too."

"Thank you." She closed the door gently.

Porter turned again to the portrait. The old man's eyes were steely gray and seemed to follow everything in the room. There was a trace of a smile in the portrait, enough to make one think he'd like to have known

Clarence Starr, to have heard him speak. Aloud, he said, "You were good to Larona. I sure thank you for that, sir. Oh, my name is Jesse Porter. I used to be a golfer. Now I don't know what I am." He casually saluted. "You wouldn't mind if I look around, would you, Clarence?"

He turned to face the pictures on his right. There were six of them, all original paintings of western scenery. Each was about three feet by four feet. Each featured kids and *kids*. "Brilliant," he muttered, "and beautiful. No wonder people wanted them."

After a few minutes, he turned to the other wall. It must have held a hundred photos. He scanned them, pausing to study some more closely. They were in chronological order, with brief captions. Someone had spent a lot of time perfecting the display. Betty Lou, maybe.

The photos clearly revealed the growth of Starr of the Prairie Pharmaceutical Company, from a small drugstore on Clydeston's South Central Avenue and a large ugly brick building that Porter decided could have been the first workplace when operations began in Clydeston. Then they showed a huge network of larger brick-and-glass building with impressive laboratories and tall structures housing scores of offices. There were photos of Clarence Starr, employees, persons shaking hands, officials presenting awards, groups at banquets and picnics, and a few at other entertainments.

There was even one of Clarence Starr with several golfers. Porter studied it at length. He identified the background as the old municipal course where he played with the one-o'clock gang. It looked much better then than now. The caption confirmed the location. The occasion had been the grand opening of the course. He recalled that Clarence Starr had donated the land.

Going back over the group pictures, Porter thought he might be able to find a likeness of Wallis, Lowman, or someone else he had met. In one photo the old man had an arm around the shoulders of Jack Karns. The caption indicated that Karns had received a cash award for some cost-cutting procedure in the accounting department. Twenty years or more had changed Jack Karns' appearance drastically. Porter actually noticed the name in the caption before recognizing the face in the photo. "Good going, Jack," thought Porter. "I wonder if you know your picture is on this wall."

He stepped back and leaned against the conference table. Suddenly a thought crossed his mind. "I'll be darned," he said aloud.

"Why is that?" *Her* voice startled him.

He whirled and found Larona just inside the door.

"Hi! I didn't hear you come in'," he said happily.

"Why will you be darned?" she repeated.

He advanced, took her into his arms, and kissed her. "Oh, I just noticed that there is not a single photo of you here on this wall. You'd think that when we have the most beautiful lady in the world among us, we'd find at least one photo of her."

Larona made a sweeping gesture around the room. "I chose to leave it this way because it shows the history of the company up until Clarence died. It's like a visual history of his endeavors. A small tribute to him."

Porter nodded toward the Starr portrait. "He was a pretty good-looking fella."

Larona studied the portrait silently. Finally, she nodded and said, "Yes, but mostly he was bright and pleasant and fair minded. He had unbelievable energy until the end. The painter couldn't capture that. He built this company on the strength of personality." She laughed. "Of course it didn't hurt when Representative Farnsworth brought in some big government contracts. That gave him the financial leverage to expand and to establish a national marketing program."

She took a seat at the conference table. Reaching out for his hand, she said, "I'm so happy to see you. I'm sorry we couldn't get together last night. I missed you, Tsunami Man."

"Are you still meeting with the Swedes?"

"Swedes? Oh no. No, they're on their way to New York by now. We went through their business quickly and they decided to go on. Mercy, I've been so busy with other matters today, the Swedes seem like something that happened last week!"

"Have you heard my news?" Porter asked. "That is, the news from the golf course and what happened to me there yesterday?"

"Someone mentioned a death...a body was found. My word! Was that you?" She put her hand to her mouth in surprise. "Did *you* find it?"

He studied her. How could she not have heard about the incident? It must have swept through Clydeston like the wind. Could she really have been so busy yesterday--so out of touch? "Yes, I was with Pastor Glenn, and we stumbled onto a body buried on a hillside--probably many years ago. Apparently the heavy rain uncovered it."

"A body? Who--Has it been identified?"

Porter walked around the table and took a seat opposite her. "Not yet. At least not that I know of. But the common wisdom seems to think it's a fellow who disappeared from Clydeston years ago." Slowly and deliberately, he added, "A fellow named Lenny Sanford."

"Lenny San--" Larona sucked in her breath and again put her hand to her mouth. "Lenny Sanford! My god, Jess, I knew him!"

"That's what I heard."

"Wait a min--" She eyed him narrowly. "What does that mean?" Her voice hardened slightly. "What have you heard?"

"Only loose conversation. I heard he was a jerk, that he had no scruples, that he may have been in several dark activities. I heard that he may have crossed swords with Clarence Starr, and...."

"And?"

"And I heard that he was quite a lady's man. I heard he may have been especially friendly with you," Porter spoke flatly.

"So naturally you believe that he and I were lovers? Is that it?" Now Larona's anger flared and her voice tightened with emotion.

"No, that's not it. I don't know anything, one way or another. But I'm very curious." He raised both hands and gestured openly. "Dammit, Larona, I know practically nothing about you... about your past, really. But I've fallen hard for you. I think about you all the time. I want to be with you all the time. I want to trust you. I know only a few superficial things about you. I'm curious as hell when someone says anything about your past."

Larona took another deep breath and faced Porter squarely. Fully under control, she said, "He was an absolute swine. The first time we met, at a large party, he tried to bed me. We were attending a dinner party, and he made an obvious pass at me, right in front of Clarence. It made no difference to that lecherous gutter rat. We had to hold Clarence back and move away. Sanford just laughed.

"Clarence already knew him and hated him. Clarence was extremely sensitive on moral issues, as you can imagine. Worst part, he was already dying.

"Sanford just stood there and laughed as we walked away. He shouted comments that he and I had already had sex together. If I'd been able, I would have killed him that night. But I did not, not then or ever! I suppose some people chose to believe him. But I swear he lied! You'll never know how sick I am of rumors like that. They have gone on even after Clarence died. I've always been viewed as a fortune hunter by...people...people..." Her voice broke and she turned her face away.

After a moment, he asked softly, "Did Clarence have an investment in a real estate development that failed about that time, maybe a little later?"

Larona expressed astonishment. "My! You really have been digging into things, haven't you?"

"I keep hearing bits and pieces of stories that intrigue me."

"As a matter of fact, Clarence did have an interest in real estate. He acquired a lot of land around here. You've seen how much property S O P requires. But that was mostly a matter of purchasing. The only promotion he dealt with, as far as I know, was with a fellow named Thomas Tipton."

"I know him." Porter said.

"You do? How in the world--"

"I play golf with him."

"Amazing!. Well, anyway, when Clarence learned that Sanford was involved, he bailed out immediately."

"What was his role in that? Clarence, I mean, was he just buying a lot or a house, or was he a principal investor?"

Larona frowned. "I don't know. In those days, I wasn't involved in things like that."

"It seems to me that if Clarence Starr had a large investment in the development, he might have been motivated to--to *remove* Sanford."

She laughed. "You mean kill him?" Larona waved her hands as though eradicating the idea. "That's preposterous. Clarence would never have considered killing anyone! Not even that lowlife. He might have found ways though. I mean, if possible, ways to thwart him legally." She added, "If he had thought there was any hanky panky between me and Sanford--or me and anyone, for that matter--he would never have left S O P to me. He would have disowned me."

"There was nothing to it then."

"Of course not. One thing you do not seem to understand is that Clarence died several years--four or five--before Sanford disappeared. Also, she added emphatically, "Lenny Sanford was a boy. I was probably twenty years older than he. He was too--" She searched for words. "He was too *slick* for me." She shuddered slightly.

"I see."

After a moment, she said, "Clarence trusted me."

"Have I led you to think I don't?"

"You have asked a lot of insinuating questions."

"I'm sorry. It's not a matter of trust."

"What do you call it?"

"It is more like--like ignorance on my part. It's just as I told you. I really don't know you very well."

"I'd say you know me intimately."

"Oh, you sweet thing, you know what I mean."

"I have a feeling that we had this conversation last week. We keep going back over the same ground. I thought we settled these concerns."

"I'm sorry. When I'm away from you, I'm eager to be with you again. Then, when I'm with you, I just seem to sense these nagging--I just cannot bury my uneasiness about...something. I'm not sure what it is."

"About what?

He stood up and looked around the room. "I don't know if I can put it into words." He pointed at Clarence Starr's portrait and waved toward the wall of photographs. "Look around, Larona. This is a big, rich, powerful company. I'm not sure I belong here. Heck, I wasn't even sure how to dress when I came here this afternoon. I'm just an ordinary old guy with a day-to-day kind of job--if I still have it."

She laughed. "I'm sure you still have it. Or your boss is an utter idiot."

Ignoring her comment, he continued. "On the other hand, you're a rich, beautiful, highly regarded pillar of the community. How can I expect to get along in your world? I don't want to become *Mister* Larona Starr."

"Oh, Jess, you big dope," she said, "I love you."

"I feel very strongly about you, too."

She repeated, with emphasis, "I love you."

"Yes, I believe you may...."

"Don't you love me?" she asked.

"I feel very--You are very dear to me."

She frowned. "Don't you *love* me?"

"Wait a minute. I didn't say that. It's just that love is a very special condition. I've been in love. I had a wonderful wife and we both knew what love means. It implies trust, which you were talking about a minute ago. And it implies a commitment. If I say I'm in love, that means, to me, that that condition takes precedence over everything else. Everything else becomes secondary to the relationship."

"That's wonderful," Larona said softly. "It's beautiful. That's how I feel. Even with this 'big company' that you keep referring to, that's how I feel. The company is secondary, Jess."

"Oh it can't be, Larona. I can't ask you to put all this behind you." He waved a hand at the wall of photos. "Just think how many people depend on you. If I say I love you, I have to join you, be with you, be part of all you do. I just don't think I can do that. I don't have the S O P know-how. And I see now it would be too much for you to give up."

"That's not all true. We can work it out." She stood and raised her voice slightly. "You are smart enough to work here without being intimidated by the company or me."

"I'm not intimidated, Larona." Porter's voice rose somewhat, too. "I'm just trying to face fact, to be reasonable. It's this whole place--this institution. I would just be trying to cope, day after day."

Larona sat quietly for a moment, then said, "I suppose Patricia is still part of the problem, too, isn't she?"

He nodded. "That, too. She is a big part of my concern. I cannot fly in the face of her clear opinion."

"What can I do? Should I talk with her?"

He shook his head. "No. It's not just Trish, Larona. It's this whole set-up. Maybe we're just moving too fast."

Larona sat down again and remained silent for a moment. "I did not expect this kind of confrontation today," she said. "It seems to happen every time we meet. I don't like that. It's not something I can look forward to."

"I didn't like it either. But this room hit me between the eyes. Your S O P company.... I'm just now fully realizing your position and power."

Larona sighed. After a moment of silence, she said, "At a time like this... I'm sorry to have to tell you that I must be out of town again. Another business meeting...somewhere. I have to check. Atlanta again? I know this is just the kind of thing.... But when I return, I promise...."

"Oh, Larona, I do care for you."

"I know my feelings," she said. "What are your plans, Jess?"

"I promised to play in the golf exhibition next week. I'll certainly do that. Then I guess...I may return to Albuquerque."

"Oh, Jess, that would be terrible...." She spoke tenderly.

"I'll make a mistake whichever way I jump, Beautiful. That's what's so tough about this whole thing."

"Your mind's made up?"

"I was told earlier today that I'm a decisive sort of person. Fact is, I've been vacillating on this matter ever since I met you. But now--heaven help me--I think I've made a decision."

He started around the table to get to the door. As he passed her, Larona said, "Jess."

"Yes?"

"I truly love you."

They looked into each other's eyes for a long time. He reached out with one hand to touch her face but stopped short. At last, he turned and walked out, growling at the world.

When Patricia came through the front door after work, Porter met her. He said, "What do you say we go out to dinner, Trish? My treat."

She smiled, "Well, what's the big occasion?"

He shrugged. "Just want to spend some time with you."

"Why aren't you with Missus Starr tonight? Is she out of town again?"

Noting the sarcasm, Porter sighed heavily. "I think you will be pleased to learn that I have broken off my relationship with Larona."

Patricia clapped her hands. "Broken off? Well, hooray for that! What happened?"

"I don't think you need to be all that happy. I'm sure as hell not."

"I'm sorry, Dad, but I'm sure it's for the best. If you're not happy, does that mean *she* broke it off? Not you?"

"No. As a matter of fact, she doesn't want to quit."

"Then why the sudden change?"

"I'll be glad to tell you all about it. But first, do you care to go out for dinner or not?"

Patricia stood in the doorway where Porter had stopped her. Now she stepped close and gave him a kiss on the cheek. "I really would like that, but Doyle is coming by any minute. I already have a date for the evening. Sorry. We can--"

"Maybe later," he said.

"I can fix something quick for you before I go."

"No need. I can do that."

She moved close and looked him full in the face. "I know this is important to you, and I'm sorry for you. But not for her. Please tell me what happened. My date can wait." She added, "if you want to."

He rubbed a hand across his face and turned away. He picked up a magazine from the sofa and sat down. Then he tossed the magazine away. "I guess it's a combination of things. I think it was all happening too fast. Larona and I don't really know each other as well as we should, I guess. Then there's her business and position."

"What are you saying?"

"I'm afraid I'd just become *Mister* Larona Starr. I couldn't handle that. She lives in a world a lot different from mine." He shook his head.

Patricia studied him for a molment. "You really care for her, don't you, Daddy?"

He smiled and nodded. "Yes. Listen, I hope this won't have a negative impact on your job."

"Oh goodness, don't worry about that." She sat beside him. "I guess I didn't realize how serious you are. You know, I've learned that we can make things work out if we give them time. My jerk of a husband taught me that. You'll be able to let go of these feelings after a while."

"Um. Maybe. Thanks, Trish."

She took his hand in hers. "It's probably best this way. So, what are you going to do now?"

"I told Larona I'll honor my commitment to play in the fund-raiser next week. Then I'll go back to Albuquerque probably."

"You're welcome to stay here with me as long as you wish."

"Thanks, Sweetie, but I think I'll need to go. I can't stay in Clydeston with Larona so close. I'd go nuts. Besides I don't have any work here. And if I stay here, there might be some blowback on you, I'm afraid."

"I'm sorry you're unhappy, Daddy. But it's really just as well. The fact that you recognize that she operates in a different world tells me that she's not serious--"

"Hold it, Trish," Porter said sharply. "I don't need to hear that."

"Daddy, I've just heard so much--"

"I know what you think, but you're wrong." He stood and stalked across the room. "You and she would never get along because you think like that!"

"Are you saying that you broke off with her because of me?" Patricia rose, and her voice rose, too. "Are you saying it's my fault? Now don't lay that on me!"

"No. I made the decision. I'm the only person responsible."

"I hope that's true because I don't think it would be fair for you to blame me for making you unhappy."

"I don't blame you, Trish." Porter hugged his daughter. "I love you, Sweetie. I just hope I haven't made your position at S O P untenable."

A car horn blared outside.

"That will be Doyle," Patricia said.

"He has remarkable timing," said Porter. "Are you expected to run out to him at his beck and call?"

Patricia opened the door and waved.

The reporter ambled in shortly. "Hi, Trish," he said. "Oh, hi, Jess."

Porter waved half-heartedly and turned away.

"So, what's new?" the reporter asked.

"Same old thing," Patricia said lightly. "I just got home a few minutes ago. Give me a minute to put my face on."

"You work late almost every day, don't you, Trish?" said Dugan. "Old Lady Starr really gets her money's worth out of you, I think."

Porter snapped at the young man. "You can refer to her as 'Missus Starr', Dugan!" There was flint edging his voice.

"Oh, you bet," Dugan said indifferently. "I forgot that you and she are--"

"Are what?" demanded Porter. Now his voice bore an unveiled threat.

Dugan backed down. "Nothing. Nothing." He put his hands up in surrender mode. "I didn't mean anything. Excuse me for living."

Both men sat down and Patricia said, "Can I trust you two not to fight if I leave you alone for a minute?"

"Sure," said Dugan.

Porter waved her away, and she left them.

After a minute, Dugan cleared his throat and said, "Heard the day's news yet?"

"What's that?"

"Two things. Chief Still has confirmed that the skeleton you found was indeed Lenny Sanford--just as I expected. On the basis of a chipped rib, the best guess is he was shot."

Porter nodded.

"Yeah, and the other thing is that Tom Tipton--You know him, don't you? Well, he had a bad episode with his emphysema today while he was driving. Wrecked his car."

"Damn! Yes, I know Tom. I'm very sorry to hear that. Do you know--"

"They took him to the hospital. You know, it's interesting that these two events come up at the same time, I mean Sanford and Tipton. They were partners in some real estate scam years ago. Funny timing."

"How is Tom doing?" Porter asked impatiently. "Do you know?"

"Oh, he died about an hour ago."

Through the early hours of the night, Porter lay in bed, trying to assess his situation with Larona and Patricia. Sleep was impossible. He turned the matter over in his mind, again and again, seeking new insight into all the relationships. But it was basically a simple picture. Like a sphere, it looked the same from all sides. He cared deeply for both women. One was of his blood. One was not. His daughter did not like Larona personally. He was not sure Trish even respected Larona from a business point of view.

Larona lived in different worlds. If he and she tried to continue their association, he could foresee great problems adjusting their lifestyles. They might be able to do it. He certainly would like to think they could. Even so, there remained Trish's animosity. And how would a marriage to Larona affect Trish's career with the company? He had said he didn't wish to become Mister Larona Starr. Now he realized that Trish would be looked upon as Larona's daughter. Unfair to Trish. At least she would think so.

He tossed and turned, trying to find an answer. In the midst of his probing for a solution to his personal life, questions repeatedly also rose about the skeleton he had found. What about this Lenny Sanford guy? Who the hell was he, really? Had Larona revealed the whole truth about her relations with the man?

Porter had thought he would inquire of Tom Tipton about the real estate development in which Tipton had joined Sanford. That had seemed to Porter as the subject most likely to shed light on Sanford's activities. Now, in a bizarre coincidence, Tipton was dead. Suddenly, unexpectedly dead. Was it merely an event arising from Tipton's emphysema? Or was there some more insidious reason for his death on the very day when Sanford's identity was confirmed? That possibility was too chilling to contemplate.

At last Porter fell asleep. Even then, however, he struggled subconsciously, dreaming, seeking answers.

Upon waking, Porter realized he needed to do one thing regardless of what else the future held. He felt compelled to contact Larona and apologize for his abrupt departure the day before. He did not expect to renew their relationship with the same intensity it had enjoyed in recent days. He knew, though, that regardless of what else might happen, he wanted to remain cordial, friendly, close. He could not and would not shut her out completely.

He showered, dressed in his running togs, and ate breakfast with Patricia. After she left for work, he waited for a few minutes, then called Larona's office.

Betty Lou informed him that Larona would not be in the office this day nor part of the coming week. "I know she intends to be back for the Harrison House Benefit though. I thought she must have told you that, Mister Porter," she said apologetically. "She's probably in the Wichita Municipal Airport right about now and departing very soon. I'm sorry."

"Oh yes, of course she told me. I forgot. Betty Lou, will you please give me her phone number? Then I'll get in touch with her later."

"Oh, Mister Porter, she gave me strict orders not to give anyone her phone number. I don't know why. She's never told me that before."

"I think it would be okay for you to give me the number," he said.

"It probably would be. But I just cannot do that, sir. I'll ask her for sure when she calls in next. I'm sure she will say it's okay, and then I can pass it along. I hope that's all right, sir." She added in a confidential tone, "You know, of course, that you can find almost anyone's number if you just search for a while with *your* phone...."

"Of course. But if she doesn't want me to have it for whatever reason, I'll just wait...."

"I expect she will call you directly as soon as she lands."

"Of course. It's okay, Betty Lou. Thank you."

He cursed himself when he hung up. Deep inside, he knew he didn't want to let go of Larona Starr. But he also clearly realized that she was inevitably slipping away.

"I appreciate your agreeing to help me in the exhibition match, Slim," Jesse said to Braun when they met outside the caddy shack at the Clydeston Country Club Friday morning.

Braun nodded. "Okay, providing I can use my Kangaroo for your clubs. I don't think I can carry them, Jess."

Porter laughed gently at his friend's concern. "We'll ride, baby! It's just an exhibition. We'll ride today, too."

"Okay. Good. Sounds like fun to me. What else is there?"

"Today I want you to help me chart this course."

"How does that work?"

Porter produced a small loose-leaf notebook from his golf bag. "Simple. We're going to take notes on every hole we play. We'll step off distances from various landmarks, and we'll plot the best positions from which to approach each green."

"Ah, I see." Braun said. "Then next week, you'll have a plan of attack!" He laughed.

"Exactly." Porter looked at his watch. "The starter said we can go off at ten-thirty. It's about that now."

"I'm surprised the course isn't more crowded today. Nice weather this morning. Where is everybody?"

"I wouldn't know, but it gives us more time to gather the information we want. We probably won't hold anybody up out there."

"Uh, Jess, before we get started, I guess you heard about Tom?"

"Yes. Man, that's too bad. I heard he had a respiratory attack while he was driving."

"Right. He lost control of his car and crashed into a telephone pole. In his condition, I guess he didn't have much of a chance."

Porter shook his head. "It's tough. You know, I...." His voice trailed off.

"What is it?" asked Braun.

"Oh nothing. Well, you'll probably think I'm nuts, but I intended to chat with Tom about this Sanford fella."

"In regard to what?"

"I've been thinking about it ever since we found his remains. Obviously he was murdered. I've heard bits of information from you guys, about him, you know."

Braun nodded. "So?"

"I understand that there was a close connection between Tom and Sanford at one time. I just thought Tom might have been able to clarify what happened."

Braun laughed. "Welcome to the club, buddy. You know, you're not the only one who thought that. I tried myself to question Tom. Finally he told me to shut the hell up. You wouldn't have learned much, Jess, I'll bet. Sanford ruined Tom's life, turned him into a pauper almost, and I think Tom was very, very bitter. He simply did not want to be reminded."

"I'm sure you're right. I suppose it's just that I've never been this close to a murder before. You know what I mean? It really piques my curiosity."

"I know. I feel the same way."

They stood silently for a moment, then returned to the matter at hand.

"Mister Porter?"

Both men turned toward the voice coming from the pro shop. A slender young man approached with a smile.

Porter nodded.

"Hullo. "I'm Morris Brent. They said inside I might be able to join you fellows. I'm alone this morning."

Porter and Braun exchanged glances, and Porter said, "Why, sure. Why not? You're welcome, but I must tell you we intend to play a leisurely round. We may take time to hit some extra balls."

Brent said, "Sort of a practice round, eh? That's good with me. I won't get in your way. I'll probably learn something. I've heard who you are, Mister Porter."

Porter laughed lightly. "Maybe we can both learn something. This is Slim Braun, Morris. And call me Jess."

They prepared to tee off on number one. Braun labeled a page in the notebook, noting the distance. "What do you want me to write, Jess?"

"I'll tell you as we go," Porter said. "Why don't you hit first, Morris, if you wish."

They watched as the young man addressed his ball and then cracked a hard, high drive straight down the right side, well over two hundred yards. Porter raised an eyebroww and nodded with approval at the well-timed, fluid swing. He said, "Nice shot. Boy! I wish my back were as flexible as yours, Morris. Nice swing."

"Thanks," said Brent.

Braun hit second, knocking his ball straight, but short, down the middle. He picked up his tee without comment.

Porter took his time, teed up toward the left marker, and swung easily. The ball landed a few yards short of Brent's. As they proceeded in their carts after the drives, Porter remarked to Braun, "He seems like a personable young man, don't you think?"

"You bet."

He has an excellent swing. It'll be interesting to see the rest of his game."

"You'll like it," Braun said dryly.

"What do you mean?"

"I've seen this fellow's name on the sports page, Jess. He's the county champ and was runner-up in last year's state amateur tournament."

"Oh." Porter looked again at Brent, this time with much greater interest.

The young man grinned as he climbed out of his cart for their second shots. "I guess you're away. You nearly outdrove me, though, Mister Porter."

Braun said, "There are gonna be a bunch of young guys like him playing here next week for the right to challenge you." He chuckled. "Young, limber, eager guys." He added, 'Age, I do abhor you. Youth, I do adore thee.'"

Porter tried to laugh, but he really wasn't amused. "If they all look like this one, they'll probably beat my brains out."

As they proceeded, Porter tried to remain indifferent to Morris Brent's play. It was difficult, however, for Brent made good shot after good shot. He chipped well and putted with authority. Porter decided Brent's long irons probably were not as accurate as his own, but the rest of his game was formidable.

Several times, Porter dropped balls into sand bunkers and hit them out, explaining that he wanted to test the depth of the sand and to see how hard it was packed. He made other observations, too, which Braun recorded for him in the notebook.

Brent commented, "You'll soon know this course better than the locals."

"I doubt that, but I have to minimize the locals' advantages, if possible."

When the two men putted thereafter, Porter noticed the trajectory of both their putts over the undulations in the greens. Before leaving the greens, he putted from several other different directions, and Braun drew them in the notebook as best he could.

When they finished playing, the three men shook hands all around and then headed for the parking lot. There, Porter put his clubs into the LeSabre and told Braun how much he appreciated his assistance. "See you tomorrow, Slim. Thanks again."

Braun said, "Before you go, would you like to hear something really wild?"

"What's that?"

"Abe called me yesterday. He is absolutely convinced that there's some big, big money buried out there by old number twelve where you found the skeleton."

"Why would he think that?"

"Don't ask me! He believes it though. There has always been a rumor that Sanford made off with a pile of dough. That idea has been bandied about all these years."

"But whoever killed Sanford would have taken the money, wouldn't they? Assuming there really was some."

"Seems that way to me, sure. But Abe is obsessed with the idea that there's a fortune out there just waiting to be picked up."

The police have been all over the area, haven't they?"

Braun rubbed his chin. "Well, yes and no. I think they looked carefully for anything associated with the body. But, you know, they probably weren't seriously searching for money. Y'know, probably just going through the motions. And Abe's got another point. He says the cops didn't do any digging. He actually went back out to the scene and looked around."

Porter shook his head and laughed. "Lord help us," he said. "So did Abe say what he wants to do? Is he going to dig up the whole golf course?"

"Well, he says the police tape is still up. But as soon as it goes down, he's going out there and start digging. I don't know where."

"That's crazy."

"That is just what I told him, Jess." Braun paused. "I asked why he told *me*, and he said he needs someone to help him dig. Says he's too old and feeble to do it by himself."

"I see. So you're going to help him?" Porter laughed again.

"Well, you know, I'm not too strong either. We thought we should find someone a little younger, with more energy than we have. We hoped maybe you'd like to help."

Porter returned to the Clydeston library Saturday afternoon. The same pretty librarian who had helped him earlier was there. This time he decided to accept her assistance rather than spend so much time in a random search. "Sure you have time to give me a few minutes?" he asked.

"You bet. Just tell me what you're looking for."

"There was a night club that opened just outside of Clydeston, I'm told, between here and Wichita, maybe in the late nineties. I believe it was called The Pretty Kitty. The owner was this man named Sanford. I'd like--"

"Oh," she interrupted, "that was the person who somebody found this week at the old golf course, wasn't it?"

"Yes, I'd like--"

"Yes! That's exciting. We've already had several inquiries about it."

"Okay. What I'd like to see, if possible, would be some articles that may have appeared at the time the club opened and--"

"That was 1995."

"Oh. Okay. And perhaps something when Sanford disappeared."

"And anthing exciting in between?"

Porter couldn't help smiling at her eagerness to help. "Sure, I guess so."

They walked toward the viewing machine where he had worked earlier.

"That's exactly what Doyle asked for," she said.

"What? Who?"

"Doyle Dugan. He's a news reporter for *The Clydeston Times*, she explained. "He wanted the same information you're asking for. I know right where it is." She pulled several cartons of microfische from a shelf and proceeded to load the viewing machine.

"I know who he is. Doesn't he have access to this sort of thing in his newspaper files?"

She smiled sweetly. "Yes, of course, but he sometimes asks me to help when he's busy or rushing for a deadline. You know, in a little newspaper, there aren't many assistants, and reporters are always pressed for time. They have to dig up all the information. And you know, Doyle really, really works very hard. Poor guy. I usually have a few minutes I can spare to help him." She giggled, "And folks like you. Like now."

Very quickly she turned to Porter. Here are the items I found for Doyle."

"Thank you, Miss--I don't know your name. You're being very helpful."

"I'm Winifred Wallingford. Call me Winnie! And you're welcome. Glad to help."

Porter quickly turned his attention to the materials she had laid out. He learned that the Pretty Kitty Club had opened June 1, 1994. Leonard Sanford was identified as sole owner. The article supplied surprisingly little personal information other than that he had served in the US Army in Iraq. His photo appeared in a full-page advertisement announcing the opening. He had been a handsome young man with black wavy hair and a flashing smile. His dark eyes hinted at something equally dark behind them. Porter decided women would probably find his looks inviting and romantic. In another photo of Sanford and Clydeston's mayor shaking hands, Porter noted a bracelet on Sanford's wrist. It was surely the same one Porter had seen Wednesday afternoon on the skeleton's bare wrist.

One old editorial commented only minimally on the development that businesses such as the Pretty Kitty Club might bring, and it strongly cautioned against the dangers of overindulgence in drinking and driviing.

The editorial comments clearly avoided antagonizing Clarence Starr and other resident conservatives, Porter thought.

As he sifted through subsequent newspapers, he found numerous advertisements for the club but little else until he reached the stories about Sanford's disappearance, for which very little factual data were involved. "The police continue to report that they have no news in the matter." Sanford had been last seen the night of March 6, 2003 by several employees of the club. He had been in his usual good mood as far as they could see. There was no physical evidence of foul play. He had simply vanished. The primary tone of the newspaper stories related to the financial side of the story. Would the club continue to operate? Who would become the legal owner? Apparently there were no locals who might have been investors. Most likely, the property would revert to a Wichita bank.

One employee had stated that she understood Sanford had a date with someone that night. It would have been late, after closing. But the employee had no idea who the girl friend might have been. Somewhat surprisingly, Sanford had kept pretty quiet about names of girl friends. Apparently that night's designated girl friend had never come forward. *That's not hard to understand*, thought Porter.

At last, he sat back, disappointed at the lack of helpful information. Realistically, he knew there was not much chance of finding something significant in a newspaper account that had been read years ago by hundreds of persons who knew far more about the affair and were closer to the people involved than he was.

He turned back to one of the ads he had already seen. It showed photos and listed names of several club employees. He jotted down the names. Then he turned off the machine.

At the front counter, he paused to thank Winifred again. "I just left the materials there. Thought perhaps you would like to put them away so they get into the right places. Hope you don't mind."

"That's fine. I'll take care of it." She smiled the pretty smile and asked, "Did you find what you were looking for?"

"I was just curious. I wondered what happened to the property where the club was located. Apparently a Wichita bank held a mortgage and they took it back."

"I see. I'm pretty sure the building is now an automobile sales lot." She added, "Isn't it exciting to hear about an old murder though?"

"Winnie, did Doyle Dugan say whether he found anything of special interest?"

"No. He was disappointed. But we found enough background for a story at least. It'll be in today's paper."

"Do you see him often?" Then Porter tried to cover his interest. "I mean, does he ask for your help often?"

"Well, y'know he's awfully busy. And he's so smart that he's into just everything imaginable, of course. But, y' know, we see each other as much as possible." Her eyes danced. "I guess one might say, y'know, we have a special understanding."

Porter said, "That's nice." But what she was suggesting surprised him and upset him somewhat as he thought about the implications for Patricia. He tried to maintain a friendly attitude nonetheless.

"Yes," she went on, "Doyle says someday he's going to move on, soon maybe. He just needs a big break--y' know, a scoop of some kind. And when he does, he'll take me with him to a big town with an important paper." She grinned. "Y' know, he expects to wind up with his own syndicated column. Or, in time, even in television news someday. He's so special, y' know, I mean, a lot of those news anchormen make lots of money, y' know. Wouldn't that be something?"

Porter said, "Yes, Winnie, I know that it surely would be something."

⸺⸺◈⸺⸺

A few minutes later, Porter pulled up to a little convenience store where he could park off the street. Remaining in the LeSabre, he unfolded the paper with notes he had made in the library. It had some names of former employees at the Pretty Kitty Club. Quickly, he determined that two of the four phone numbers were useless. Presumably those people were no longer in Clydeston.

The third name was James Barrow. Porter punched the number, and when a male voice answered, he inquired whether this was the same James Barrow who used to work at The Pretty Kitty about twenty years ago. He was told immediately and impatiently, no, this James Barrow was only twenty-six years old and there weren't any other James Barrows around. Nothing more. The man hung up.

He shook his head and tapped the fourth number.

A sleepy female voice said, "Hullo."

"Hello. Audine Mahon?"

"Yeah, hon. Who wants to know?"

"Hello. Are you the same Audine Mahon who worked at The Pretty Kitty in the nineties or perhaps more recently?"

Porter's question was greeted by silence for several seconds. Then she cautiously said, "Mebbe I am. Who wants to know?"

"My name is Porter. I was--"

"Porter! Like re-porter? I don't want--"

He laughed. "No no. My name is Jesse Porter. I'm not a reporter. I'm just a guy wondering if it would be convenient if I came by for only a few minutes to ask some questions about the club and Leonard Sanford."

A few seconds passed. Then she said, "I heard he's dead."

"Yes, I know."

"Are you a cop?"

"No. I--"

"Well then, why do you--"

"I'm just curious, Audine. This is not about you. You see, I'm the person who found his--uh, remains. Out at the golf course. I'd simply like to learn what sort of person he was. I won't impose on you in any other way."

"*You* found him? I read about that, hon." The caution seemed to lift from her voice. "Sure, you come on over and we'll talk. I'd like to hear *your* story."

He asked for directions to her house, which she gave, along with a request for a bottle of Jack Daniels.

He found her house with no difficulty. It was only a block away from a street with large, well-maintained houses. By contrast, hers was a small place, a simple rectangular frame building. The porch was slightly atilt, and the white paint had long ago lost is luster. Porter pulled into the weed-filled, gravel drive and stopped behind an old rusty Ford pickup. There was no garage or carport.

His knock rattled the screen door. He recognized the voice from the telephone conversation. "Com'on in, hon."

The door opened directly into the front room. Blinds were down, and Porter found the room eerily dark and musty. There was a card table in front of a lounging chair where a blowzy blonde sat.

"Audine Mahon?" he asked.

"That's right."

He took one step into the room and said, "I'm Jesse Porter. I called--" He stopped short: as he noticed in addition to the cards she had arranged on the table there lay an automatic pistol within easy reach of her right hand.

"Have a seat, hon." She gestured toward a straight-backed chair

"I'm not sure I should stay," he said, eyeing the weapon. "Perhaps I've made a mistake. Wouldn't want to intrude."

Audine laughed boisterously. "Don't wory about the pistol, hon. I won't shoot you if you don't shoot me."

Cautiously, Porter sat on the front half of the seat without leaning back. He raised his hands in a gesture of openness. One hand held a brown sack with a bottle in it. He laughed. "I don't have anything to shoot with. Except this...." He jiggled the bag.

She said, "Well, y'never know." She reached over and took the paper sack with its contents and set it on a small table at her side. "Some dude calls outta the blue. I never met you until now, y'know. You mentioned Lenny Sanford on the phone. For all I know, you could be some kinda shooter, comin' back here, tryin' t'collect Lenny's loot after all these years." She laughed, "Hell, If I had his money, I wouldn't be livin' like this."

Porter laughed with her, but he shook his head in disbelief. He tried to speak with sincerity. "I assure you, Miz Mahon, robbing you is the farthest thing from my mind. Farthest that I can imagine."

"Okay. I believe you. Y'don't look like a thug, fer sure. But a lady can't be too careful, y'know. Lenny ran with a very mean, low-down crowd. I mean, some of those guys would grind you up without, well, hell, y'know."

Porter now studied the woman before him. She was somewhat overweight, probably ten to fifteen years younger than he, but so worn that it was difficult to be sure. Her eye makeup was overdone. Even so, she bore an expression of honesty. Her general appearance was one of an amiable, once-pretty woman who lacked both training and finances to make herself as attractive as her natural features might allow.

He plunged in. "I'm one of the men who found Sanford's remains. On the golf course. I'd simply like to know something about the man I found. My name is Jesse Porter. I'm in Clydeston visiting with my daughter. That's all. It's a simple request, if you care to talk about him."

She toyed with the cards before her and then laid them down with a slap. "Yeah, hon, I know you. I mean, it just came to me. You're the fella Larona Starr has been foolin' with for the last coupla weeks, ain't you?"

Again Porter felt the sense of disbelief at how many Clydeston citizens must be aware of his relationship with Larona. He nodded. "We're friends, that's right."

"I'll bet you are, Mister." She snorted. "I mean--Well, I don't blame you, hon. That's some catch, that Larona. She's really loaded, and you must have somethin' on the ball, too, 'cause over the years, she's had lots of opportunities to find a man. Y'know, I don't think she has ever paid much serious attention to anyone, though. I mean, leastwise not here in Clydeston. We'd all know if that happened!" She added, "I work for her, y'know."

"You do?" he said with surprise.

"Sure. That's how I heard about you. At the plant. It's been an important topic lately."

Porter grimaced at the thought. "At the S O P plant, you mean?"

"Yeah, on the packaging line. That's how everbody keeps up on the gossip. Otherwise we'd keel over with boredom!"

"I should have known."

"Yeah. For a lot of years," she continued, "I lived with a truck driver. When he finally run off for good, he left me this crummy little house, and I got a job with S O P. I'm on the packaging line. Night shift."

"I see." Porter searched for words. "That sounds, uh... I was a little surprised to find you, Miz Mahon. I thought you might have a different name, a married name, and my source of information was nearly twenty years old."

"How *did* you find me, I mean, why me?"

"I found your name in an old newspaper ad for Sanford's club, The Pretty Kitty."

"The Pussy Club, he always called it." She laughed.

"Yes, well, anyway, I found your name and three others. You are the only one still around town, as far as I can see."

"Jeez, you're a regular Sherlock or somethin'. I mean, that's good. Well, whatta you wanta know, hon?" She picked up her cards again, shuffled them, then began to lay them out in a pattern for solitaire.

"Whatever you can tell me about how and why he disappeared. Is there anything that did not appear in the newspapers at the time? That is, something you might have heard or seen that wasn't generally known, any personal suspicions about some mysterious amount of money that you heard of at the time? Did he have a number one girl friend among the ladies? Anything along those lines."

She squinted at him. "Y'know--I don't really have to tell you nothin', do I?"

He shook his head. "No. You don't have to. And I promise I won't repeat anything you tell me. But I'd appreciate...."

She studied him for a moment longer. "Damn, hon, I hardly know where to start. Let's see. Lenny's outstanding trait was that he was a terrific womanizer. He really loved the girls at the club. I mean, y'know, he scrawnched about every woman he met."

"He what?"

She grinned. "He scrawnched 'em. You know: laid 'em, bedded 'em. banged 'em. He always called it scrawnchin'. When us gals at the club realized he had scrawnched about all of us at one time or another, it got to be funny. Hell, he fired any lady who wouldn't come across. Y'know, I mean we all pooled our information and kept score. I reckon ol' Lenny hardly ever missed a day--or night. He had a helluva lot of energy, that boy!"

"I--uh, don't know if that is--"

She laughed. "Din't mean t'embarrass you, hon. Hell, I'm jist tellin' you about the guy. There was close to two dozen female employees at the club at any time. I mean, more than that, I suppose, over the whole time the club operated. I may be the only one who still lives in Clydeston. I don't know for sure. We all went our separate ways when the club closed.

"Let's see now. I remember the night he disappeared. I mean, I remember it well. I'll never ferget it. It was a Saturday night in October. Kinda chilly. It was a normal business night except we closed a little early for a Saturday. That's because he had a date, of course.

"It was a long time ago. I mean, ordinarily I wouldn't remember much. But there was so many questions at the investigation and all. I mean, you don't forgit stuff like that. What I'm tellin' you is stuff none of us ever told the cops. You're not gonna--"

"No, I promise. I won't repeat any of this. Promise."

"Well, it was a pretty ordinary night, like I said. I left a few minutes before most of the gang. Alone. I suppose Lenny was last t'leave. He was always last. I mean, he wanted to lock the place hisself. That was somethin' he insisted on doin'.

"I know he didn't have none of us club girls lined up that night, 'cause we talked about that afterward, y'know? But he never limited hisself t'just employees. He almost never went a night without a piece, y'know. I always figured he had some lady waitin' outside for him. He often did that--had 'em wait out in the parkin' lot 'til he locked up 'cause some of the classier ladies in town didn't necessarily want it known they was scrawnchin' him." She laughed. "Especially the married ones."

Porter nodded but said nothing, waiting for her to add anything more that was on her mind.

At last she said, "You mentioned money. The official story was that there wasn't no shortage in the books. But I'd bet everything I have that Lenny stashed some on the side that dint show up in the books. Something for an emergency, y'know? Hell, he was too *slick* not t'keep books the way he wanted 'em. I always thought that." She patted the pistol that lay before her. "I mean, that's why I keep this baby around, 'cause I believe there was money involved." She paused briefly. "You know, one thing--"

"Yes?" Porter prodded softly.

Audine frowned. "Lenny had a family friend who helped him with the books. I always wondered why his name never came out. I mean, he would of known if there was missin' money. I used t'wonder if there was a Mafia connection there. Except this guy dint seem like Mafia t'me."

"How is that?"

"You know. Like Sicilian or Eye-talian. I mean this friend was an old family friend, I was told, part-timer, not a full-time employee at the club. He jist helped out, I think. Moonlighted. I think he had been a friend of Lenny's dad or something like that. Y'know--they was both from New Jersey originally. He may still be around town. Name is Jack Karns."

That information struck Porter like a hammer. "I know Jack Karns."

"Oh well, mebbe you oughta check him out," she suggested. "But don't tell him I told you."

Porter nodded, then asked, "Is there anything else you can think of?"

"Nothin' important...."

"Any other names?"

She shook her head.

"Is there any reason you think organized criminals might have been involved? I mean, other than what you said, that Sanford ran with a rough crowd?"

"Well.... Y'know, the newspapers always said Lenny jist disappeared. But at the club we figured it was more than that."

"What do you mean?"

"Because a rug from his office was missing."

"A rug?"

"Yeah. Y'see, we figured he probably went out wrapped up in that rug. I mean, that could be why nobody found any blood. We didn't think it was a valuable rug. Why else would anybody take out a rug, unless there was blood or mebbe to help carry a body? At the time, the newspaper didn't mention a missing rug. But you'd think the cops would have noticed it, wouldn't you?"

"Very interesting," Porter nodded. "Yes, I'd be very surprised if the police overlooked that. Very surprised. I really appreciate your input, Miz Mahon. Anything else?"

"I don't think so. No."

He rose to leave. "Thanks again.

"It was a long time ago--just an average night, I'm afraid, other than Lenny--He was there one night and gone the next. Y'know?"

Porter pulled out his wallet as if to find money to give her for her information.

"No no!" she said and waved him off. "That bottle of Black Jack you brought is plenty. "Jist put in a good word to Larona Starr for me sometime."

He looked at her sharply.

"Jist kiddin'," she said. "But good luck with her, hon. She's okay in my book. She's a bit of a hard-headed lady, I guess, but I like her. She helped me a lot after my man ran off. Gave me a job. Y'know?"

Clydeston's buff brick police station was about six years old. It was an addition to the red brick building which had been built about three-quarters of a century earlier and was used now solely as a jail. The casual observer would find little to connect the two buildings architecturally. Apparently, the appearance of the addition had been dictated by cost, with little consideration to visual compatibility.

It was late Saturday afternoon when Porter entered the police station. He found a small, brightly-lit lobby with several heavy plastic benches. A counter crossed the middle of the room. Behind the counter were four desks and three small, glass-fronted offices. Porter saw Chief Still's name on the door farthest to his left.

A lady in uniform at the central desk asked, "Can I help you, sir?"

"Thanks. I just dropped in to see if I can catch Chief Still."

"What's the name please?"

"Porter. He knows me."

The lady went to the office door and spoke to the Chief. Very shortly, she turned and motioned for Porter to come over.

The chief looked up and motioned Porter to a chair when he entered. "Hullo, Mister Porter. "How are you? Can I get you a cup of coffee?"

"No thanks, Chief. I didn't know whether you would be here this time of day on a Saturday. Just wanted to chat for a minute or two."

"I'm almost always here. Hard to get away from this place. What's on your mind?"

"I'm not sure how to start. It's about that body that we found at the golf course."

"I suppose that you know we made a positive identification. It was a fella named Sanford, as I had expected."

Porter nodded. "That's what I heard. And since I was the one who found him, I'm just naturally curious to find out what--who he was. Can you tell me anything about him?"

"I reckon that's a normal reaction." Chief Still laughed lightly. "You don't exactly uncover a body every day, do you?"

"No." Porter wasn't certain how to proceed to the questions he really wanted to ask. He didn't want to appear too inquisitive. "I've talked with several of my golfing friends who said this Sanford fellow was a pretty unsavory character."

"Oh. They knew him, huh?"

"Well, I suppose that word got around pretty fast."

Still leaned back in his swivel chair. "Um. Unsavory. That's a fair description. Lots more things he could be called, too."

"What do you think happened to him? How did he get out there on the golf course?"

The Chief pressed his fingertips together and studied Porter for a moment. "What did you find out about him at the library?"

Astonished by the question, Porter said, "How did--Well, just the old newspaper reports. They really didn't say much. How did you know I looked it up at the library? You haven't been following me, have you?"

Still chuckled again in a friendly manner. "I often go to old news reports myself when we're dealing with events that took place a long time ago. I have the official records, of course, but the newspaper tends to provide a more conventional wisdom and a different point of view."

"I see. Makes sense."

"And I happened to ask the librarian whether anyone else had been after the same information. She said you and Doyle Dugan had been there."

"Ah." Porter nodded, and they fell silent for a moment. Chief Still didn't appear likely to volunteer any unsolicited information.

"In my opinion, Chief, that 'conventional wisdom' didn't offer much.

No mention of suspects by name. Only vague theories and a reference to organized crime. Whatever that is."

"Yeah. I didn't find much either."

"So what do you think really happened?"

Still sighed and looked at the ceiliing. "I'm not sure what to tell you, Mister Porter. There really isn't much to tell you."

"What's the big deal?"

"No big deal. It was just a long time ago. At the time Sanford disappeared, I had been on the force for only a few months. I knew very little about the ins and outs of the investigation that took place. So when I read the files this week, it was almost like going through the affair for the first time."

"What's in the files?"

Still leaned forward and put his elbows on the desk. "Not much. Really not much. I got to thinking about that, too, you know. There's nothing more in the file that what you might expect from a minimal effort. Actually, *a very minimal effort.* I've tried to remember what I thought and heard at the time. Not much there either. Only a couple of today's people were on board at that time. I've asked them and they don't seem to know any more than I do."

The conversation was going around in circles. Porter could not help thinking Chief Still was withholding something. He didn't want to play cat and mouse with the Chief, so he decided to dive in. "Who were the suspects at that time, Chief?"

"There was no strong suspect, Mister Porter, because Sanford was only missing. Nobody could say for sure that he had done anything wrong or that anybody had done anything wrong to him. He had simply disappeared. There was no evidence of a crime other than some folks didn't get pay that was due them."

"Who did the police interviews? Do you know?

Still chuckled again. "I don't think we need to go into that."

Porter shrugged. "I'm just curious. You have a body now. There's grounds for a more intense investigation now, seems to me. I've heard there might indeed have been a woman involved. Do the files mention any women?"

"*Someone* said that? Look, Mister Porter, I'll tell you what I can. You don't have to keep probing."

"Thank you."

"This Sanford felllow was actually thought to have some connections with some crime syndicate in Mexico or South America. Mafia? Who knows what? He had been in Vietnam, y'know. Lots of drugs came from there, or so people say. When he disappeared, the Department didn't worry much about it beyond what had to be done to satisfy the letter of the law and the financial side. You know--Like who got the building and things like that. We all figured we were well rid of him. I believe that attitude prevailed with most of the townspeople, too.

"We watched carefully to see if anyone rose up in his place. Nobody seemed to want it." He added, "I think you may have a misguided concept of that place. It was not a huge gambling hall like the Las Vegas clubs. Not a hotel with hired entertainers. Just six or eight slot machines and a small, convenient dance hall where a couple could get simple foods--sandwiches and such--and dance in dim light."

"What sort of security?"

Still laughed. "Very little. Some simple electronic gizmos. There were a couple of big guys, enough to throw out drunks if necessary. A couple of old retired fellas, too, as needed. If the weather was good, someone might walk around outside once in a while, I suppose. No leads there, I assure you.

"You've probably heard a rumor that a woman might have been with Sanford that night. But we could never pin that one down either. Ladies don't jump up and say they've been playing around, you know. Husbands don't like that." He leaned back and smiled.

"Porter said, "I suppose if suspects were influential, they may not have been interrogated as thoroughly--"

"Hey!" The Chief leaned forward and put both hands on his desk as if he might spring at Porter. "What do you mean by that? Don't say that!"

Porter smiled pleasantly. "I merely meant, for example, someone who may contribute substantially to the town's economy and welfare. I thought that might be what you were implying. Sorry, Chief." Porter wondered if he had gone too far.

Still sat back and drummed a pencil on his desk. "Remember one thing, Mister Porter, and this is important. Sanford had only disappeared. He was *missing*. I pointed that out a minute ago. There wasn't any need for a full-blown murder investigation. We didn't know until this week that he was actually dead. That makes a huge difference."

Though the Chief was clearly losing his patience, Porter could not resist tossing one more dart. "Okay. Sanford was only missing back then, but now there is evidence of foul play. That will prompt a thorough investigation, won't it?"

"Yeah, Now we know he was shot."

"I'm referring to the other evidence."

Still sat upright. "What are you talking about?"

"There was a rug."

"Yeah, he was wrapped up in it. So what?"

"There was a rug missing from his office."

Still's eyes narrowed. "You mean you think he was killed in his office?"

"Sure."

"Nobody mentioned this at the time."

"Think about it. He was shot in his office. He fell on the rug. If he was bleeding, the shooter wanted to leave a clean room. Also the killer could have carried the body out much more easily wrapped in a rug. And could have kept his or her car clean."

"Who said there was a rug?"

"I promised not to tell. But look at photos and ask around. When a bloody rug was carried out, it also removed evidence of violence."

"That's pretty good, Mister Porter. Your story also says there was probably more than one killer. And--if one was a woman, she could not have done it by herself."

"Could be he was wrapped in a different rug."

Porter chuckled. "Be serious, Chief."

He stood up as if to leave. "By the way, were there any other marks on the skeleton, other than a chipped rib?"

Chief Still shook his head. "Look," he said, "When you came in here, I thought you just wanted to find out what sort of guy Sanford was. What else have you got?"

"I don't know, Chief. I just hope I haven't offended you. By the way, who was that prominent person we were talking about?"

Still just chuckled again and shook his head. He stood up, too. "You're pretty persistent, aren't you! Well, I will tell you something else, Mister Porter."

"What's that?"

"If you tell me who you're really concerned about, I'll tell you if he or she was suspected of anything."

Porter hesitated a long time. He could not bring himself to mention Larona. Finally he said, "One of the fellows I golf with is Abe Lowman."

"I know Abe."

"I know Abe thinks this Sanford guy may have had his son beaten until he was critically injured. I wonder if--"

"Abe Lowman was never seriously considered to be implicated. He had motive all right. But he also had a strong alibi, according to our files."

Porter shook his head. I'm glad to hear that, but it was not what I was going to ask. I wondered about his second son. Was he checked out?"

"Yes, his other son was cleared. He had been at a party that night clear up at Atchison, far from Clydeston and the club. His time was fully accounted for."

"That's good. I'm glad to hear that," said Porter. "And the other person I've heard about was Tom Tipton. Anything there?"

"Tipton was a good candidate. He had gone through a sour real estate deal with Sanford. Sanford was supposed to supply funds but renegged, leaving Tipton holding the bag. Tipton certainly had a motive."

"What does your file say about him?"

"He was home that night. No evidence one way or another." The Chief sighed. He was clearly tiring of this conversation. "You need to know that Tipton was a paragon of virtue, Mister Porter. He took the real estate loss upon himself and spent the rest of his life trying to pay off the people who got swindled."

Porter saw that it was clear that the Chief was not going to implicate anyone. He turned to the door. "Thank you very much, sir, for your patience and understanding."

Still said, "Did you know that Tom Tipton died Thursday?"

Porter nodded. "Yes. I was very sorry to hear that."

"Maybe I'll see you at the funeral."

As Porter and Patricia parked near the entrance to the country club shortly after noon Sunday, she said, "This looks really swank. It's much fancier than I expected."

"I've been here a couple of times now. It's a nice place. They take good care of it. This will be the first time I've tried the restaurant. We'll see how good it is." Porter opened the door for her and steered her toward the dining room. "If you're going to live in Clydeston, Trish, you need to get acquainted with the amenities that are available to you."

"I know, Dad. Not to mention the socially elite, eh? I just haven't had the time yet. Aside from the people I work with, I may actually know fewer locals than you do."

They had already ordered lunch when Walter Edwards spotted Porter and came to the table. He beamed, "Aha! Decided to get a really good meal, I see! We have some great fried chicken today. New recipe!"

"Thanks. We've already ordered." Porter shook hands with him and introduced Patricia.

Edwards welcomed her and said, "We're pleased you came to see us, Patricia. And of course, we're pleased that your father came to visit you, so we can have his expert assistance with our Harrison House fund-raiser next weekend. His contribution will be invaluable!"

"Thank you. Dad and I have had a nice visit." She refrained from looking at Porter as she added, "I know he has enjoyed it much more than he expected. On the other hand, he probably would have left town by now if it were not for your golf exhibition."

"Really?" Edwards turned to Porter. "I'm surprised to hear that. I thought perhaps you would be staying longer."

Porter smiled. Obviously Edwards knew of his association with Larona Starr. "No, I have to get back to work. I'm sure you understand how that is." He added, "But I'll do the exhibition before I go. As promised."

"That's good. I mean, I'll be sorry to see you leave. But we're certainly glad to have you stay for the golf. We're going to be ready for you Saturday.

All indications are that we'll have a great competition and a great crowd. Lots of people from out of town have requested information about the event. Anything you need before then? Anything at all?""

"I'll probably practice here another day or two this week."

Edwards nodded. "Good. Well, anything at all that we can do to help you get ready, just let us know." He turned to Patricia. "Very nice to meet you, dear."

"Thanks," she smiled.

Edwards took a step away, then turned and said, "You'll be on hand to watch your dad, won't you, Patricia?"

"Oh yes," she replied. "Couldn't miss that!"

"When you come, you tell the attendants that you're my guest, so you don't have to pay for attendance." Edwards was again about to leave, but he hesitated. "Is Missus Starr going to join you here this afternoon?"

Porter said, "No. She's out of town. Some business meeting." Edwards slapped his hand to his forehead. "Oh, of course! I knew that. I wasn't thinking. Guess I forgot what day this is. As a matter of fact, I was thinking of calling her about some arrangements for next weekend."

"Do you have a phone number?" Porter asked.

"Yes. She left a number where she could be reached. She wanted to know whether one of the banquet speakers could make it or if she needed to find someone else."

Porter said, "Would you mind giving me the number?"

Edwards frowned, then smiled. "Of course. I'll get it for you. Enjoy your lunch." He turned away and left the dining room.

"You need to call Larona?" Patricia said icily.

"Not what you think, Trish. I haven't changed my mind about what I told you. I still intend to leave. Probably Monday after the golf Sunday. It's just that I thought about how I left her the other day. I was abrupt with her, and she may have thought I was rude. I want to apologize. I don't want to leave our friendship on a note like that."

"I see." With obvious insincerity, she added, "Oh, of course you must."

They finished their meal with minimal conversation. Finally, Porter said, "If you're ready, I'll show you the pro shop and the golf course."

With a smirk, Patricia said, "Oh boy! I'm just dying to see the pro shop. I wouldn't want to miss that!"

"Okay. We'll skip the pro shop. But this is a pretty nice place. You should at least have a quick look around."

The waitress came as they were about to leave. She gave Porter a note from Edwards with Larona's phone number in Atlanta. He stuck it in his pocket. "I'll call her when we get home."

He led Patricia out the back of the restaurant onto a wide veranda decorated with many large terra cotta pots of geraniums and impatiens. Steps ran down to a patio and a large pool with a small fountain in the middle. Beyond the pool, the green lawn fell away toward the eighteenth green. Several tables on the patio were occupied by couples seated under large multicolored umbrellas, enjoying the fresh air. They had unobstructed views of the green and the fairway below.

"That's the final hole," Porter explained. "It's a long par five. I'll probably be worn out when I reach there next Sunday." Without thinking, he added, "There's a sharp dogleg down there that hides a maintenance area." He pointed to a row of walnut trees and cottonwoods far down along the right side of the fairway. And that's a tough, steep slope up to the green. I'll probably need to...." His voice faded away.

"Goodness! You're really involved in this exhibition, aren't you?" observed Patricia. With some surprise in her voice, she softly added, "I think perhaps I've never quite realized how much golfing is in your blood."

He looked at her and nodded. "Sorry. I got a little distracted. I guess you're not terribly interested in these details, are you? I get carried away because I don't want to look like an ass out there next week. Let's move on. He took her arm and gestured toward the steps at her right.

"You're pretty obviously wrapped up in this place, the course, and how to play it," she said. "But I detect some strong vibes that say you don't really want to play. I don't understand that. If you don't want to, why are you going to do it?"

He sighed. "You're right, Trish. I'm just going through the motions. With that talk a moment ago about the eighteenth hole, I was probably just trying to talk myself into something. I haven't competed in such a long time that I'm very uneasy about playing in public. The last time I did that, years ago, I looked like Ned in the Primer. I have no confidence about this thing. But I promised to to do it. I promised," he repeated. "I cannot run away from it at this late date."

He tried to change the subject as they came around a corner of the building. "Over there is the entrance to the pro shop. You sure you don't want to look inside? They have some good stuff...."

"If you wish, Daddy."

He saw that she truly wasn't interested. "Well, no need really. Let's just go on to the car. There's a walkway around to the front."

Someone called Porter's name. He and Patricia both turned back toward the pro shop. Morris Brent was there waving. He was in his golfing togs. "Hullo, Mister Porter!"

"Hi, Morris. How are you today? Are you starting out or coming in?"

"I'm just about to start." The young man walked over to Porter and Patricia and extended his hand. "Hullo," he said to her. He removed his cap when he spoke.

"This is my daughter. Patricia. Trish, meet Morris Brent. He's one of the outstanding golfers in the area. County champ."

"Really?" She smiled and they shook hands. "Are you going to play with Daddy next week?"

"That depends on how well I play Saturday. There's a little one-day playoff with some other people, you see, and Saturday's winner gets a crack at your father Sunday."

"Oh, I see." She smiled broadly and shaded her eyes against the sun and studied Brent closely. She liked him immediately. No rings, she noted.

"Are you a golfer?" he asked.

"No. 'Fraid not. Daddy tried to teach me years ago, but I'm just a duffer. The last time I tried to hit a ball, he was lying on the ground laughing so hard I thought he would have a heart attack!"

She laughed happily.

Brent laughed, too. "I'd be happy to take up where he left off. Sometime," Brent offered. "Any time, actually! If you'd ever care to."

"Oh, that would be *very* nice," she replied. "What sort of business are you in, Mister Brent?"

"Please call me Morris," he said. "I have a little office supply business here in Clydeston. What do you--"

"I work at Starr of the Prairie," she said. "Quality control right now."

Porter was amused and pleased to see how these two obviously liked each other. There was electricity in the air between them. They couldn't take their eyes off each other and were carrying on the conversation as if he were not there. He said, "We don't want to hold you up, Morris."

"No, of course not." Brent suddenly turned to Porter. "I mean, that's okay." To Patricia he said, "I do need to move on. The time, you know. Will you be here for the exhibition, Patricia?"

"Wouldn't miss it!" she said emphatically. "I just love golf!"

"I sure hope to see you then," Brent said.

"I'll look forward to it," she said. "Very much."

Brent nodded to both. He seemed reluctant to take his eyes off Patricia, and as he moved away, he bumped into a large pot of geraniums. He laughed self-consciously. "See you soon then," he said and went on toward the first tee.

"My--He's a very...nice...." Patricia said. "Did you notice his eyes? And he actually removed his cap when you introduced us. When was the last time you saw anyone do that?"

"Yes, I like him, too," said Porter. "He needs to work on his long irons, though."

She said, "Oh, Daddy!" and punched him on the arm.

———————⬦———————

While Patricia was occupied with laundry, Porter tapped his cell phone with the number that Edwards had provided. As he waited for an answer, he flattened the notepaper with the pencilled number on it. He was aware of the eagerness he felt. He realized he was breathing faster. God! He wanted to hear Larona's voice again!

A young woman answered. "Thank you for calling the Hyatt-Regency. How may I help you?" There was a pleasant soft Georgia accent.

"Yes. I'd like to speak with one of your guests, please. Miss Larona Starr."

"Just a moment, sir." After a few seconds, the voice said, "I'm sorry, sir. We have no one by that name registered."

"Oh? Well, she's there for a meeting. Do you have names of people registered for a Pharmaceutical Manufacturers Association meeting--or something like that? Pharmaceutical companies?"

"I'll check, sir. Please hold for a moment."

He exhaled heavily and studied the note paper with the number on it. This must be correct. It's the right hotel.

The operator said, "Sir, I have no record of such a meeting here. I checked with my supervisor and she says that group met here a year ago."

"What!"

"I'm sorry, sir. I have no other information about a Miz Starr."

"Okay. Thank you." Porter hung up. If Larona wasn't there, where was she? Damn! He kicked himself for not getting her personal number long ago.

He was disappointed not to talk with her. Beyond that, her absence raised questions he didn't wish to face. Why would she have given Edwards a wrong number? Could she perhaps not have gone to a business meeting? Could she be involved in some activity associated with Lenny Sanford? To his murder?

No. Of course not. That's ridiculous. Absurd.

He wished now he had not even tried to make the call.

Tom Tipton's funeral service was held in the Baptist Church on Central Avenue Monday morning. Porter climbed the front steps and entered the sanctuary from the right rear. Already there were some fifty to sixty persons present. He saw Slim Braun and a woman he assumed to be Missus Braun and slid into a seat behind them.

Slim turned around when Porter touched his shoulder, and in a subdued voice he introduced his wife.

Porter looked around the congregation. After a few minutes, he located all the members of the one o'clock gang, some with wives, some alone. Nancy Grimsby was there, too, with a handsome young man that Porter assumed was her husband.

Pastor Glenn conducted the service jointly with a fellow pastor. The ceremonies were brief but sincere. Pastor Glenn obviously felt a personal regard for the decedent. He referred to having played golf with Tipton and to the latter's courage to continue to participate in activities such as golf despite severe physical problems. He also alluded to Tipton's determination to make things right to clients who may have been hurt inadvertently in business dealings. Clearly the reference was to the Walnut Acres debacle although it wasn't mentioned by name.

Porter found Glenn's presentation surprisingly powerful. The man spoke in a more articulate and confident voice than Porter had heard on the golf course. Preparation, Porter decided, and experience in the pulpit. Glenn also sang a solo, *Nearer My God To Thee*. He possessed an unexpectedly wonderful, well-trained baritone voice that amazed Porter. Afterward, outside the front entrance, he found an opportunity to congratulate Glenn on his eulogy and his singing.

Glenn looked at him seriously. "Thank you, Jess. It was easy to be sincere about Tom Tipton. He was a fine man. He had an unfortunate business episode that became a major part of his life, but he faced it with great integrity. I just hope I wasn't out of line by referring to it."

Later, at graveside, Porter stood beside Ray Wallis, Jack Karns, and Karns' wife. When these people stepped over to Missus Tipton to offer condolences, he moved alongside, but stood a step away because he had not met her. She wore a dark dress and a broad-brimmed hat which drooped over the upper part of her face.

When she saw him, she stepped close and said, "You must be Mister Porter."

"Yes, ma'm, Missus Tipton. I--uh--want to tell you I'm very sorry for your loss."

"Thank you, Mister Porter. I'm so glad to meet you." She clasped his hand in hers and squeezed hard.

"I really didn't get to know Tom very well. We played golf a few times together. I admired his dedication to the game and to his friends. I've heard a lot of very favorable comments about him."

She turned her tear-streaked face up to him, and she seemed to throw off her pain momentarily. "Oh, Mister Porter, I'm very glad you came today. Tom talked a lot about you, you know."

Surprised by her unexpected comment, Porter was at a loss for words. "We only--we didn't talk much. I'm truly sorry I didn't get to know him better."

"I know. Except for business, Tom was always quiet until he got to know people well. But he talked to me about you. He said you were the very best golfer he ever played with. That was a great joy to him. He said you were the best he had ever seen except perhaps for a few on television. He loved golf. He was thrilled and proud to play with you." Her eyes sparkled with pleasure.

"Missus Tipton, I--" Porter hesitated. He felt a tremendous sense of gratification at this unexpected praise. "I don't know what to say. Thank you very much," he said softly.

Slim Braun put his hand on Porter's shoulder. "Com'on. We have something to do."

"What's that?"

"Were going to the golf course," said Wallis. "We'd like for you t'join us if you will."

All the members of the one-o'clock gang showed up within a few minutes of each other at the municipal course. Doctor Jensen was present, too. He had closed his office early to attend the funeral. Now he was here even though it was Monday, not his usual Wednesday. All the men were still dressed in their funeral clothes. No one had changed to golfing togs. Porter asked what was going on. Braun said, "We have a little ceremony."

Porter silently hoped he wasn't going to be the butt of some outlandish gag.

Nancy Grimsby arrived from the cemetery and unlocked the pro shop. After a couple of minutes, she came out with a golf club and a box of new Titleists.

Three of the men had driven golf carts to the first tee, and everyone climbed aboard, including Nancy. They started down number nine fairway, angling left toward number seven green.

Porter squeezed alongside Doctor Jensen. "What's going on, Nate?"

Doctor Jensen said, "Our gang is an informal club, as you have seen."

"Yes... So?"

"Well, it was even more informal when we first started playing together. Over the years, several men have played with us and quit for one reason or another. A few moved away. Four have passed on. Five now. Tom was the fifth."

Braun, who was hanging on the side of the cart, said, "Chuck Dunkan, Bill Noffer, Danny Harris, Roberto Salas, and Tom Tipton."

"Yes," said the Doctor. "All those were players who have passed on. The first of our group who died was Chuck Dunkan. Before the end, he asked us to perform a little ceremony in remembrance. Since then, we've done the same for each man who has passed."

They drove the carts past number seven to the edge of the pond, about halfway between the seventh and sixth greens. The rim of the pond lay at that point under an embankment that overlooked the water. A steep, bare expanse of red dirt ran down to the water where cattails stood. A sparrow flitted there.

Nancy opened the box of balls and handed one to each man. She took one herself and teed it on a tuft of grass. Then she raised the old golf club she carried so Porter and the others could see it. The handle had been heavily taped with black tape. "This is Chuck Dunkan's nine iron. Here's to camaraderie," she said. With that, she addressed the ball and struck it into a high, gentle arc over the pond. It landed near the middle with an audible splash.

She turned away and solemnly handed the club to Doctor Jensen. He placed his ball on the ground and then knocked it into the pond.

He passed the club to Ray Wallis, who pitched his ball into the water.

Abe Lowman followed the same wordless procedure.

Slim Braun plunked his ball into the pond.

Pastor Glenn topped his ball, so that it skipped on the surface of the water before going under. Then he handed the club to Porter, who, without instruction, followed the others and crisply hit his ball into the center of the pond.

Jack Karns was last to hit. Then Slim Braun soberly said, "'They shall grow not old, as we that are left grow old. Age shall not weary them, nor the years condemn. At the going down of the sun and in the morning, we will remember them.'"

Pastor Glenn's voice sounded softly, as though far, far away, "So be it."

With no further comment, the group reboarded the carts and returned to the clubhouse.

Porter wondered about what they had done. If an outsider had observed them, he or she might have found the ceremony amusing, but Porter had been impacted by the deep feelings these men--and Nancy--held for each other and the great pleasure and bonding they had achieved for each other over the years as they had played the game together. He was humbled by their acceptance of him.

There would be no round of golf today. Each of these old-timers was too full of thoughts of his mortality, driven home by the demise of their friend and the others who had gone before.

When they dismounted from the carts, no one spoke until Abe Lowman approached Porter. Speaking very quietly, so as not to be overheard, he said, "Did Slim speak to you about diggin'?"

"What?" Porter was taken aback by the question.

Lowman frowned and raised a finger to his lips to caution Porter to speak softly. "Did Slim say anything to you about diggin' up the money?"

"Are you serious?"

"SHHH! Yes, I'm sure Sanford's money must be right near there, where you found the bones. I wanta look for it."

"Abe, I don't know...." Porter could see that Lowman was in earnest. He did not want to embarrass the old man nor rile him by telling him he thought his idea was preposterous. "Look, Abe, the police have been through that area. They didn't find any money."

"Hell no, Jess! Of course they didn't find no money. That means it's still there! They weren't lookin' fer it. They jist scratched the surface around the body. Mebbe you haven't noticed, but the cops have taken down those yellow tapes. They're finished over there. Now we can go in and look fer ourselves. We might have t'dig a little, but it's *there!* I jist know it is! It has to be. You can bet other people will be lookin' fer it soon, too. Fer years, everbody in Clydeston has said Sanford took it with him. I wanta find it before someone else does."

Porter looked around at the others to see if Lowman had any support or opposition from them. Slim Braun was the only one who was paying any attention to Lowman and him. Porter gave Braun a questioning look. Braun winked and grinned. Porter nodded.

At midnight, Porter slipped quietly out the front door and seated himself on the swing on the porch. He had agreed to accompany Lowman and Braun on their treasure hunt if they would pick him up. He really didn't expect them to come by. They must surely be joking about this business. It crossed his mind that he might be the butt of some practical joke. The others in the gang were probably already waiting at the golf course where they could spring out and laugh at him. For now, however, he figured he would simply wait here, outside, for a few minutes and then go inside and try to get some sleep.

The night air cooled his face--quite a difference from the hot daytime wind, he noted. The moon hung high, still rising, three-quarters full, and it illuminated the few small clouds dotting the sky. *Wouldn't it be nice to have Larona beside him*, he thought. What a fool he must be, to find himself sitting here alone under this wonderful starry sky, wondering why he was shutting her out of his life.... He would try again tomorrow--later today, actually--to call her. But why should he? Nothing had changed. She still lived in a world far different from his. And Trish couldn't tolerate her. He had made a decision to walk away from her. Why was it so difficult to fight that decision?

A car approached. It could be Abe's, though the headlights kept him from seeing it clearly. It pulled up to the curb in front of the house, and he made out Braun in the right front seat, motioning to him.

Porter neared the car, shaking his head. "I didn't think you guys would actually show up. This is the craziest thing I've done since I was a teenager stealing watermelons."

Braun said, "God rest you merry, Golfer. Let nothing you dismay."

Lowman drove west on the road bordering the north side of the golf course. On that stretch of road they saw only one other car, which passed them in the opposite direction. Almost involuntarily, Porter turned his face away from the headlights as the vehicles passed.

At the northwest corner of the golf course, they turned south and proceeded about a quarter of a mile. This narrow road paralleled the old number twelve fairway, which rose up a steep hill. Their destination was near the bottom of the hill, on the east side.

Lowman pulled onto the right shoulder and stopped. "Okay, men," he said.

Braun asked, "Why are you stopping here? We can get a lot closer. It's another hundred yards to the top."

"I don't want nobody t'see where we're goin'," Lowman replied.

Porter snorted with amusement. "You have license plates on this buggy, haven't you? Somebody may report the deserted car."

Braun said, "Who is gonna see us--for Lord's sake? Hell, there's nobody within a mile of us."

"You never know," Lowman explained. He climbed out and opened the car trunk. He handed a long-handled shovel to Porter and kept a sharp shooter for himself. "Here," he said simply.

"I get the idiot stick, huh," Porter observed.

"What do I get?" asked Braun.

Ignoring Braun, Lowman said, "I've got some lamp black." He pulled a small round package from his shirt pocket and offered it to the others.

"What's this?" Braun asked.

"To put on your face. Like in the army. When they do commando raids, they darken their faces so's no one can see 'em."

"I'll pass," said Braun.

Porter shook his head. "No thanks."

"Well, if you guys ain't gonna do it, I guess there's no sense in me doin' it. Com'on. Let's get goin'." Lowman started up the right side of the road. He bent over as he proceeded. "Keep low and single file," he ordered.

Braun clapped Porter on the shoulder and laughed softly. "You didn't know this was gonna be a military operation, did you? Aren't you glad you came?"

"I wouldn't have missed it for anything. But I hope it's just a bad dream and I'm about to wake up."

"Keep it quiet," Lowman called over his shoulder. "You don't wanta be heard, do you? Sound travels farther at night y'know!"

Braun and Porter fell in behind Lowman and obediently followed him up the hill. They tried to refrain from laughing as they moved along the shoulder of the road, which was bordered by a ditch on their right.

At the top they stopped. Lowman carefully surveyed the road. It crested about fifty yards ahead.

Porter could see Clydeston's lights spread out to the east and south. The moon provided excellent illumination to the road, the field beyond the bordering fence nearby, and the golf course across the road to the left. It was a vista that emphasized the natural beauty of the prairie and the quiet town.

Porter was amazed at the size of S O P, well defined by night lights.

Lowman interrupted the silence. "This is a good place to cross."

Braun said, "Why don't you turn up your hearing aid first and see if any bad guys are coming?" He elbowed Porter.

Lowman replied hotly, "You think this is a gag, don't you! Well, you'll change your tune when we dig up thousands of dollars. You'll--"

"Shhh!" Porter cut the other two off. "Someone is coming up the road. There." He pointed ahead of them.

Just coming into view at the top of the hill, a dark figure shuffled aimlessly but steadily toward them. He made a strange, jingling sound.

Lowman ordered, "Com'on! Get down!" He slipped immediately into the roadside ditch and lay flat. Somewhat reluctantly, the others followed. He whispered, "Now you see why I brought the lampblack! If we had that stuff on, this character wouldn't see us. Keep yer faces down."

Braun grunted something unintelligible.

The figure on the road approached. Only a few yards away, he stopped to view the lights that Porter had admired minutes earlier.

The three men in the ditch tried not to move, tried to breathe as quietly as possible. Porter shielded his face with one hand as he sneaked a look upward.

Ominously dark in the shadows of night, the newcomer appeared tall and thin. He was dressed in dark summer clothes and carried what seemed to be a large plastic trash bag.

He dropped the bag and the sound suggested that it was full of cans and bottles. Then the man turned to face the cornfield beyond the ditch and fence. Now he stood only a few feet away and almost directly above the trio. Casually, he unzipped his trousers and without delay began to urinate into the ditch:

Lowman, closest to the offending stream, shouted, "Hey! Look out!" He leaped up from his concealment, followed closely by Braun and Porter.

The man, heretofore totally unaware of their presence, jumped backward, barely keeping his feet under him. Absolutely terrified by the dark figures seemingly rising to attack him from the black depths of the earth, he exclaimed, "Holy shit! What? Who? God damn!"

"Hey, watch where you spray that thing, man," shouted Lowman.

Now the man saw that the figures from the ditch might be human after all. Still, he took another cautious step backward, prepared to flee for his life if necessary. "Who, who are you?" he cried out.

"None of your damn business!" shouted Lowman. "Just some guys!"

"What are you doin' in that ditch?"

Lowman groped for an answer. He shouted, "We're lookin' fer golf balls!"

"Golf balls?" the stranger repeated incredulously. "Golf balls? In there? At night?"

"Yeah," said Lowman. "And what are you doin' out here at this time of night yerself?"

"I'm jus' hikin' the road, man." He had caught his breath now and seemed to see some humor in the situation. "There for a minute I thought I was gonna take a piss, but I didn't expect no midnight golf ball hunters."

"What's in yer bag?" Lowman demanded.

"Aluminum cans. I collect 'em to sell."

"Well, you might like to know that golf balls are worth a lot more than aluminum cans."

"Is that right?"

"Absolutely."

The man said, "Well, I think you oughta do that in the daylight when you kin see better."

Braun replied, "Ah, my friend, 'We do not what we ought; What we ought not, we do.'"

Baffled, the stranger frowned and took another step away. "Well, if you don't mind, I'll jist stick with aluminum cans." He waved a half-salute and picked up his bag. He stepped to the middle of the road as if to continue his journey. "See you fellas around."

"Good night," Braun said.

"That your car down there?" the man asked, pointing down the hill.

"Yeah," said Lowman.

"You leave it locked up?"

"Yeah."

"Well, that's a good idea," said the man, "'cause you never know what kind of weirdos you might meet out here at night!" He laughed and moved on.

Braun and Porter laughed, too, and Lowman muttered, "Wise ass."

As the stranger strolled away, they heard him mumble to himself, "Huntin' golf balls at night with shovels. Now I've saw everthin'!"

Lowman watched until he was certain the man had passed his car and wasn't going to break into it. Then he said, "Com'on. Let's go."

The trio hurried across the road and climbed through the three strands of barbed wire that bordered the course. They found themselves near the old twelfth hole, overgrown with weeds, at the top of the hill. Carefully they began their descent on the far side. Very shortly, they neared the place where Sanford's remains had been uncovered.

They looked around and satisfied themselves that there was no one else nearby to interfere with their search. "This is it," said Lowman. His voice was crisper than usual. He was clearly excited at the prospect before them.

"What do you want to do now, Abe?" asked Braun.

"Well, let's see," said the little man, stroking his chin. He pointed at the area where the police had done some digging already and where weeds and grass had been trampled flat: "That's about where Sanford was at, ain't it?"

Porter and Braun agreed.

"Well, if someone buried him there, where would they put the money?" asked Lowman.

"I would have put it in my pocket," said Braun, "and taken it with me."

"Aw hell, Slim, com'on!" Lowman insisted. "We've come this far, dammit! It's here. Close! I can feel it. Can't you feel it?"

Porter said, "I know you don't think the cops looked for money. At least not very hard, Abe, but I'd guess they probed around the immediate vicinity pretty thoroughly. Let's try a few feet farther away."

"Okay! Now you're talkin'."

Lowman and Porter held the shovels, so Braun set about turning a few stones and nosing around small shrubs in the area.

Porter began digging under a mound of loose dirt that had clearly slid down from the face of the hill. After watching him for a few minutes, Lowman found a similar spot and began to dig there.

After turning only a few shovelfuls, Lowman said, "Damn! I'm too old for this. I'm winded already. I don't have no stamina."

"I'll take your spade," offered Braun.

"Naw, I don't want you t'have a heart attack, Slim." He called over to Porter. "You doin' any good, Jess?"

"This dirt is eay enough to move, Abe, but I'm afraid we'll need a bulldozer to move enough to search the whole area." He leaned on his shovel to catch his breath." It's hard. It's had years to settle, you know."

"I didn't expect it t'be so much work," Lowman said. "It's too slow. Yer right, Jess. Dammit!" He sat on a rock and watched as Porter resumed his dig and Braun continued to poke around fruitlessly.

At last Porter said, "I think we're wasting our time. We'd have to work for a week here to uncover the whole area. I'm just not up to this kind of labor, I'm afraid." Trying to lighten the moment, he added, "I could use this shovel better if I could use an overlapping grip."

Braun laughed. "Yeah, right. I should have brought my wedge, and I could take some big divots."

Lowman ignored them. "You know what I think?" he asked.

"What's that?"

"If the guys who buried Sanford's money did leave it here, somewheres, they prob'ly left it where they could find it fast. Prob'ly left it where there's some sort of landmark. You know what I mean?"

"Makes sense." Porter nodded, a little surprised by Lowman's logic.

"If he or they didn't take it with them at the time," said Braun. "How do you know they haven't already come back and picked it up? Hell, they've had all these years, haven't they? They could have picked it up last year, five years ago, ten years ago--"

"It's still here. I know it," said Lowman. "I can almost smell it!"

"That's me," said Braun. "I just farted."

"Dammit, Slim, be serious," Lowman said. He stood up and studied the area. "Where would you leave it?"

Braun shrugged.

With sudden animation, Lowman cried out, "I'd leave it over there!" His voice filled with excitement as he answered his own question. "Look there!" He pointed at a young elm tree. "Look, that tree would have been a little sapling back then, right? You'd want a marker that would last for a long time mebbe. And there's a pile of rocks around the base. That don't look real natural to you, does it? Those rocks were placed there by someone who wanted to be able t'find this spot again!'" He rushed to the tree for closer inspection.

Porter and Braun followed. "You're really something, Abe," said Braun chuckling. "You know that?"

"Let's look, Slim. He's not going to be satisfied until we check it out. Here, Abe, I'll help you move some of this stuff. But if it's not here, let's call it a night. If it's not here, we just don't have the energy or tools to search this whole place. We'll have to plan a different approach."

"Okay," said Lowman. "If it's not here, we'll go home. But you agree, don't you, that logic tells you it might be here?" His eyes flashed in the moonlight.

"Sure," laughed Braun, "your logic tells us!"

Porter thought the rock pile at the base of the elm tree did indeed resemble a man-made cairn, yet the rocks were so overgrown with weeds that one would scarcely find them remarkable. "That's very perceptive of you, Abe. I never would have singled out this as a landmark."

"Yeah," said Lowman. "This looks like the real thing t'me."

The little man was already pulling up weeds and clawing to dislodge the smaller stones. He worked with sudden energy. His face shone with sweat.

"Take it easy, Abe," cautioned Braun. You'll have a stroke or somthin'. We'll help."

The three men worked for several minutes without talking. They quickly removed the smaller stones and then found themselves facing two stones of a size and weight that would require much greater effort to remove.

"Do you really want to go on with this?" asked Porter. "These things are going to be tough to get out. And there may be more underneath that we can't even see,"

Lowman stepped in front of him, impatiently edging him back. "Here! I'll do it if you don't want to." There was a grit of frustration in his voice bordering on anger.

"Take it easy, Abe. Let me work on them. You'll strain something," Porter said. "Let's be patient."

He put the long-handled shovel under one stone and tried to pry it loose, using a smaller stone as a fulcrum. But the large stone only rocked slightly.

Braun took the spade and hacked at a nearby sapling. After a minute or so, he had a pole which he edged in alongside Porter's shovel. Together they moved the larger rock a couple of inches.

"Look!" exclaimed Lowman. "Look! There's a hole under there."

"Probably a skunk's den," gasped Braun as he labored.

Lowman leaned his weight on Braun's pole, and the three men strained as hard as they could. The rock moved again but fell back into the same position. Braun swore. They tried again and were able to wedge the shovel and pole farther under. Porter dropped another flat rock under his shovel for greater leverage.

At last the big rock turned over. Now they were able to grasp it and pull it completely out of the hole. Lowman collapsed on top of it. He was panting hard. Then he twisted around to peer into the vacated space.

"Can you see anything?" he gasped.

"It's dark. Too dark. I'm not sure," said Porter.

"There is a cavity," Braun said. "A big hole!"

Lowman was breathing hard. "Here, let me clear it out," he demanded. On hands and knees, he scraped out several handfuls of dirt and pebbles. Finally he fell back out of breath.

Braun got down and continued to probe by hand. "By God, guys," he said quietly, "there is something in here. I hope it's not a snake." He stood up and said, "Let's get this other rock out of there."

Again they pried and lifted, finally removing the second large rock.

Then Lowman fell on his knees and frantically clawed at the soft earth they had just exposed.

The Clydeston Coffee Pot Cafe stood directly across South Main Street from the Clydeston State Bank. During early morning hours, a dozen or more Clydeston business men and women routinely gathered there before opening their various shops downtown. Most of them had left the cafe by the time Porter, Braun, and Loman arrived.

These three ordered coffee. Then they talked in subdued tones for about fifteen minutes. Then Braun and Lowman left together, and Porter ordered breakfast. Eggs, biscuit, and more coffee.

While he ate, he silently reviewed what he and his two colleagues had done.

About one a.m. Abe Lowman had pulled an oversized leather briefcase out of the hole at the base of the elm tree. Then he popped it open with his pocket knife. To Porter's astonishment, the briefcase contained bundle after bundle of U S currency in various large denominations clearly totaling many thousands of dollars.

Braun had suggested that they should take the bag and money elsewhere before handling it or counting it. He had been concerned about getting fingerprints on the bills.

Lowman immediately stated that the police weren't going to see this money, so who gave a damn about fingerprints? He agreed, however, that they should leave the site before anyone saw them, and they needed to go elsewhere to count the money and dispose of it.

They had worked hard to uncover the treasure and were very tired. But somehow the thrill of finding the loot gave them enough energy to fill the hole, replace the rocks, and generally cover the evidence of digging. It wasn't a perfect cover-up, but it was the best they could do. All three were about ready to drop when they left the scene.

From the golf course they had driven to Lowman's house. His wife was asleep, so, in the kitchen, as quietly as possible, they counted the money they had found. Lowman counted. He had no qualms about fingerprints. Porter and Braun carefully avoided contact with the currency. They watched with great relish, however, as well as a deep sense of disbelief.

The total came to two hundred eighty-seven thousand, four hundred and twenty-five dollars.

"That was a helluva lot of money twenty years ago," declared Braun.

"That's a lot of money today," agreed Porter.

"Could it be counterfeit?" asked Braun. "No," snorted Lowman. He held up a one hundred dollar bill and stared at it against the kitchen light.

"Looks good to me. It looks great!" He laughed. "And the best part is it's tax-free!"

"You mean you intend to keep it?" asked Braun.

"You bet your ass!" declared Lowman. "My share, at least. You guys each get a third."

"But this is evidence in a murder case," said Porter. "We must inform the police."

"Why do you say that?" Lowman's voice rose, and when he realized it, he lowered it, speaking in a hoarse whisper. "This money is lost money.

It don't belong t'nobody. It was prob'ly loot from some crooked scheme. Where else would that scumbag Sanford have got it? If you give it to the police, the county or state or some damn lawyers will git it all. We won't git none of it, by god!"

They had all fallen silent, just looking at one another. Finally, Porter said, "Any comment, Slim?"

"He has a good point, Jess. The legal system would probably eat it all up. I'm not sure what we should do."

Seeing that Braun could be swayed, Lowman had tried to push his advantage. "Look, I really need a share of this dough. I've got a son who's in business, and he's hurtin' financially. And one more thing--"

"Yes?"

Abe had clenched his fists and rancor filled his voice. "Jist remember that that son-of-a-bitch was responsible for the death of my boy Jamie. He still owes me a whole lot more than this money!"

Now, hours after Lowman's plea for the money, Porter washed down a bit of sourdough biscuit and brown gravy with strong, hot coffee. But it did not remove the scene from his mind. Three very tired guys at a poorly lighted kitchen table, looking at an almost unreal pile of money. He could still hear Lowman's voice as the little man had stated his claim. There had been anger, frustration, hope, sorrow, and a cry for understanding.

Finally they all agreed to wait before making a firm decision. Lowman wanted to keep the money. Porter still thought it should be reported. Braun was somewhere in between.

Porter had suggested they take a couple of days before disclosing their discovery. After thinking about it, perhaps they would be able to come to the right decision. "What do you want to do with it in the meantime?" He had asked.

Braun immediately shook his head. "I can't keep it at my place."

Porter simply shook his head.

"That's okay," Lowman had said. "I got a lot of boxes stored in my garage. We can put it out there and nobody will ever notice it." He had immediately left his seat and darted through a back door that the others assumed must be the garage.

Braun commented, "Not any worse than leavin' it out at the golf course all this time, I guess."

Lowman returned very soon with a big cardboard carton that bore advertising for paints. It looked almost new. He also placed two rolls of tape on the table. He was grinning. "I know how t'tape a box so it's good and see-cure!"

I'll take you guys to breakfast as soon as you're ready," offered Porter. "If you want to. Maybe you take me to pick up my car first."

Porter found himself in a quandary undreamed of a few hours earlier. Who needed to know about the money? He felt a duty to inform the authorities, but Abe was adamant that they did not have to do so. Who should have it? The three of them couldn't simply split it up among themselves, could they? What if by some far-reaching coincidence the money had not even been Sanford's? And even if it had been in his possession, was it legally his? Very doubtful.

He sighed. Well, at least the money was safe for the time being. Perhaps in a day or two, Abe would be more amenable to the idea of reporting it.

Porter yawned. The caffeine in the coffee had done its job, but he was really very tired. He had been up all night, and he wasn't used to that. He smiled as he thought that spending a night with Larona was a totally different matter.

He checked his watch and decided that he had sat in the cafe long enough for Patricia to have left for work. He would try to dream up an explanation for his absence, to give her later, if necessary.

As he left the cafe, a police black-and-white pulled up to the curb and the driver hailed him. "Morning, Mister Porter. How are you today?"

Porter felt a shock of guilt, just short of panic. He leaned down and looked into the car window. "Oh, hello, Chief. I didn't recognize you there for a moment. I'm fine, thanks. How are you?"

"I'm doing okay," said Chief Still. "Looks like you've already put in some work today."

Porter glanced down at the clothes he wore. They were soiled with dirt and sweat from the night's activities. "Oh! Oh, yes. I, uh, I did a little gardening work for my daughter and then came down for some breakfast. Guess I should have cleaned up first."

"It's good to do that sort of work early, before the day gets too hot."

Porter nodded, unsure of what the Chief was really thinking.

"Well, take it easy, Mister Porter. I'll see you around." Chief Still smiled pleasantly and drove away.

Porter stared after the departing officer. He had the impression that that was one smart cop. He wondered if Still could have seen him earlier with Lowman and Braun. *My gosh! What had he gotten himself into?*

———— ❦ ————

Shortly before noon Porter awoke. The same questions he had faced before sleeping rushed through his mind. Now the questions seemed more sharply defined, but the answers were not.

Prior to shaving and showering, he called S O P. He wanted to catch Betty Lou before she went to lunch, if possible. He recognized her voice when she answered. "Hello, Betty Lou. This is Jess Porter. Larona isn't back from her trip yet, is she?"

"Oh, Mister Porter, no, she isn't due back until Wednesday. I'm so--"

He cut her off. "Perhaps you can clear up a question for me."

"Certainly, I will if I can."

"I have a phone number where I was supposed to be able to reach her. But the hotel said she is not registered there. Can you tell me just exactly where she has gone and how I can reach her?"

"Of course. I'm so sorry. Yesterday I could have given you the hotel number. I got confused, I guess, when I said I couldn't. I thought you wanted her personal number, and that was what she had said not to give out. I'm so sorry!"

"That's okay, Betty Lou, I was partly at fault, too. Anyhow, let's try again. Walter Edwards at the country club gave me a number and I called it. But they said she was not there."

"What number do you have?"

"It's for the Hyatt Regency in Atlanta. Area code four-oh-four--"

She interrupted. "Oh no, Mister Porter. The meeting is in Philadelphia! They were in Atlanta last year. Missus Starr probably gave Mister Edwards that information a long, long time ago. I'm so sorry for this mix-up."

She gave him another number, and he felt a tremendous sense of relief.

The vague concerns that had arisen about Larona when he had failed to reach her now evaporated. He knew they had been silly anyway.

As soon as he could say goodbye to Betty Lou, he punched the new number she had given him. This time a hotel desk clerk in Philadelphia promptly connected him with Larona's room. Impatiently he waited for her voice. But the phone rang without answer. He checked his watch. She's out to lunch, he griped silently. These business meetings usually include group lunches. *Maybe they do*, he laughed at himself. *How would I know what business meetings like that include?* He could only imagine. That's another one of the reasons that he and Larona should go separate ways: her world was so different from his.

Nevertheless, he would try to reach her later. Again.

At one p.m. Wallis, Lowman, Karns, Porter, and Glenn teed off. Porter decided Slim Braun was probably home sleeping after a very arduous night. He said to Lowman, "I thought you might be resting instead of playing today, Abe. How do you feel?"

Lowman quickly turned to face Porter. He looked very tired. In a quiet voice, he said, "Keep it down, will you! You want the world t'know?"

Porter nodded and backed off. Obviously, Abe was antsy, wrung out, probably had not rested at all since they had parted.

As the men waited their turns to putt on the first green, Porter spoke to Pastor Glenn. "I want to tell you again that I think you conducted Tom's service very well yesterday."

"Why, thank you, Jesse. Actually, I thought it went well."

"You thought it went well!" Lowman mimicked loudly.

A little surprised, Glenn turned to the little man. "Yes, Abe, I did. Is there--"

"Hell, you preachers are all alike! What difference does it make how the service went? You're jist concerned about your performance. What about the dead man? Do you think Tom liked the service?"

Wallis said, "Hey, Abe, lighten up, fella."

Lowman ignored him. He stepped closer to Reverend Glenn. He looked as though he wanted to fight. "You think if the words are right and the music is pretty that the dead man gives a damn? Huh? He's jist dead meat, Cal, and his wife is left all alone!" He cupped a hand behind his ear. "How about singin' one fer me--now--while I can still hear it?"

Karns said, "Get a grip, Abe!" He stepped between Lowman and Glenn.

The Pastor tried to maintain his composure in the face of this unexpected assault. "We try to give solace to those who remain, Abe. You know that."

Lowman waved him off. "It's all a bunch of crap. The only solace Annie Tipton could have would be t'have Tom alive and with her! The rest of the folderol is phoney. If you were honest with yourself, you'd admit it."

"It's tradition, said Glenn. "If you don't believe in the theology, at least you must concede that most of our lives are based on tradition, actually."

Karns backed Lowman away a step or two, then turned to face Glenn. "But that kind of tradition is a cop-out, Cal. Religion is all hypocrisy. If something good happens, you say it's God's will. If something bad happens, you say it's God's will. That's a cop-out!"

Lowman was surprised by this unexpected support. "Yeah, we do things most of the time 'cause it's easier t'go along with what's expected than t'face the truth! I'm tired of it! I'm too old t'put up with the damned games everybody plays."

Wallis said, "I think you're jist tired, period. You act like you've been up all night. Go home, buddy. Get some sleep."

"Yeah. You're right I'm tired. Mostly I'm old. I'm gettin' older every minute. I'll never be younger than I am right now." Lowman was panting. "And you guys ain't gettin' younger either. Don't you know that? We're all gonna be dead meat soon. Jist like Tom. And then somebody can say nice things over us. And sing songs, whether it does any good or not."

Pastor Glenn said simply, "There's little we can do about aging or about death, Abe. Actually. It comes to all of us."

"Well, Cal, that's what I been tryin' t'tell you. And I want t'do somethin' more with the time I have left than jist go t'funerals and listen to bull about the hereafter. I still have a few days left, by damn!"

"Hey, com'on, guys," Wallis intervened. "We're all gettin' older. But that means we've been together long enough not to have this kind of fuss."

"That's another thing," said Lowman. "This one-o'clock gang is gettin' on my nerves, too. I've had enough of all this buddy-buddy stuff!" He picked up his putter and thrust it into his golf bag, which he unstrapped from the cart he had been sharing with Willis.

The group stood, nonplussed, unable to find words.

Porter was fully aware of the cause of Lowman's tirade, but he could say nothing.

The little man stalked away a few steps in the direction of the clubhouse. Then he turned around and addressed Porter. "You're not as old as the rest of us, Jess Porter. You don't know yet how it feels t'be weak and tired all the time, unable t'do simple things that you take fer granted now. You won't always hit a golf ball as far as you do now. I'll promise you that." His voice dropped to a harsh whisper. "Well, you can have my place in this dumb little gang. And the gang can go to hell! I'm gonna enjoy my remainin' days. I'm gonna do things I've always wanted t'do. While I still can."

He turned again and walked away.

Wallis called after him, "Abe! Wait a minute! I'll give you a ride."

Without looking back, Lowman just waved and continued up the fairway.

"Why did he jump on you?" Glenn asked Porter.

"He's awfully upset about something. I think Tom's death has affected him. More than we realized.

"I can't play today after listening to that," Wallis said. "I'm goin' in. I've never heard him talk like this. Damn!"

Porter gestured weakly with both hands. "I hope I'm not the cause of this."

Glenn asked, "Why would you ever think that? You heard what he said about the funeral service and all that."

Porter said, "I'm sure he is very, very tired."

Wallis said, "He's sure frustrated about something."

Karns said, "He's also *right!* To hell with golf and everything else for today. I'm going home, too."

<hr />

Once again, Porter called Larona at the Philadelphia Marriott. The hotel operator rang her room, as before, and, as before, there was no answer.

161

Porter glanced at his watch. Eastern time zone. It would be about eight p.m. there. "May I leave a message please?"

"Yes, of course."

"Just leave a message for Missus Starr, saying Mister Porter called and requests that she phone him at her earliest convenience upon her return. She has my number. Okay?"

"Yessir. She's to call Mister Porter as soon as she returns."

"Thank you." He hung up. He really would like to have spoken with Larona. He wanted to hear the sound of her voice and its distinctive vitality. God, he missed her!

The telephone rang shortly after Patricia left for work Wednesday. Porter's heart quickened in anticipation. He snatched up his phone in the middle of the second tone. "Yes! Hello?" But it was not Larona. Instead, he heard Abe Lowman's weary voice.

The harshness that had scathed the golfers the day before had faded away. Now he spoke slowly, cautiously, like someone in a television thriller who feared his phone might be bugged. "Listen, Jess, we gotta decide what we're gonna do. Have you thought about what we should do with the--you know...?"

"Hello, Abe. Of course I've thought a lot about it. I have not changed my mind, though. I still believe we have to report it to the police."

Lowman instantly flared. "To hell with that! We all agreed--"

Porter tried to respond calmly. "That's my understanding, Abe. All three of us agreed to agree on what to do before anyone does anything."

Neither man spoke for a few seconds. Then Porter added, "We can figure this out, Abe. Just be patient a while longer. Please. Listen, I expect to leave town next week. I promise you now I will not take one dollar of the--uh, of the *swag*, with me. At that time you and Braun can do whatever you see fit."

Porter had not consciously formulated this idea before he stated it. It simply spilled out, a concession that surprised him as much as it did Lowman. Now that he had said it, he knew he would have to stick with it.

"Well, I guess that's all right," Lowman said. "Meanwhile, that stuff might as well be buried out on the hill. If you're willin' t'give it up in a week, why not now? What difference will another week make anyhow?"

"Just let me think about it a while longer, Abe. I'm trying to meet you halfway. Have you talked to Slim today?"

"Aw, t'hell with it!" said Lowman and hung up.

***

Porter waited at the golf course for the gang to show up, unsure whether anyone would come after Lowman's big blowup. His thoughts now dwelt on Larona. He had waited all morning for her to return his call. Neither his cell nor the house phone made a sound. He wondered if she had received the message he had left for her. He wished he had talked with her, before she left on this trip. He wished he could hold her in his arms.

He could think of nothing to do but wait. It occurred to him that his feelings for Larona were not unlike Abe Lowman's feelings for the money. Very frustrated. He wondered how long it would take him to get over his feelings for her when he got back to New Mexico.

He pulled out his driver and swung it to loosen up. After a few swings, he checked his watch. Five minutes until one. Since he had started playing with this gang, someone had always shown up by this time. He took several balls and his putter from his bag and started in the direction of the putting green when he saw Doc Jensen's white Cadillac pull up by the cart sheds. He returned the balls and putter to his bag and waited.

Shortly, the doctor's golf cart appeared around the corner of the sheds and approached Porter.

"Hello, Nate," Porter called.

"Hello, Jess," the physician answered with a smile. "Where is everybody? In the clubhouse?"

"No one here today. Just me."

"Hmmph! That's darned unusual."

Porter picked up his clubs again and walked toward the first tee.

Doctor Jensen drove his cart alongside. "This is such a pretty day, I thought we would surely have everyone out here."

"You know, Nate, yesterday there were--let's see--six of us, I think, and we broke up early. There may have been--were--hard feelings. After a moment, he added, "Abe was most upset."

"Broke up? Hard feelings? What are you talking about?"

"I don't think there was truly ill will. Everybody was still a bit downcast after Tom's funeral. But Abe seemed awfully tired... irate about something, and the rest of us..."

Doctor Jensen had stopped his cart, and Porter stood beside him. The physician held up his hand. "I have to stop you. I cannot play ignorant about this. I know, Jess. I had a conversation with Abe yesterday evening."

"Really! What did he say?"

"Let's just say he was anxious. Maybe a little angry. And you're absolutely right that he was very tired."

"I guess you do a lot of counseling in your practice."

The doctor nodded. "Tom Tipton just died. Now Abe says he doesn't want to play anymore. I hope the whole gang wasn't upset." Sadly, he continued. "This group has been very important in my life."

"Karns was upset, too. Ray Wallis didn't seem upset with the golf, just about Abe's behavior. He'll be back, I'm sure."

"I notice he's not here today."

"I'd hate to think that I've been responsible for this--this coolness among your friends," said Porter.

"You? Why should you think you're responsible?"

"Maybe not *responsible.* But I have been involved with Abe in something that I'm not at liberty to discuss. I think that matter is at the root of his problem."

Doctor Jensen looked away, as though collecting his thoughts. Then he exhaled slowly, audibly. He faced Porter and said, "You mean about finding Sanford's money?"

Astounded, Porter stuttered. "Y-you mean Abe told you about that?"

Doctor Jensen nodded. "He said it was you, Slim, and him."

"Damn, I am surprised! That was supposed to be a total secret!"

"As far as I know, it still is. Just happens to be one more person in on it." The doctor laughed. "It's still a secret...if four people can keep a secret."

Porter stared at the sky, not knowing how to deal with this revelation. "Yes, well, I guess you're right. Four is no different from three, really. It doesn't change anything."

"Do you know what you fellows will do about the money? That's what Abe is most upset about."

"Not for sure. But I think he and Ray--and now maybe you--will decide after I leave town next week. I just hope that whatever action they and you decide to take doesn't follow me to Albuquerque. My involvement might raise some legal questions that I don't need."

"Yesterday Abe sounded like he wants to go on a world cruise." He smiled. "Actually, Nate, I find it's a bit of a relief to know that he told you. How did he happen to discuss it with you?"

"I've been his private physician and friend for many years. Our children were once very close. He was bursting to tell someone what was on his mind. He needed to share it. He knows I won't discuss it with anyone who is not already involved."

Porter nodded. "Okay. So you know. Okay with me."

Doctor Jensen asked, "Did I just now hear you say you're leaving town next week?"

"I expect to, yes."

"I'm awfully sorry to hear that, Jess. I was hoping you would stay longer, maybe even decide to live here indefinitely. This community would be better with you here."

"Thank you very much, Nate. But it's just not in the cards."

"What about Larona Starr?"

"What do you mean?"

"I have heard--Well, let's say I had the impression that you and she-- that you are fond of her."

"Oho, yes, I'm very, very fond of her," said Porter. He nodded. "But I'm afraid that ship has sailed. I believe that from now on we're just going to be good friends."

"I see...or maybe I don't really see. I'm sorry. None of my business. I just know you would be good for her, and I believe you two would be good for each other. I like both of you and was hoping something would develop there."

"Thanks, Nate. Larona's about the most special.... Well, you know Larona. I've never met anyone like her. Hell, there probably *isn't* anyone else like her! Trouble is, she moves in an entirely different world. I'm afraid it just can't happen."

Doctor Jensen removed his eyeglasses, wiped them on a sleeve, and nodded. Then he continued. "Larona is a patient of mine, you know. She has long been a favorite of mine. She has had a hard life in some respects, though spectacular in others. Over all...well, she certainly has all the worldly goods she needs.

"One thing you must understand is that her marriage long ago to an older man was merely a matter of accommodation at best. She needs a few years with a good man like you, Jess."

He chuckled and replaced his glasses. "How's that for trying to run your life?" he asked.

"I think that in addition to the worldly goods you mentioned, Larona is very lucky to have a friend like you, Nate."

After a moment, the doctor said, "It's after one o'clock. You want to play golf or not?"

"Let's hit a few. This may be the last time I play this course. From here on, I have to play at the Country Club--for the fund-raiser, you know."

"Have to?"

"Yes. I've committed to play there. An exhibition round. I'm not very enthusiastic about it, though. In my state of mind, I probably can't beat anybody."

"And what else?" asked Doctor Jensen.

Porter looked at him, hard. "You're a sage old guy, Nate. You read me like a book, don't you? 'What else?' you ask. Sure. It's Larona Starr's event. I'll die a little every time I see her there. Two days of that. How in the world am I going to concentrate on golf?"

Porter pulled out his driver. "Com'on. I need to hit something. In my frame of mind, I might just put a ball into orbit!"

Normally, when Porter drove away from the golf course, he turned right, toward Patricia's place. This afternoon, however, he chose to turn left along the northeast corner of the golf course. Then he turned left again at the first crossing, toward Starr of the Prairie Pharmaceuticals.

He rationalized that if, by chance, Laronna had returned, he might be able to see her Continental. Slowly, as he approached the main gate, he peered toward the parking lot in front of the administration building. He could not spot her car. He gave the LeSabre some gas.

Almost instantly a horn sounded, repeatedly, close behind. He braked instantly, fearing he had pulled out in front of someone. He glanced at his rearview mirror and saw that Larona's Continental had stopped behind him.

He jumped out immediately and saw that Larona had already reached the front door on the other side of his car. He quickly climbed back in and unlocked the door for her.

He realized that he was grinning from ear to ear. Larona was chattering something about being able to catch him as she returned from the airport. They squeezed each other's hands. Vaguely, he realized that she had sent the chauffeur away. Her car had disappeared. They were alone together again. He wanted to hug her and smother her with kisses and tell her he adored her.

But he said, "I was cruising by, looking for your car to see if you had returned yet."

"I just landed in Wichita and Marty met the plane and brought me here. I'm awfully glad to see you, Jess."

"I'm glad to see you, too. I needed to apologize for the abrupt way I left you the other day. I tried to reach--"

"Don't I get a welcome-home kiss?"

"He released her hands. "I--we shouldn't do that here in full view of the company buildings, should we?"

Somewhat reluctantly, she sat back. "Perhaps not." She frowned.

"I tried to get in touch with you while you were away," he said. "First I tried to call you in Atlanta, but they had no record. Walter Edwards gave me that wrong number."

"Oh goodness! I probably gave him that wrong number some time ago. We went to Atlanta last year."

"Yes, I learned that later. Then I called you in Philadelphia and left a message."

"They gave me your message. It said to call when I got home. I would have done that if I had not seen you here first."

He shook his head. "No. I meant to call as soon as you got to your hotel room. I wanted to talk to you. I wanted to hear your voice."

The frown disappeared. Her eyes sparkled. "Then you've changed your mind since we last talked. That's wonderful. I had a terrific idea while I was away, Jess. Listen. S O P has a department which produces educational symposia for physicians. We hold about twenty meetings a year in different cities all over the country. Doctors can attend and fulfill their state and national requirements for continuing medical education. Hundreds attend. Many of them would be tickled to death to take an afternoon after the meetings to play golf with someone like you. You would be a perfect P R representative for the company. We could make it one of--"

"No. Just wait a minute." He shook his head. "I can't stay. That's a truly inspired idea, Larona, but I can't do that. I feel as strongly as ever about you. God! I can't tell you how much you mean to me. But my common sense continues to tell me that you and I could never find a way--"

"Yes, we can, my love." Larona spoke urgently. The spark fled from her eyes as she realized what he was saying. Tears suddenly welled there instead. "I know that I want us to find a way."

"Sweetheart, you just do not seem to understand that we live in different worlds," Porter said softly but as firmly as he could manage. "I came here today to drink in the vision of you and to hear you. I will always care for you, but that has to be the extent of it. I just want you to know that we can continue to be...best friends."

"Of course, Jess." She gathered her disappointment and flatly said, "We will always be friends." She daubed at her eyes with a tissue. "I told you I never cry. I'm not going to now. *I'm too old for that.*"

"Oh, Larona it's not about ages--"

Before he could say more, she unlatched the door and stepped out of the car.

"Larona," he called.

But she had started walking, almost running, away from the car and back to the main entrance to Starr of the Prairie, her company and her world.

Porter met Slim Braun at the country club Thursday morning to continue preparation for the golf exhibition. The bright sky and low humidity promised a beautiful summer day.

Braun greeted him jauntily. "'Good morrow to the day so fair: Good morning, Sir, to you.'"

When Porter failed to respond, Braun said, "Oh, we're a little dour today, are we?"

"Sorry, Slim. It is a pretty day, but I didn't get much sleep last night. I just want to get this fund-raiser thing done. I haven't played a really competitive match in years. My game's not in synch. I know I'll find a way to screw up. Just the way I've been screwing up a lot of other things lately."

"Well then, I don't suppose you want to talk about the money either?"

"I have not changed my mind about that. But I told Abe that he and you can do whatever you wish after I leave Clydeston next week. Just as soon as this golf match is over."

"I'll be sorry to see you leave, Jess."

"Thanks. By the way, did you know that Doctor Jensen knows about Sanford's money? Abe told him."

"What? Dammit! I don't believe it! Soon everybody will know! If we don't decide what to do, we may all wind up in hot water. Or jail!"

"Do you know any good quotes about that?" asked Porter.

The two men soon found themselves on the course. With no one playing immediately behind them, they took their time. Porter tried to work on his shots. If he failed to hit a ball as he wished, he dropped a second ball and hit it. Frequently, he made observations about the rough, about distances, about angles of approach, and Braun entered them into the notebook he had started.

They proceeded methodically in this manner without much conversation. Porter tried hard to concentrate on his golf, but his mind continually returned to Larona Starr and the murder of Lenny Sanford.

When they picked up on the eighth green, Porter said, "Slim, do you have any idea what really happened to Sanford?"

Braun shook his head. "I wondered a lot about that at the time he disappeared and off and on ever since. I never had a clue. And I never heard anyone say anything that made much sense. He ran with some undesirable people, I understand. Most folks around here thought some mobster-types did him in. And he had a lot of girl friends, I understand. One of them could have had a jealous boy friend. Or husband."

"It seems to me," said Porter, "that the money may be the key to understanding it."

"What do you mean?"

"Well, why was the money left out there near the corpse? Why didn't the killer take it with him?"

"Hey, I see what you mean." Braun stroked his chin. "Until we found that money, you know, it was only a rumor. Some people suspected Tom Tipton might have done a job on Sanford because Tom had a good motive. Sanford had cheated him on the real estate development."

"That's what I've heard," said Porter.

"Over the years, Tom made an effort to pay back people who had lost money. He couldn't pay it all, of course, but he'd give back a small percentage of what they lost. At least that's what I heard. I also heard some folks blame him and say he was paying back with money stolen from Sanford. Now we know that wasn't true."

"Did Tom ever take bankruptcy?" Porter asked.

"Naw. He came from another generation that didn't care much for that. Bankruptcy used to be considered an admission of failure--something sort of sinful, you know. Nowadays if someone stubs his toe, he files for bankruptcy cause his toe hurts. The guy who files gets away with all his assets, and the people he owed have to absorb the loss. Nowadays you don't have to be responsible for what you do 'cause it's so easy to bail out. Tom wasn't like that. He figured that if he gave someone his word on a deal, he should stand behind his promise to the end, come hell or high water."

"Okay. Then Tipton surely wouldn't have left the money out there on the golf course."

"Yeah, I believe that. He would've used it to pay people back. He would have figured it belonged to the people who got cheated."

Braun added, "If you had known Tom longer, you'd know he would never have killed anybody. Not for any reason."

"I'm still in the dark as to why the money was stashed out there," Porter said.

"Well," mused Braun, "I'd say, at least, the murderer didn't need it. Right?"

"Someone who was already well off financially?"

"Yeah. Or perhaps was afraid the money could be traced if he or she spent it."

Porter froze at that reference. "She? Why did you say 'she'?"

Braun shrugged. "Persons unknown. He or she. No special reason."

"A woman wouldn't have been likely to drag a body out there on the golf course and bury it, would she?"

"Well, I guess not, not by herself anyway. But if Sanford were forced to go out there before he was shot, he didn't have to be dragged."

"I think he was shot in his office at the nightclub," said Porter. "Remember, he was wrapped in a rug when we found him. That's likely how he left the club. I talked with a woman who worked at the club, and she said she always thought there was a woman waiting outside for Sanford that night. If so, it might have been a couple who did it."

"Really!" said Braun with surprise. "You talked to someone from those days! Man! You really have been digging into this thing, haven't you!"

Porter nodded. Yeah, *digging* more ways than one."

They were startled by a voice. "You fellows mind if we play through?"

Braun and Porter looked around to find three men and a woman who had caught up with them while they stood talking.

"Sorry to hold you folks up." They laughed and waved the foursome to go ahead. Porter added, "We just got absorbed in conversation here."

While the others stepped up and teed off on nine, Porter said, "All this murder, money, and mystery have been on my mind a lot, Slim, as you can see. Like you, I expect. I find it difficult to concentrate on golf. What say we call it a day and ride back in?"

"Okay. I've had enough, too."

As they drove back toward the clubhouse. Braun said, "I agree about the money, Jess. I guess the killer just didn't need it."

"If he didn't need it, why take it from the office in the first place? Why not just leave it there? Same for the body." Porter feigned great seriousness and said, "Slim, you're always well attired and appear pretty affluent for a retired school teacher. Did you do the crime?"

"My wife's daddy left her well off," Braun laughed. "But not that well off. I would have taken the money."

Braun left for home immediately after returning to the clubhouse.

Porter showered leisurely, enjoying the stinging hot spray followed by a sharp, cold rinse. After dressing, he ate a barbecued beef sandwich with iced tea in the club restaurant.

On the way out of the club, he stopped by Walter Edward's office to see if there were any special instructions he needed to know about for the Saturday event. Edwards wasn't in, but his assistant assured Porter that they would be in touch. Porter thanked her and walked out into the bright sunshine.

The shower and food had greatly refreshed him. For the first time in several days, he did not feel totally weighed down by anxieties about Larona, or the mystery surrounding Sanford's corpse, or finding the money, or the impending challenge on the golf course. He enjoyed the sun's beating on him as he approached the LeSabre.

Before he could get in, Doyle Dugan's Bronco II swung alongside and the reporter popped out. "Hi, Jess," he called jauntily. "Hey, I need an interview. What say we take a couple of minutes?"

Immediately, Porter felt a temptation to say no, but he restrained the impulse. "What is it about, Dugan? I'm about to leave."

"Hey, I just want to give our readers an update on your affairs." Dugan grinned and pulled out a recording device. "*Some* of your affairs, that is."

Porter's earlier opinion of Dugan had not changed. He frowned. The reporter struck him as abrasive and inconsiderate. Porter's mind jumped to Phyllis, the pretty librarian, who had implied a special relationship with Dugan. "Maybe you should do your interview at the library'" he suggested.

"Huh?" Dugan squinted without understanding. "Naw, I want to hear about the golf match, and maybe ask how you feel about finding that body. You know, for a newcomer to Clydeston, you really have gotten involved in some interesting activities."

Looking at his watch, Porter sighed. "What do you want to know?"

"We'd like to have a summary of your career as a pro golfer. You know, which tournaments did you win and so forth? What was your biggest win? Why did you quit the tour? Why don't you play in public anymore? Why do you just play with a bunch of old stumblebums who can hardly get around the course? How do you feel about this fund-raiser? Why do you--"

"That's a lot of personal stuff that I don't need to go into, Dugan. My golfing history should be available to you in your paper's sports department files."

"I just--"

"As far as my reasons for playing this weekend are concerned--and be sure your recorder is on--you can say I'm happy to do it for charity, for the kids of the Harrison House."

"I hear...." Dugan's voice trailed off as he realized that Porter did not intend to answer anything in depth. "Hell, Jess, why are you so touchy?"

Porter rose somewhat and leaned toward the reporter. His voice hardened. "Dugan you can print this: I think you are a jerk. You are disrespectful, two-faced, and inconsiderate."

"What? What do you mean? Hell, I--"

"You can print this: *Stay away from me and from my daughter.*"

"Trish? What's she got to do with this?"

Porter climbed into the car and slammed the door.

At that moment, Larona Starr's Continental swung into the parking lot and slowly passed in front of Porter and Dugan. She sat in the back seat. As her car moved past, she glanced toward Dugan. She saw Porter, too, at the same instant he recognized her. Surprised, she smiled, then seemed to withdraw.

Porter raised his hand to wave, but the moment passed quickly, and he wasn't sure whether she saw him or not. For an instant, he thought about leaping out of his car and following her to the front door of the club....

"That's another thing," Dugan said with a sneer. "That's something the people of Clydeston deserve to know about you, Mister."

Porter barked, "What's that supposed to mean?"

Dugan poked his forefinger through the car window into the vicinity of Porter's nose: "I'm talking about your shenanigans with Larona Starr. The whole town knows what you're up to, and *we* don't like it."

Porter brushed Dugan's finger aside and said, "Oh, we don't, huh? Just what is it that you don't like, hotshot?"

Dugan stepped back at the anger he heard, and he hesitated briefly before he went on. "We all know what you're up to--everybody in town--Larona Starr is a wealthy and influential lady, and you're here trying to sweep her off her feet. We think you're a fortune hunter, and we don't want to have some--some deadbeat, some has-been, like you come in here and mess up the biggest industry in the county.

Porter's eyes flashed angrily. Then he realized that the reporter was actually frightened as he had blurted the accusation. Porter laughed. "That's what you think, eh?" He eased back into the car seat and switched on the engine. Shaking his head, he added, "You're a two-bit twit, Dugan. You know that?"

"Oh yeah?" Dugan recovered his courage when he saw Porter was about to leave. "I've looked you up, Mister. I checked you out. I know you don't have a permanent job. I know you haven't played a tough round of golf in years. You're in this event under false pretenses. I know that you'll get your butt whipped Sunday--no matter who you play. You'll fold up like a--like a cracker box! And that's what I'm gonna predict in tomorrow's paper!"

"You do that, dummy. Just remember that this exhibition is a community fund-raiser. You do anything negative that makes it unsuccessful, and the pillars of the community will be on you like hawks on a sneaky little garter snake."

Porter shoved the gear shift and tromped on the accelerator.

Out of Dugan's hearing, he added, "But, dammit, you're probably right about my chances of coming out of this thing a winner."

Porter's cell phone rang as he reached Patricia's house. Some unknown driver crossed in front of him and diverted his attention, so he did not answer before the caller hung up.

He parked and then checked for a message. Immediately he recognized great tension and impatience in the voice. "Hullo, Jess Porter. This is Abe. I need t'hear from you. We need t'decide something about what t'do with the--the stuff in the garage. Tomorrow's Friday and I don't think it's fair t'drag on this way. Well...call me. Let's talk." He added a phone number.

Porter went inside and sat down, intending to return Abe's call, but he stopped in mid-dial. What could he say? He had already told Lowman that next week Lowman and Braun could do as they wished. After he left Clydeston.

Doc Jensen knew about it, too. Those three could settle the matter.

Also, Porter had been intrigued by the idea that he needed to understand more about the role of Sanford's money. *Why had it been taken from the office and buried?* He believed that the answer to this question would unravel the mystery. Somehow. Maybe. He wanted to think about that a little while longer.

He erased the message and put the phone back into his pocket.

<hr />

Restless all night, Porter rose with the sun. Without wakening Patricia, he donned his jogging clothes and slipped outside.

Pink clouds layered the eastern sky. There was no wind, and the humidity was low. Both would rise later. The day would be clear and hot, he knew. He hoped the weekend weather would be good for the fund-raiser tourney. Or, he mused, perhaps a storm will come from a guardian angel and rain out the golf. He could be saved the ignominy that he believed must lie awaiting him. A rainout? "Haw! No such luck!"

He ran through a small city park shaded by mature elms. There was a litter-strewn bandstand in the middle of the park. A hundred yards beyond, he turned and followed a railroad track that ran down the center of the street. The tracks appeared unused, being rusty except at the street intersection, where they were kept brightly polished by crossing auto traffic.

He crossed them, too, and shortly found himself on South Main Street. It was early, and only two cars were parked in the next block. He jogged on the sidewalk. Since there was practically no traffic he ran through a red light. As always, running loosened and invigorated him. The dark thoughts that taunted him during the night faded in the warmth of the sunlight and the pleasure and vigor of exercise.

Porter reached the bank that was across from the Coffeepot Cafe, where he intended to eat. He stopped and stared at the front window. Venetian blinds shielded the interior from view. He speculated about the wisdom of bringing Sanford's money here for safe keeping.

Suddenly someone asked, "Thinking about robbing it, Mister Porter?"

Startled, Porter looked around. "Hey, Chief, I didn't hear your car! That's really a smooth-running Ford!"

In his cruiser at the curb, Chief Still smiled pleasantly. "Nice morning, isn't it?" commented the officer. "You jog every day?"

"Most. Not all." Porter stepped toward the vehicle. "Yes, I agree. Looks like it'll be a pretty day. How are you, Chief?"

"I'm just fine, thanks. Pretty busy these days. And speaking of *busy*, how's your investigation coming along?"

"My investigation?"

"You were nosing around about Lenny Sanford's death the other day. You remember, I'm sure, how you were asking me all sorts of things. Did you learn anything that I should know?"

"Oh that--" Porter said, "I'm afraid I didn't learn much. The trail is too old." He laughed.

"That's just as well. I wouldn't want you to stir up something that makes more work for me. I'm busy enough."

Porter nodded, trying to show how much he agreed.

"I understand you have a big weekend of golf coming up."

"That's right. Will you be attending, Chief? At the country club."

"I'd sure like to, if I can get away for a while."

Somehow Porter felt that Chief Still's encountering him in front of the bank smacked of more than coincidence. Had the Chief been following him? Nothing in the officer's demeanor suggested anything more than a chance meeting and a casual greeting. But Porter believed this cop saw and knew a lot more than he let on. "You'll be welcome, I'm sure."

"Yeah. Well, I wish you luck, Mister Porter." He shoved the gear shift into Drive. "I've gotta move on. Be seeing you." He waved.

Porter returned the gesture as Chief Still drove away. He hoped he didn't have to confront that cop when the others decided what to do with the money. He wished he had not accompanied Braun and Lowman the night they dug it up. All this concern could have been avoided.

He crossed the street to The Coffee Pot Cafe and entered. It was still too early for many of the merchants who usually gathered every morning. He found fewer than a dozen customers inside. He sat in a booth by the front window. From this seat he stared across at the dark window of the bank and thought about money.

For the thousandth time, he mulled over the things he had learned about Lenny Sanford and his mysterious death. He made up scenarios which might fit the events of that night long ago, scenarios involving the people and faces as he had learned them. He mentally massaged the information, twisted it, tried to make one piece fit with another. Always he found that he knew too little or that one piece of information conflicted with another, negating a conclusion. He was merely a stranger here, after all. Years ago the mystery had been probed thoroughly by people who were much better qualified than he. If *they* didn't know what happened, how could he figure it out?

The waitress took his order for a sweet roll and coffee. As she walked away, he overheard two more customers entering the shop. They were arguing at the tops of their voices about something a second baseman had done in Kansas City the night before to beat the White Sox.

"How could that be?" one man asked.

"It jist couldn't be, but the umpire let it go," said the second.

They continued enthusiastically with their debate, but Porter heard no more. Their words echoed words he had heard elsewhere. Something that had eluded him had now suddenly, unexpectedly, fallen into place. Like a row of falling dominoes, other pieces of his puzzle clicked in a neat pattern. A scenario with which had had previously struggled unsuccessfully now appeared simple, clear, probable, and supportable.

Without waiting for his coffee and roll, he laid a ten dollar bill on the table and darted out. He needed to get home and make a couple of phone calls.

ASAP!

Doctor Jensen's professional suite was alone on the fourth, and top, floor of an old, red brick building on North Main Street. Three other physicians and a dentist occupied suites on the lower floors, but most of the building was vacant. Previous professional tenants had opted for more modern office space nearer the hospital in the middle of Clydeston. Doctor Jensen's space was clean and neat, but many layers of cracked white paint on the window and door frames shouted the structure's age.

Porter waited impatiently for the doctor. He watched a thin, gray-haired nurse--probably as old as the doctor--shuffle papers at a reception counter.

At last Doctor Jensen appeared at his office door, ushering out an elderly man in blue overalls. When the patient left, Porter stood. Doctor Jensen smiled and said, "Hello, Jess. How are you, this morning? Missus Briggs here said you called. What can I do for you?"

"We need to talk, Nate."

Missus Briggs thrust a clipboard toward Porter. "Here. Fill out this patient history," she ordered.

Porter waved her off. "No need for that." To the physician he added, "This is not a medical matter, Nate."

Doctor Jensen showed no expression. "Okay. Come on in, Jess."

To the receptionist, Porter said, "Mister Abe Lowman will come along any minute. When he arrives, please tell him to join us."

She looked to Doctor Jensen, who nodded. Then he waved Porter into the office and closed the door. He gestured to a chair for Porter, then sat in his own worn leather chair behind his desk. He adjusted the position of his crippled legs with both hands after sitting down, grunting with the exertion. "Sounds as though you have something on your mind."

Porter nodded. "Afraid so. Sorry to barge in this way. I'm not sure how to begin."

Receiving no comment from Doctor Jensen, he plunged ahead. "You told me that Abe told you about the money we found at the golf course the other night."

"Yes."

Porter waited a moment, but received nothing more from the doctor who, clearly, was not going to volunteer anything until he heard why Porter had come to him. "Okay, first, the money is still in Abe's garage. As far as I know, that is. Abe desperately wants to take it out and split it up. I think it should be reported to the authorities. Slim Braun will go either way, I think."

"I see." Doctor Jensen placed his finger tips together and stared hard through his thick lenses at Porter. "What do you want from me, Jess?" he asked softly.

Porter decided to plunge in. "Nate, I've become very fond of you and your golfing buddies in the short time I've been in Clydeston. I wouldn't do anything to offend any of you if I can avoid it. I hope you know that. I have something on my mind, however, that I just have to spit out."

The doctor nodded again without changing expression.

Porter said, "Ever since we found the body of Lenny Sanford, I've had concerns about how he died and who might have been responsible."

"That was a long time ago, Jess. Many people have come to Clydeston and many have left since then."

"I understand that. But I have heard some things--strange comments-- that have been unsettling to me. Things I can't get out of my head. Possibly just coincidences, I'll grant you. I have to tell them to somebody, though. I know that Abe has confided in you with his problems. I'm sure many other people come to you, too, at one time or another, for one reason or another. You're the one most likely to be able to tell me whether what I'm thinking is true or not."

"Very well."

"Do you remember when Ray Wallis spotted that mannequin in the golf pond?"

"The mannequin? Sure." Doctor Jensen chuckled, the first change in his expression since Porter arrived.

"Well, when Abe saw it--before it was identified as a dummy--he said something like 'How can he be here?' and you said, 'He can't be' Those may not be the exact words, but they're close. And Abe didn't speak those words to Wallis. He spoke them to *you!* I didn't think anything about it at the time. Now I realize that if Abe knew Sanford's body was somewhere on that golf course, his first thought upon seeing the mannequin might have been *How did Sanford's body get clear over here into the pond after we buried him up on that hill?*"

"But it wasn't Sanford's body," Doctor said.

"Right. But Abe didn't know that for a few minutes. At the time he said it, he thought he was looking at a real body."

Porter paused. He and the doctor looked hard into each other's eyes.

"And your comment, Nate--You said, 'It couldn't be.' What did you mean by that?"

Doctor Jensen looked away. He shifted in his chair. Before answering, he rubbed a finger alongside his nose and removed his glasses. "I'm not at all sure I remember saying anything like that, Jess. If I did, I probably just meant that the mannequin surely could not have been a human body."

"That's all I thought at the time, Nate. But later, after we found an actual body--Sanford--the comments by Abe and you can be taken another way. They may mean that you two guys knew there was a human body out there, somewhere in the vicinity."

"Are you serious, Jess? How would either of us have known a thing like that?" Doctor Jensen sounded mildly amused.

"If you had buried him, you would know."

"Look at me!" The doctor struggled to his feet. "Do you think a man with my legs could climb around a hill and bury anybody?"

"You were much younger in those days," Porter said. "And if I were a policeman, I'd insist that an orthopedic doctor should check and see how bad you are really crippled."

"That's a heinous accusation!" Doctor Jensen waved a hand and nearly fell across his desk.

"Oh, damn it, Nate, I'm sorry. I'm just--"

Doctor Jensen caught his breath and smiled. "I can see that you are really caught up in this thing. And I can see your point of view. It's all right. But your conjectures are quite a reach. You must know that when Sanford disappeared years ago, the police checked on both Abe and me. Along with many other persons. They thought both of us had motives. They were satisfied, however."

"I know you both had motives because of Sanford's relations with your kids."

"The police didn't--"

Porter butted in: "The police didn't pursue the investigation because Sanford was only missing. I know that. They didn't know he had been murdered, and they were happy to have him gone. You and Abe had alibis for each other. You had been giving him a physical or something. When I first heard about Sanford--y'know, after I arrived in Clydeston--I sort of suspected Abe had done him because of the beating Abe's son had gotten. It wasn't until today that I realized the two of you were working together."

Doctor Jensen shook his head. "No, my friend, it's quite a coincidence, but those remarks about the mannequin were truly innocent, I assure you."

The door to the office opened, and Abe Lowman entered. "Hullo, Jess. Hullo, Doc," he said. Jess here called and said I should come over here as soon as possible. I guess you're talkin' about the money. Have you decided how t'handle it? Kin we split it today?"

"Sit down, please," said Doctor Jensen. "It appears that Jess thinks you and I were responsible for the death of Lenny Sanford."

Surprised, Lowman whirled toward Porter. "What! How do you--I mean, why do you say such a damn thing?"

Porter repeated what Lowman and the doctor had said when the mannequin was first spotted at the pond and what he thought that meant.

Lowman flung up his hands. "Hell, that's nothin', Jess. I don't remember sayin' nothin' like that anyway."

"Well then, how about the fact that you knew where to dig for the money, Abe?" Porter asked in a quiet voice.

Lowman snorted and paced around the end of the desk. He looked to Doctor Jensen before answering. "Heck, that was jist a lucky guess," he said finally. "You were there. We tried t'figure where someone might have hidden it, remember? Jist lucky, that's all."

"Pretty lucky all right, I agree. We could have dug around there for days without finding the money. But when we were nearly ready to quit, you pointed out the right location."

Porter turned to Doctor Jensen. "You weren't there, Nate. At the time, I thought Abe had made a good, logical guess. But these little pieces of the puzzle are coming together. After we found Sanford's body, the remarks you made at the pond earlier sound pretty significant."

Lowman fell silent and sat down. He and Doctor Jensen exchanged glances. The physician said, "These things you're saying are mere speculation. Coincidences. They aren't proof."

"Dammit, Nate, I don't want to prove anything," Porter declared. I'm not a cop. I'm just trying to figure out what happened that night."

Lowman said, "Does that mean you're not gonna report the money to the police?"

Porter considered the question. "We've already discussed that. You know how I feel." Very deliberately he added, "If you tell me everything that happened, you can do whatever you wish with the money after I leave town. But if you don't tell me, I will go to the police."

Again Lowman looked for guidance from the physician. After a moment, Doctor Jensen sighed ponderously and nodded.

Lowman laughed nervously. "I guess it had t'come out someday, huh? Tell him, Doc."

"It appears that he has already figured out most of it, Abe."

"I believe Sanford had caused your son to be beaten almost to death, Abe. Apparently, he also ruined your daughter's relationship with her fiance', Nate. Both of you clearly had powerful reasons to do him in."

Unexpectedly, Doctor Jensen said, "My daughter, Jennifer, was raped by Sanford. She was pregnant."

"What!" Lowman cried out.

Porter was speechless.

"She was at her wit's end when she took Jamie from the hospital and ended both their lives. I have a note from her which I received in the mail two days after she died. She explained it all in writing before she went to the hospital that night to get Jamie," Doctor Jensen said. He opened the drawer in his desk and brought out an envelope which he handed to Lowman. I never showed this to anyone until now."

Abe read the note quickly then handed it back to the doctor. He removed his glasses and wiped his eyes. "That son of a bitch got what he deserved. We didn't intend t'kill him, though. Not at first anyhow."

Doctor Jensen said, "We went to him, you see, to confront him alone and try to force him to admit to the police that he was responsible for having Jamie beaten up.

"We went to The Pretty Kitty--that damned place--that night and accused him and tried to force him to admit it. But he just laughed at us. He said we would be happy to know that he was leaving Clydeston. He had a bag of money with him. He laughed and showed it to us. He taunted us and pushed me aside. He was younger and bigger than either of us. When I realized that he was about to get away without punishment and that he would be beyond our reach, I shot him. Just like that. I just pointed the pistol and pulled the trigger. God! It was easy!

"I had taken a little twenty-two caliber target pistol with me, you see, but I had not expected to use it. Truly. We just wanted to scare him into confessing. Christ! I just removed him from this earth as easily as I would remove a splinter from your finger." He shook his head sadly.

After a moment of silence, Porter said, "Tell me about the money."

The buzzer on the desk intercom interrupted them. With some irritation, Doctor Jensen answered, "Yes?"

"Missus Hackett is on the phone, Doctor. She wants you to--"

"You take care of her, Missus Griggs. Give her an appointment or whatever you need to do. And I want you to cancel the rest of today's appointments. I don't want to be disturbed. Tell them I'm sick. Then you go home. Thank you." He flicked off the intercom. After readjusting his legs, he leaned back in his chair and sighed. "Damn! Where were we?"

"I'd like to know why you took the money and buried it," Porter said.

"He didn't take it," declared Lowman. "I did. Sanford had it with him. He was skippin' out of town, he said. I figured it was money from south of the border or some other illegal money, and I didn't see no reason t'leave it fer cops or lawyers t'git their hands on. I jist picked it up as we left. Doc didn't even know I had it until we got outside of the club."

Doctor Jensen said, "I thought we should not keep it. I was afraid that somehow our possessing it or spending it would give us away. We didn't have time to discuss the matter. So Abe agreed to bury it and leave it indefinitely. I said the survivor between us could do whatever he wished with it."

Lowman said, "Later on, we figured that most of the money rightfully belonged to Tom Tipton, but we didn't know how t'return it without gettin' him or us into trouble."

"I see," Porter said. "But when the body was discovered last week, you decided--"

"Yeah," said Lowman. "I figured everything would come out, and we might as well try t'save the dough fer ourselves."

The three of them sat silently thinking about what had been disclosed about these events that had transpired about twenty years ago. Lowman looked to the doctor as though wishing to be told he had acted properly.

Doctor Jensen stared at the top of his desk, seeing only the ugly events of years past.

Porter respected their feelings. They had suddenly, without planning, purged themselves of secrets held for many years. Now the story flooded into the open. They had trusted him to hear them, but they had little idea about how he might handle the revelations.

Doctor Jensen said, "Things are different now from what they were when Sanford died. Abe and I still had productive years ahead of us then. We were concerned about keeping the secret. Today, things are much different...."

"Yeah, Doc had a lot of influence in this town in those days. Still does, I reckon. He was head of the school board, practically ran the hospital by himself, lots of stuff like that. He doesn't need to go t'jail fer what happened to that skunk."

Jensen said, "My wife committed suicide as a direct result of Jenny's death. I've lived without family for a long time. I'm an old man. I don't have a helluva lot to live for anymore."

"My wife is all I have," said Lowman, shaking his head. "It doesn't make much difference what happens t'me, I guess, but I don't want her t'have trouble that's my fault."

"Don't worry," Porter said. This information will go no farther than this room, as far as I'm concerned, gentlemen. I promise."

Lowman nodded and Doctor Jensen said, "Thank you, Jess."

"There is one more thing, however," Porter said.

"What's that?"

"It's something as important to me as what you've already told me. I understand that there was a woman present that night. I want to know who she was."

"Ahh," said Doctor Jensen. Suddenly his mood had changed and he grinned. "I see." He nodded at Lowman, who shrugged. Then he turned back to Porter. "That's why you've been knocking yourself out trying to solve this whole thing! Well, we won't tell you who it was.

"She was a friend of Jenny's. We asked her to help. So she made a date with Sanford to meet him when he closed the club. He was always last to leave. She told him she would wait for him in the parking lot. But as he came out that night and was ready to lock the door, we stepped up, instead of her, and forced him back inside. When we did that, the young lady drove away. There's absolutely no need to tell you who she was."

Porter said, "But--"

Doctor Jensen laughed. "I promise you, my friend, that the young lady was not the one you're worried about!" He went on. "The lady you're concerned about never did anything underhanded in her life. Take my word for it. She not only has more money than anyone else, she probably has more integrity. You may have heard otherwise, Jess, but, believe me, the gossip about her is only gossip, grown primarily out of envy and ignorance."

"Well!" Porter stood up and smiled. "I don't know what else to discuss. I thank you both for your candor and for trusting me with this tale."

Lowman stood up, too. "Jess, As we been talking, I've felt a great relief. Now I know I'd like t'get out from under the weight of this damned money. Fer the last few days I've acted like a real jackass. I was tired. I couldn't get no sleep. I insulted you, and maybe broke up the one-o'clock gang, all 'cause I've been so greedy.

"Doc, I'll bring the money to you, and I'll tell Ray. I think he'll be relieved."

All three men shook hands.

Outside the office building, Porter took a deep breath. Most of the dark questions that had hung over him for days had now been dissolved. Best of all being rid of the insidious doubts he had dreamed up about Larona Starr's past.

Thanks to Doc Jensen's word for that. His elation dimmed, however, when he remembered that he still did not belong in her world of high finance wheeling and dealing and pharmaceuticals.

Moreover, Patricia still held the lady in low esteem. These problems had not changed.

As he started to climb into the LeSabre, he noticed a police car slowly pass in the street. The seemingly ever-present Chief of Police waved cordially as he cruised by.

Porter wondered if that guy might be just one of a set of triplets!

At about twelve fifty p.m. Porter arrived at the municipal golf course. Nancy greeted him and said that no other players had arrived. "None of the regular bunch have been here for a couple of days. I don't know what has happened." She seemed downcast. "I've been here for years, you know, and somebody always shows up unless the weather is terrible. And the weather today is good. Do you intend to play?"

"I guess not." Porter had not truly wished to play. He had told himself he might loosen up in preparation for the weekend activities. Now, however, he decided a day off with some rest might be more beneficial. If his game were not ready now, it never would be.

The thought that the one-o'clock gang had broken up disturbed him just as it had Nancy. For these men to give up golf was for them to concede that a major part of their lives had ended! Somehow he could not let go of the thought that he had caused this situation. At least partly. If he had not nosed around about Lenny Sanford and the missing money, Abe would not have blown up the other day. Some harsh words would not have been spoken.

"Are you all right?" Nancy asked him.

"Sure. I'm okay."

"I guess you'll be having a big time at the country club this weekend, won't you?" She smile amicably.

"Who knows? I'll just be glad to get it done. I know that. I have a feeling it may be a disaster. For me, that is." He got off the counter stool where he had been sitting. "I don't expect to be around Clydeston much longer, Nancy. I'd like to thank you for your help and good service while I've been here."

"You're welcome, Mister Porter. I--"

"Jess," he said.

"Okay, Jess. Anyhow, we'll all be sorry to see you go. It's been a real pleasure."

"Well.... Thanks again."

As he passed through the doorway, she called after him, "You'll be great this weekend. I know you will."

At Patricia's house a phone message from Walter Edwards stated that Porter need not come to the country club until Saturday, but to be there by eight a.m. if possible. And all he needed to do was "bring your sticks."

There was a second message. It came from Dave Curtland, Porter's employer in Albuquerque. He wanted to know when Porter expected to return. They needed the LeSabre he had borrowed. They might have a customer for it.

Porter placed a call to Albuquerque and, in Curtland's absence, left a message for him stating that he expected to return with the Buick by the middle of next week.

Then he phoned Slim Braun and asked if they could meet for a few minutes.

The Clydeston Times carried a boxed story Friday evening on the front page.

Annual Gift-Of-Love-Fund-Raiser
Features Pro Golfer
by Doyle Dugan

The heart-warming annual fund-raiser for Clydeston's Harrison House features an exciting special attraction this year. A one-day play-off Saturday will be conducted with the winner competing Sunday against former great professional golfer Jesse Porter. It promises to be a tough match for the one-time PGA star.

Contestants include four of Kansas' top amateur linksmen. Will Stanley of Topeka, last year's state amateur champion, has promised to be here. Also competing will be Jack Partee from Ottawa, Chris Clouston, state junior college champ from Dodge City, and Clydeston's own Morris Brent, county champ and runner-up in last year's state tournament. Bonnie Oursler, state women's champ from Salina, will be here, too. These and many other fine golfers promise to produce a worthy contender to vie with Porter.

Golfing fans will remember Porter as a shining star who burst upon the PGA tour in the late 1980's. Though he had to give up professional competition for personal reasons, he told this reporter that he is now at the top of his game and itching to do everything he can to help the gate in this worthy charity event.

Porter has been visiting here in Clydeston with his daughter for several weeks. Therefore, he has had plenty of time to get tuned up for this weekend's bash. Porter's daughter is the attractive Patricia Porter Cameron, currently employed at Starr of the Prairie Pharmaceutical Company.

Here is your opportunity to see great golfers in person and in action, folks! Come out to the Country Club Saturday and Sunday for this extravaganza. Remember, it is for one of Clydeston's worthiest causes.

I wouldn't miss it! See you there!

For complete information about GOLF-R, see advertisement on page 4.

A photograph of Porter accompanied the article. Its background included the eighteenth green at the country club. Porter didn't know when Dugan had taken the picture, but assumed it had been sneaked during one of his practice rounds.

Patricia woke her father early Saturday morning. "Golly, Dad, I'm surprised you would oversleep today. I should think you would be awake early if anything."

Groggily, he noted the time. Seven o'clock. "Um, well, I was awake half the night. Couldn't sleep. Seems like I just dropped off a few minutes ago."

"Breakfast is ready."

Porter rushed through breakfast, showered, and dressed. The country club was no more than fifteen minutes away. He made it with a few minutes to spare.

Several young men in red shirts busily directed traffic. The main parking lot had almost filled, but he found a space and pulled in. He hauled his clubs from the trunk of the Buick and started for the pro shop. As he walked, he noted that an open lot across the road also had parking signs posted. If all that space got used, it would certainly assure a good crowd for the day.

Pastor Glenn met him near the pro shop with outstretched arms. "Good morning, Jess! My! Isn't this a glorious day? I haven't seen you for several days. How do you feel?"

"Hello, Cal. I'm fine," Porter responded much less enthusiastically. "How are you?"

"Actually, I wanted to ask what you may have heard about Lenny--about the body we found. Do you know how the investigation is progressing?"

"I guess the state police are looking into it, Cal.' I haven't heard of any new developments." Porter found himself trying to avoid Glenn's eyes as he avoided the whole truth.

"I know we're going to have a glorious success here today," Glenn exclaimed. He laughed, "I think you may have your hands full tomorrow. Actually, there are some really good golfers participating." He wouldn't wait for Porter to reply. "Here, you need this." He pinned a large black-and-gold GOLF-R button on Porter's shirt. "If that interferes with your swing, just move it."

"Thanks, Cal."

"I suppose you want to get dressed and all. I have to meet some folks inside. Actually, Walter asked me to tell you to be at the first tee at eight-thirty. Okay?"

"Sure."

"Oh yes. Larona Starr is here already. I'm sure you will want to say hello to her, too." He winked knowingly.

"Sure," Porter replied softly.

"Well, I have to run. Have a great day. God bless you for helping us."

"Have you seen Slim yet, Cal?"

"Yes. He's in the pro shop, I believe. Glenn waved and hurried off toward the front entrance of the club.

Porter pulled off the GOLF-R pin that Glenn had pinned on his shirt and stuffed it onto a nearby table. He found Braun in the pro shop, and Slim greeted him eagerly. "How you feel, Jess?"

"Oh hell, Slim, everybody has been asking how I feel, and I don't even know. Everybody else seems full of energy and disgustingly happy. One minute I'm up and the next I'm down. I just want to get through this day. And tomorrow."

"Yep. I can only imagine. They have some crackerjack golfers competing today."

"How are *you* feeling?"

"I'm okay. A little nervous, I reckon. I've never done anything like this before. You just let me know what I can do to help."

"Stick around close, and we'll go one step at a time."

189

"Okay."

"By the way, thanks for giving me a hand. I probably sound so depressed that you may think I don't appreciate having you here, but I do. I really do."

"Nothing to it," Braun laughed. "As long as I don't have to make any shots for you. 'I have nothing to offer but blood, toil, tears, and sweat.'"

Porter prepared himself and they moved out to the first tee on time. Walter Edwards was there with half-a-dozen men and women. As Edwards introduced everyone, Porter became aware that other persons nearby were pointing at him, identifying him as the advertised celebrity. A chill passed over him even as he smiled and waved at them. How in the world could he live up to this billing?

Edwards was saying "--and these folks are looking forward to your company for an hour or so."

Porter understood that he was supposed to accompany a foursome and make small talk with them. They had made large contributions to the fundraiser for the privilege of golfing with him. Perhaps he could give them a pointer or two. They'd be happy merely to say they had played with an honest-to-goodness professional golfer. He wondered how much they had paid for the dubious honor.

Smiling broadly, he said, "Good to meet all of you. This is Slim Braun. He's going to accompany us today. Fact is, Slim is the guy who tells me which clubs to use." He laughed at his small joke, and the others laughed politely and a bit impatiently. After all, Braun wasn't the celebrity.

Edwards said, "Jess, if you will be back at the practice green about ten, you're scheduled to give a little demonstration there at that time, as we discussed. Have fun, everybody." He waved and marched away.

The two couples teed off, and Porter watched them closely. They all had such flawed swings that he could have coached them for an hour nonstop. But he said, "You people do so well that I don't think you need me at all." They laughed self-consciously and proudly. Then he teed up and drove a ball more than a hundred yards beyond the longest ball any one of them had managed. Among the *ooh's* and *aah's* he heard a smattering of applause from other persons who had gathered to watch.

One boy in the crowd hollered, "Did you ever beat Tiger Woods?"

Porter laughed and said, "I was a little before his time, pal."

Another voice asked, "How about Tom Watkins?"

Porter answered, "He was awfully good," and walked a little faster.

An hour passed quickly, and both Porter and Braun found themselves actually enjoying the company of these folks. They seemed pleasant, friendly, and totally aware of their shortcomings as golfers. Porter entertained them with brief stories about his play earlier with legendary stars. After three holes, he signed autographs for them and shook hands all around. The foursome thanked Porter profusely for his tips. Then he and Braun headed back toward the eighteenth hole and the practice green nearby.

As they proceeded up the ninth fairway, they got a look at several golfers who were actually competing for Sunday's final match. Porter recognized Morris Brent. He watched as the young man hit a dazzling approach shot on nearby number two. The ball arched high and plunked down less than a club's length from the cup. Porter caught Brent's eye and waved. "Good shot, Morris," he called.

Brent grinned and waved back. Cupping a hand beside his mouth, he shouted across the fairway to Porter. "We're gonna make it tough for you tomorrow, Mister Porter."

"That fellow is pretty damn good," Braun said respectfully.

"You better believe it," Porter nodded.

About seventy persons had gathered at the practice green. Walter Edwards introduced Porter to the group, and Porter, as advertised, provided a short lesson in how to play out of sand traps. He dropped several balls into the bunker at the edge of the green and proceeded to chip or blast them up onto the green. He explained between shots how sand varies from hole to hole and with different degrees of moisture. The onlookers seemed appropriately impressed when several of his shots bumped into the flagstick. Twice he holed out. They applauded when he ended the demonstration. Several asked for autographs, which he scribbled quickly.

"Hey," said Braun, "you were really homing in on that flag!"

"It's not so hard, Slim. When you shoot ten or twelve in a row, from the same place, you get the feel and the rhythm. The hard shot is when you're out on the course and get only one try, without practice."

Walter Edwards materialized again. "That was just great, Jess. Just great. Exactly what we wanted! Boy, you'd make a great club pro! Hey, that's an idea, isn't it? We could really use you here! Seriously!"

Porter shook his head. "Thanks, Walter, but I have other plans. How is everything else going? Looks as if you have good attendance."

"It's terrific! We already have almost as much in the till this morning as we did in two days last year! This is one charity event that's a sure-fired howling success!"

"That's good to hear."

"We have another foursome reserved for you to take out for an hour. And we'd like for you to repeat the same routine this afternoon that you did this morning. Okay? Are you up for it?"

"Sure."

"Meantime, if you want to take a break for a few minutes or get something to eat...."

Porter nodded. "I'll pick up a snack."

Edwards clapped him on the shoulder. "Good. Then we'll see you on the first tee in a few minutes and again about two-thirty. Okay?" Without awaiting an answer, he hurried away.

Porter turned to Braun. "Do you want to--" He stopped when he saw Larona Starr walking directly toward him. Transfixed by the sight of her, he felt as though clouds had parted to allow the sun to shine for the first time.

She stepped very close to him and studied his face. "Hello, Jesse Porter."

Braun spoke her name and touched his hand to his cap. Then he turned and walked toward the pro shop, leaving the couple alone.

Porter said, "Hello, Larona." His voice seemed to come from somewhere outside his body.

They faced each other for several seconds. She said, "I wanted to ask how things are going today."

"Fine. I understand--from Walter--that the contributions are very good."

"Yes. They are. They're excellent."

"That's good."

"Yes."

"How are you?"

"I'm...all right."

They stood silently for some time. Several passerbys who knew who she was noted with amusement the apparent awkwardness between them.

Finally Larona said, "Is there anything I can--That is, do you still feel the same way about us?"

He nodded. "I care very deeply about you, Larona. But I'm afraid I still must leave." He added, "Soon."

She took a deep breath and exhaled. Then she took a step backward. "I see. I'm so very sorry. Well, I hope you have a great game today. Or tomorrow. Or forever." She averted her eyes and walked away.

The afternoon program took place much as the morning program had. Porter played three holes with a group of four more persons who had made significant contributions to GOLF-R. Then he gave another brief demonstration. This time he provided putting tips.

Afterward, he and Braun bought beers and checked out the leader board. Several players were already under par. Partee from Ottawa was leading with a sixty-nine.

"It's a tough group," observed Braun.

"Too tough," said Porter.

"Oh hell, Jess, you're too pessimistic. You can shoot with any of these guys. Just speak softly and carry a big stick."

Porter shook his head. "You don't understand, Slim. I just don't have the old confidence."

"I watched you today, Jess. You were great," Braun declared.

"It's not the same, Slim. As I told you, there was nothing on the line today. It's one thing to put on a little show that doesn't mean anything. It's something else to really compete and find a way to win when there's no margin for error. Every shot has to be right. Every move. Every detail. I just don't think I have what it takes any more. I've gotten a lot older. I feel alone out there."

"I'll be pulling for you, Jess."

Porter looked gratefully at his tall friend. "Thanks, Slim. I appreciate that more than you know."

Sunday dawned like a clone of Saturday. Bright. Cloudless. Hot. Calm. Porter was able to prepare more leisurely, however, since he was not expected at the country club until nine. He was scheduled to tee off at ten. Nine holes in the morning. Nine holes in the afternoon.

There had been a banquet Saturday night which he should have attended, but he had declined, claiming he needed to rest for the match. He reminded everyone he was no longer used to playing eighteen. Walter Edwards was upset that Porter would not attend, of course, but he acceded.

The truth was that Porter could not tolerate the idea of spending the evening at the speakers' table in the presence of Larona Starr and having to keep telling himself he should not want her now or ever.

Since he had left the club early Saturday, he did not see the final scores posted for the day, so he didn't yet know who his opponent would be.

Patricia fixed a large breakfast for him, to give him lots of energy, she said. He poked at a plate of eggs and potatoes but ate little more than a frosted roll and coffee. She wished him well and informed him she would not be able to make the starting time. She had promised a friend two weeks ago that she would go shopping with her today. But she added that she would get to the golf match as soon as possible. Thus she sent him off alone.

When he arrived at the club, Porter learned that Morris Brent's sixty-six had held up. So the local champ would vie against him. He liked Brent and was glad the young man had won. Brent's score--six under par--indicated the talent Porter would face, however, and--he felt certain--would most likely succumb to.

In the locker room a burly young man approached. "Mister Porter?" he said.

"Yes."

"Sir, my name is Max Graham. I'm supposed to caddy for you today."

Porter frowned. "No. I have a caddy, son. Mister Braun. He may already be here." He glanced around for Slim.

The young man shook his head. Obviously ill at ease, he said, "No sir. Mister Braun called and asked for you. He left a message that he's not feeling well this morning. He can't come." Trying to ease the situation, the young man forced a laugh. "I guess he had too much exercise yesterday. Anyhow, Mister Edwards said I should caddy for you today."

"Damn!" Porter spat out the oath through clenched jaws. "What else can go wrong!"

Graham said, "I'm sorry if you think I'm not--"

Porter put his hand on the young man's arm. "Oh, it's not you, Max. I'm just very disappointed that Braun won't be here. He had taken a lot of notes to prepare me for this. And I don't have a copy."

"I can help, Mister Porter. I'm a student at Clydeston Community College, and I play on the golf team. I know this course pretty well."

"Good. I apologize for the way I reacted just now," Porter replied. "You look more like a football player," he added.

"Yeah, I play defensive end," the young man grinned.

"Well, you certain look big enough to carry my bag. I'm sure you'll do fine. I'm glad to have you along, Max. Thanks for stepping in."

Graham said, "Is it really true you won some tournaments as a professional--a long time ago?"

Porter looked at him for several seconds before answering. "We can talk about that later, Max."

Morris Brent entered the locker room and greeted Porter warmly.

Porter congratulated him on his win Saturday. "You had a lot of competition."

"I hope I can do as well today."

"If you do that well today, I won't look good," Porter laughed. "You know, you're supposed to let the celebrity win."

"Well, I'll just do my best to keep up with the celebrity, sir. I'm just an amateur here. No pressure on me. I'll see you on the tee in a few minutes." He grinned, looked at his watch, and walked out.

Porter turned to Graham. "Max, I feel awful. My belly's in knots."

"Are you sick, too, Mister Porter? Like Mister Braun?" Graham spoke with great concern.

"No. I'm just up-tight. I've got to loosen up. I want to go hit a bucket of balls. Com'on."

"Do we have time?"

"We'll take the time. I have to work the kinks out."

Graham grabbed a bucket of balls from the counter in the pro shop and followed to the driving range, only a short distance away.

Porter did a few back-stretching exercises and tried to limber up. He swung a five iron and it felt like a great thick log. The balls flew out when he hit them, but he felt as if he were outside himself, dully watching some mechanical man swing the clubs.

A few spectators recognized him and gathered to watch. Porter felt conspicuous and uneasy. When he swung his driver, he hit a tremendous hook, and the spectators commented on it. One man said to his companion, "That was probably intentional. These pros can make the ball go wherever they want to, y' know."

Porter began to sweat, but it wasn't from exertion. Under his breath, he said to Graham, "I'm really in trouble, Max. I just can't seem to hit the damned ball!"

"You'll be all right, sir," the young man encouraged. "It's probably just butterflies. I get 'em myself before a big game." He didn't know what to make of Porter's behavior. He had expected a confident, professional attitude, and Porter's complaints confused him.

"I knew this would happen." Porter thrust his driver into his bag. "Let's go try to putt a few."

"It's about time to get started, sir."

"No. They can't start without me. Com'on."

The putting green lay close by the first tee. A number of spectators who had gathered to await the start of the match hurried to the green to watch. Porter felt no better here. The eyes of the onlookers bored into him. His putter seemed like a croquet mallet. He missed repeatedly at various distances. From the onlookers he heard several snickers.

"Brent will have this old clown by lunch," someone predicted.

Walter Edwards strode onto the green obviously checking his watch. "Hello, Jess. About time to get this show on the road, eh? How you doing?"

"Hello, Walter." Porter heaved an immense sigh of resignation.

"I see that Max found you. I'm sorry your man couldn't make it today, but Max is a good caddy. He'll help, I'm sure. You know, he's a terrific football player."

Porter bit his lip to keep from explaining to Edwards that this was not a football match, but he let it pass. Submitting now to his fate, he said, "Okay. Let's go."

On the first tee, Edwards announced the start of the competition over a public address system. He spent several minutes thanking the assembled guests for their participation and generosity toward the fund-raiser, and he gave credit to a number of persons who had played major roles in producing the event.

Porter studied the crowd. He was somewhat surprised to see that more than three hundred persons, by his quick estimate, had gathered here. He saw not a face that he recognized. Patricia had not shown up yet. Braun had failed to arrive. He felt totally alone in a sea of strangers.

Edwards was saying "--not the least, and without whom, we could never have achieved this success, Missus Larona Starr!" He clapped his hands.

Porter spun instantly to where Edwards pointed. He saw her: drop-dead-gorgeous! Coming through the throng, Larona stepped up to Edwards' side and waved genially to the assembly. They applauded politely. She turned to Morris Brent and wished him well. To Porter she said, "And the best of luck to you, Mister Jesse Porter." Though she spoke formally, her eyes were filled with emerald warmth. The familiar smile played at the corners of her mouth. "Always," she added softly.

Porter took her hand, offered to him ostensibly as a gesture of goodwill and held it. Her touch thrilled him. For the moment it dispelled his anxiety. "Larona," was all he could say.

Someone called out, "Let her go, Jesse! You can do that afterward!" Several persons laughed.

She jerked her hand free. "Good luck, Tsunami Man!" she whispered. Then she stepped quickly back beside Edwards.

Next, Edwards introduced Pastor Glenn, who spoke briefly on the goals of GOLF-R. Then he, too, congratulated the competitors. Porter was pleased to see Cal again. "Good luck, Jess," his friend said. Then Glenn shook hands with Brent and wished him the same.

Finally, Walter Edwards introduced the golfers to the crowd. He presented Morris Brent first, to thunderous applause. The young man appeared mildly embarrassed by the support. He waved a hand and grinned at the crowd. He pointed at someone he knew.

For Jesse Porter the applause was polite but moderate by comparison. Porter heard it, but his eyes were still locked on the sea-green eyes of Larona Starr.

"Good luck to you both, gentlemen. All our thanks for a great event." Edwards pulled out a coin and flipped it. "May the better golfer win." He caught the coin and announced, "Morris Brent will hit first."

The crowd cheered.

Brent extended his hand to Porter. "Good luck, Mister Porter."

Thanks, Morris. Same to you."

"Uh, I wonder, is Patricia is going to be here today?"

"Not yet." Porter felt like laughing for the first time all day. "But I expect her to be along shortly."

Brent walked the few paces to the first tee. He drove the ball high and far down the right side. Perfect placement. Applause followed with cheers of approval.

"Go get him, Mister Porter," urged Max Graham.

Porter carefully teed up his ball. He glanced around at the crowd. Larona had disappeared. A few voices offered support.

He drove the ball poorly. It flew out with a slight hook. Rolling on hard ground, it stopped considerably short and to the left of Brent's ball in a somewhat inferior location. A smattering of applause rose from the crowd, but the tenor of excitement that had followed Brent's shot was absent.

Porter sighed with relief. "Well, not so good, Max, but at least we're underway."

Most of the gallery followed the golfers or ran ahead of them alongside the fairway. Porter noted that on other fairways golfers were playing and paying no attention to his contest with Brent. A far cry from the pro tourneys of his past, he thought.

He hit a fair wood to the edge of the green. A cheer acknowledged the excellence of Brent's approach, however, which put him on in two.

"Hey, this guy is really good!" exclaimed Graham.

"Thanks for the tip," Porter replied coolly.

"Oh, sorry, sir."

Porter chipped inside of Brent, so Brent putted first. He took his time and rolled the ball firmly into the middle of the cup.

Already down one stroke to Brent's birdie, Porter could not afford a miss. He lined up his putt carefully. His stroke was heavy handed, however, and the ball rimmed the cup without dropping. He shook his head wearily. "Down two after only one hole," he muttered to himself.

"You'll be okay," his caddy promised.

As they walked to the second tee, Porter heard voices around him indicating the spectators' disappointment. "I thought this old guy was supposed to be good," someone said.

"Yeah, Brent will beat him by twenty strokes," said another.

Both golfers parred the second and third holes. On the fourth green, Brent holed a long putt, and Porter again rimmed out.

Someone in the ring of onlookers called out, "Put it in the hole, Porter. Pretend it's Larona Starr!" Several people laughed. He whirled at the sound of the voice but could not identify who had spoken.

A marshal called for quiet.

Porter walked to the marshal and told him to watch for the foul mouth.

Brent, embarrassed by Porter's discomfiture, said, "Your putt's a gimme, Mister Porter. Pick it up. Let's go on. It's just an exhibition."

Porter waved him off without a word and tapped the ball into the hole. Scowling now, he was furious about the comment from the gallery. He continued to glare at the spectators, trying to fathom who had hurled the insult.

"Com'on, Mister Porter, what's the matter?" asked Graham. "Jist concentrate on the game."

"Don't tell me how to play golf," snapped Porter. Immediately, he regretted his loss of composure. "I'm sorry, Max. Damn it, you're the only person out here on my side, and I'm jumping on you. Sorry."

Graham said, "It's okay. Jist keep your focus, sir. We still have a lot of holes to play."

Porter tried to concentrate, but he hit his next shot into a fairway bunker.

Several onlookers muttered their disappointment, and Porter observed that a number of them had turned away and begun the trek back toward the clubhouse.

At the end of seven holes, Brent was ahead by five strokes. He had played exceptionally well, with three birdies to that point. The gallery had diminished appreciably, with no more than forty of the original spectators remaining. They all appeared to be supporters of the local champion.

After driving on eight, Porter finally heard a familiar voice. It was Patricia, who came to his side, somewhat short of breath. "Hi, Dad. Sorry I'm so late. How's it going?"

"Pretty bad, Trish. I'm really glad you're here."

Brent stepped up and smiled at Patricia. "Hi. Maybe you remember me? I'm Morris Brent." He held out his hand.

"Of course I remember you," she said, returning his smile and shaking his hand. "Very nice to see you again."

As the golfers began to walk into the fairway, she asked, "Can I walk with you fellows, or must I go with the gallery?"

"Sure you can come with us," Brent said instantly.

"There's hardly any gallery left now anyhow," noted Porter.

Patricia looked around. "Why, there must be fifty people following you guys! That's good, isn't it?"

Porter laughed. There were several times that many when we started. But Morris has been trouncing me so badly, a lot of them gave up and went somewhere else.

"Oh," Patricia asked cautiously, "what's the score?"

"I have a little lead," said Brent modestly.

"He's five strokes ahead," Porter told her. "I'm not playing worth a darn, and he hasn't missed a ball yet."

After the golfers hit their next shots, Patricia said, "You seem to have a lot of supporters out here, Morris."

"I guess it's just natural for them to root for the local guy, the underdog."

Porter said, "I'm sure glad you got here, Trish. I needed one fan at least."

"As a matter of fact, Mister Porter," said Brent, "I'm a fan, too."

"Okay, so I have two supporters. That helps." Porter eyed Max Graham trudging beside him. "Three maybe."

Both golfers parred eight. On nine Morris Brent pitched close to the pin for an easy putt, and at the halfway point of the match, he led by six strokes.

Walter Edwards greeted the golfers as they came off the ninth green. "Pretty rough out there this morning, eh, Jesse? Well, don't let the youngster get you down. After a good lunch, you're sure to do a lot better." To Brent he said, "Good shooting, Morris. You're making a mark for Clydeston golf, fella!" Jovially, he clasped the young man's shoulder.

Porter declined Edwards' invitation to lunch, saying he would prefer to rest before the afternoon session. Edwards offered his office, where Porter took a beef sandwich and a glass of iced tea.

Patricia happily joined Brent Morris in the main dining room.

At the door to Edwards' office, Doyle Dugan accosted Porter. I told you would get your butt whipped, old-timer."

"Get lost, Dugan."

The reporter backed away when he saw the pent-up fury in Porter's face. He cast back a parting shot as he left. "You're a has-been, Porter, cashing in on the rich lady's generosity and--"

Porter slammed the office door, cutting off Dugan's jibe.

He wanted to hit something, break something, but he restrained himself from damaging Edwards' things. "Damn!" he shouted, then plopped into the oversized desk chair. After the beating he had received on the course this morning, after hearing the catcalls from a disrespectful gallery, after finding himself alone in this unpleasant situation, he felt truth in Dugan's accusations. This visit to Clydeston, which had started with such pleasant events, had now become a shambles. He sighed wearily and wished it were over.

Grateful that Patricia had shown up, he was nevertheless sorry she had to witness the debacle of his pitiful golfing. How he had let her down over the years! He had done little for her, it seemed, compared to his expectations of earlier years. Now, at least, she had a good job and her future was assured--if he had not messed up her life along with his own. At least she was having lunch with Morris Brent. She seemed to be enjoying that.

He sipped on his tea but pushed the sandwich away. He desperately hoped to make a better showing this afternoon. Leaning back in the comfortable chair, he closed his eyes and tried to think. Within a few minutes, he dozed off.

Porter wakened with a start. Checking his watch, he saw that he had only a few minutes until the scheduled start of the second nine. He gobbled his sandwich and found the office restroom where he splashed his face with cold water. He shook his head at the reflection in the mirror. "Let's get it over with, Ace," he said aloud. "Take your medicine like a man!"

The scene at the tenth tee was much the same as it had been at the first tee. Walter Edwards and Pastor Glenn were there. The gallery was smaller, many morning fans having given up. But Porter had the impression that many new faces were present. Apparently, many persons who had not been there in the morning had come for the afternoon finale.

Edwards repeated his brief speech from the morning, greeting and thanking the assembly for their support. He predicted that the afternoon match would be much more exciting than the earlier play. Several negative comments from the crowd followed his statement. The jeerers were still present.

"How do you feel, Dad?" Patricia asked. "Did you eat?"

"Yes, I had some lunch. I'll make it okay."

She smiled and winked at her father. She made a gesture with her fist as though urging him to get tough. He nodded and smiled gratefully. "Do you know," he said, "when you smile like that, you look just like your mother?"

"Oh, Daddy!" was all she could say.

"I think we are ready for the match to resume," announced Edwards.

"It's about time," a raspy old voice cried out. "It's one o'clock. Let's play golf!"

Porter whirled at the sound of the voice. To his delight, he found Ray Wallis grinning just a step away. Wallis wore his Cardinals cap, which he immediately jerked sideways on his head. Beside Wallis stood Abe Lowman, Jack Karns, Doctor Nate Jensen, and Slim Braun. They all shouted, "It's one o'clock. Let's play golf!"

Pastor Glenn pumped his fist in the air, then, embarrassed, he stepped back. He mumbled something.

"Your honors," said Porter to Brent. The sight of the one-o'clock gang filled Porter with fire. His awareness that they were present to support him was like emotions he had seldom, if ever, felt before.

Braun spoke up. "Sorry I couldn't make it this morning, Jess. I was too pooped after yesterday. Felt a little nauseous."

"It's okay, Slim. How are you feeling now?"

"I'm fine. I don't think I can caddy though."

"That's all right. I have a very good man here." He winked at Graham, then introduced him to the gang.

Brent started the afternoon with another impressive drive. Porter stepped up without thinking about the mechanics of his swing. With renewed confidence, he swung easily, naturally. For the first time all day, he outdrove his younger opponent.

The one-o'clock gang cheered.

Max Graham yelled, "Hey! Way t'go!"

Others in the gallery--some very surprised--joined enthusiastically.

Brent turned to Porter. "What did you eat for lunch, Mister Porter? You really tagged that ball!"

"You didn't think I'd be that shabby all day, did you?"

The old-timers ignored the marshals' efforts to keep them back. They joined Porter as he strode up the fairway.

Wallis said, "How come you're so far behind, Jess? This kid's really been hittin' the ball, huh?"

"He's awfully good, Ray. But I feel better now. Damn! I'm glad you fellas showed up." He lightly punched his old friend on the shoulder. "Thanks for coming."

"Wouldn't have missed it," said Karns.

"They oughta provide carts fer us t'ride in," Lowman said.

Porter smashed a tremendous three iron that homed in on the pin and stopped only thirty inches from the cup.

Brent shook his head with admiration. Then he hit a good approach but left himself a long putt. On the green he took an unusually long time to line it up. His friends in the gallery shouted their support, then fell silent as he stroked the ball. It ran and ran, broke gently to the left but died a few inches short.

Porter knocked in his own short putt to cheers from the spectators. He noted that he had considerably more support now than he had heard in the morning--in addition to the one-o'clock gang, who were ecstatic in their acclaim. It seemed a little bit like old times.

Brent said, "Looks like you got one back, Mister Porter."

"Let me tell you something, Morris." Porter looked the younger golfer in the eye. "I once played in an exhibition with a great pro that I really looked up to. I kept calling him 'Mister'. Finally he said that I could never beat him as long as I called him 'Mister.' It showed that I considered him to be my superior."

Brent squinted as he considered what Porter was saying. "I was only trying to be polite."

"I know that."

"Well...did you have him down five strokes with only eight holes to play?"

Porter said. Two minutes ago you were ahead by six. Son."

Brent raised his eyebrows. "Son? *Son!* So now you're gonna treat me like a child?"

"Just an expression."

"All right, Mist--*Jess!* We'll see how it goes from here on in. Jess."

Porter chuckled as they reached the eleventh tee. He stepped in front of Morris. "I believe I have honors here."

Number eleven was a long par three, over a small pond. Porter hit a high four iron that reached the green.

Brent said, "Good shot. *Jess.*" He, too, was obviously pumped after their brief conversation. He hit his ball fat. The line was perfect, but the ball died as it reached the embankment on the far side of the pond. It plunked on the slope, then rolled back into the water.

As everyone walked around the pond, Braun edged close to Porter.

"What did you say to that guy, Jess? You threaten him, or somethin'?"

Porter said quietly, "I just let him know that there are games and then there are *games.*" Then he stepped up his pace and Braun frowned.

The crowd was growing louder. Several persons shouted encouragement to Brent. Someone else said maybe now there would be a contest after all. Porter also heard the ugly voice that he had heard earlier. Someone was saying Larona Starr had probably fixed the event so her boyfriend could win. He bristled when he heard it, but could still not identify the speaker.

Porter took three on the eleventh. Brent, shaken by his shot into the pond, missed a medium putt and found his lead suddenly shrunken to three.

Karns shouted to Brent, "He was just toyin' with you this morning, Brent."

Porter tried to shush his friends. He realized, however, that he was now playing with the confidence that had eluded him for years. His strokes were fluid. He was full of fire. His next drive excelled even the blow he had struck on ten. The gallery erupted in cheers and cries of admiration.

Halfway down the fairway, Pastor Glenn joined the one-o'clock gang. Though he drove an electric cart, he was huffing and breathless with excitement. "Someone came back to the clubhouse," he said, "and told us Jess is actually making a comeback. I wanted to see it."

"You're not the only one," said Lowman. "Look!" He pointed back in the direction of the clubhouse, whence the preacher had come.

A number of persons were rushing to catch up with the contestants. Even more were cutting across toward the thirteenth green, where they would await the golfers' arrival.

A couple of carts cut across the tenth green in their rush to catch up. The marshals could not control the excited fans.

Glenn invited Doctor Jensen to share his cart. The elderly physician gratefully climbed aboard, saying he could not have walked much farther. Lowman and Wallis climbed on, too.

Both players parred thirteen. Brent sank a long putt. He had put his ill fortune at the water hole behind him and resolved to hang onto his lead.

Porter recognized the young golfer's determination, and it hardened his own resolve to catch up. There was electricity in the air between the two men. The gallery sensed it, and their reactions grew louder.

At fourteen, Porter rolled in a chip from the bunker, nearly sixty feet from the pin. The crowd went wild with shouts of praise and wonder.

Braun said, "'And they say miracles are past.'"

Wishing not to intrude, Patricia had moved away from her father and Brent when afternoon play commenced. She simply followed the gallery, applauding both men for good efforts. As she worked her way through the crowd, moving to the fifteenth tee, she saw Larona Starr.

Following along with other spectators, Larona seemed to make no attempt to get close to the play. It appeared to Patricia that the woman tried to keep someone or some knot of persons between herself and Porter. As the gallery moved along the fifteenth fairway, Patricia watched Larona with fascination. She confirmed that Larona, for some reason, was trying to avoid being seen by Porter. Yet, when Porter made his shots, Larona clapped and appeared as excited as anyone.

Patricia approached her. "Hello, Missus Starr."

Larona turned with surprise, as if she had been caught doing some forbidden thing. "Oh, hello Miss--Patricia." She was at a loss for words.

"You seem to be enjoying the match."

"Yes, I'm--It's wonderful! Jess--your father plays extremely well."

"Are you with someone, Missus Starr?"

"No." Larona Starr turned around. "I'm alone. Please call me Larona."

There was no haughtiness in her expression, Patricia noted. Nothing but friendship and sincerity.

"May I join you, Larona?"

"Of course." Larona smiled and reached out for Patricia's hand. "Oh look! He just hit another marvelous shot. My god! How does he do that! He's wonderful!"

Instead of looking at her father, Patricia stared at Larona as if seeing her for the first time.

"How long have you been out here?" she asked.

"What?" Larona frowned slightly. "You mean today? Why, since the first tee this morning, of course. Do you think I would miss a moment of this?"

"But Daddy doesn't know you're here, does he?"

"No. I didn't want to bother him. There are people yelling terrible things at him about me. I didn't want to make it worse. He has enough on his mind without my getting in his way."

"My god!" Patricia exclaimed with sudden insight. "You really do love him, don't you." It was not a question.

Larona looked squarely into Patricia's eyes. "Of course," she replied very simply.

Patricia said, "I didn't know--I've had you all wrong!"

"We could establish a very large club for all the people who misunderstand many things about me."

"I've been a fool!"

"Be quiet, dear. He's putting."

Pars on fifteen by both golfers left the contest as it had been. Porter remained three strokes behind with three holes to play. He knew now that the only way he could win would be through his own efforts. He could not rely on Morris Brent to fold. Clearly, the young man had a backbone.

On each hole, Porter continued to hit first as the two men battled evenly. He sent a massive drive down sixteen. It faded slightly, coinciding with a small dogleg right.

Before Brent could take his turn, Patricia burst through the throng and strode up to her father. She pulled with her a reluctant Larona Starr. "Daddy!" she called.

Porter turned to shush her, for Brent was addressing his ball. Then, astounded to see Larona, he spoke her name. Immediately, he said to Brent, "I'm sorry, Morris."

Brent stepped back and grinned at Patricia. "No harm. Hullo, Trish. Excuse me for a moment." Then he hit his ball every bit as well as Porter had just hit his.

"I'm sorry to interrupt," said Patricia. "It's important."

The gallery stood by, closing in, watching and listening to this sudden diversion.

Porter said, "Larona, what are you--"

"Daddy, she has been here all day. Watching you. She didn't want you to know."

Larona now felt embarrassed.

"Is this true, Larona?" Porter asked.

She nodded.

"Why didn't you want me to know?"

"I didn't want to distract you."

"Distract me? My gosh, woman, I'd have given anything to have known you were with me!"

"I thought you didn't want to see me any longer."

Doctor Jensen was hanging onto the golf cart to maintain his balance. Awkwardly, he stood and from that perch he called out, "Seems to me that you two children ought to be a lot smarter than you act!"

Glenn added, "Yes, actually!"

Without taking his eyes from her, Porter said, "I've been a darn fool, haven't I?"

Larona smiled and nodded.

All the emotions Porter had dealt with for days swirled and suddenly evolved into one. "I love you, Larona," he said. "Will you marry me?"

"Of course."

Porter drew her against him and they kissed long and passionately, as though they were miles away from the scores of persons who pressed close around them, shouting and cheering enthusiastically, all totally astonished by this unexpected event they were witnessing.

Without thinking, Patricia hugged Morris Brent, who was more surprised than anyone. He grinned at her, and she pulled back slightly but held onto his arm. Her eyes brimmed with tears of joy.

Porter shook his head, utterly amazed at this development. Grinning from ear to ear, he said, "Well, Mister Brent, what do you think?"

"I'll tell you, Mister Por--uh, Jess. I think we still have a golf match here. That is, if you can control your hormones."

Porter's next shot reached the green. Brent's long iron was pin high, ten yards off the green. The young man chipped on but took two putts to get down. Porter narrowly missed his putt and tapped in.

One stroke regained. Two down.

Porter felt more alive than he had for years. He could feel the salt air of Saint Andrews, smell the dogwoods of Augusta, hear the crowds at Baltusrol. He had regained heaven.

Seventeen was a short par three. Porter almost knocked the pin out of the cup. Brent was about twelve feet away.

Porter, birdie. Brent, par. One down.

Porter basked in the glow of Larona's sparkling green eyes. His clubs were weightless. He felt like a nineteen year old. His shots were pictures of fluidity. The crowd now cheered every move by both players. Everyone was having a blast.

Brent refused to cave in. He felt a sudden elation from Patricia's unexpected but obvious attitude toward him. He tried not to think about it, to focus on golf. All he had to do to win the match was to stay with Porter stroke for stroke on eighteen.

After teeing his ball on the final hole, Porter spoke to his caddy. "Max, get a marshal and go down around the dog-leg and up the fairway beyond those middle cottonwoods and watch to see where my ball comes through."

"Wait a minute," objected Brent. "What are you talking about?"

The crowd edged closer and became silent as they strained to hear what was going on.

"Go ahead, Max," said Porter. "Go clear around the corner and up the fairway." Graham started off as he had been instructed. He collared one of the marshals and took him along.

To Brent, Porter said, "Morris, I have to make up one stroke on this hole to tie. Two strokes to win. The only chance I have is to take a short-cut across that maintence area and--"

"Wait a minute," said Brent. "Nobody has ever--I'm pretty sure--tried to cut across the dog-leg. You'd have to pass over the maintenance area and still clear those trees. That's at least five hundred yards. Maybe more." He shook his head. "You're crazy!"

"You're right, Morris. I can't drive *over* them. But that maintenance area is paved in there. And there is no fence on the far side. If I catch a break, I can maybe bounce the ball and *go through* the trees and reach the fairway."

"Nobody has ever played this hole that way," Brent scoffed. He turned away as though refusing to be a party to such idiocy. "It can't be done. You're just giving up the match."

"It's my only chance of catching you. I've run out of time and holes. I can't just wait around for you to make a mistake."

As members of the crowd began to understand what Porter intended to do, their voices rose. Arguments began immediately. Some persons laughed, thinking the idea preposterous. Most simply stood, not sure what would ensue.

Larona said, "I'm not certain I understand, Jess."

"I'm going to hit the ball *out of bounds* and hope that it will bounce on the pavement over there and continue through those cottonwoods and wind up *in bounds.*"

"Oh my! Can you do that?"

"I don't know. If the ball hits a truck or a shed or something over there, it won't go through." He grinned. "There's only one way to find out."

She looked at him with admiration.

He said, "Do you think I should take a drink of *Koff-Off?*"

"Am I going to marry a crazy man?" she laughed. "Well, we promised the fans a good show, didn't we?"

Brent merely shook his head.

Then Porter stepped up to his ball.

The crowd grew quiet in anticipation. Several persons whispered, still trying to determine what might happen.

Porter hit the ball hard, with a slight hook, over the wall of walnut trees. It rose high and then dropped out of sight into the maintenance area, clearly far short of the tall cottonwoods farther away.

No one saw it bounce.

Porter stood very still, watching intently. After a few seconds, he turned

EIGHTEENTH HOLE AT
CLYDESTON COUNTRY CLUB.

to Braun, who stood nearby. "What do you think, Slim?"

Braun shrugged. "Dunno. I didn't see it come up."

Lowman said, "Musta hit a shed or somethin'."

The crowd noise rose. Everyone had an opinion about the play. Several persons called out, "You'd better hit another one, Porter. You're out of bounds."

Larona tugged at Porter's elbow. "Look," she said, pointing down the fairway.

Max Graham had run into view at the point where the fairway turned right. He jumped up and down excitedly and pumped his fists vigorously into the air. He pointed up the fairway toward the eighteenth green, beyond the vision of those on the tee, yelling something inaudible.

"By god," said Lowman, "He's claimin' you made it through the trees! You're back in play!"

"How do you know what he's yelling?" asked Braun. "You can't hear him!"

"I read his lips."

"Hell, you can't even see his head, much less his lips," Wallis declared.

The crowd picked up the information and roared. Eagerly, several persons started to run ahead to see for themselves whether the ball was indeed in play.

Porter called out and held up his hands, asking for quiet so Brent could drive.

Someone called out, "Take the short-cut, Brent!"

Without looking up, he gritted his teeth and replied, "No way! I'm not that lucky." He now assumed that the score was essentially tied. It would take him one shot to get to the turn and then one more shot to reach the approximate position that Porter had obtained with one stroke. He swung tentatively, but his ball reached a playable position near where Max Graham waited at the bend of the fairway.

Now the remaining crowd rushed noisily to see the finish. Ray Wallis edged close to Porter. "Was your shot legal, Jess?"

"Heck, Ray, why not?" He laughed. "It's not really different from hitting a tree or rock that's out of bounds and rebounding into the fairway, is it? Anyhow, it was the only chance I had."

Karns said, "Everybody who plays here from now on will want to try it. Those poor guys in the maintenance shed will be bombarded with golf balls all day long." He laughed at the thought.

When they reached Graham, he grinned with delight. "We were just standing by those two big cottonwoods there, like you said to do, sir, and all of a sudden, your ball just came screaming through. You musta leaned all over that shot! It came dead center between those two biggest trees. You got a perfect lie. The marshal is up there standing over it."

The turn of events obviously shook Brent. His lead was gone. He took a long time girding himself for his second shot. Finally he hit a three iron about ten yards short and left of the green. He grinned sheepishly at Patricia. "I choked on that one," he admitted.

Porter found his ball as Graham had promised, in a perfect lie. He looked at the cottonwoods where the ball had passed through. Shaking his head, he said "I could try that ten more times and probably never get through. Just dumb luck!"

"Sometimes it's actually better to be lucky than good," said Glenn.

Brent said, "It's best when you're both. Porter acknowledged the comment with a nod. Then he hit his second shot, a three wood, onto the front edge of the green. The ball hopped several times and rolled in a straight line toward the flag, stopping about fourteen inches from the cup.

Again the crowd erupted with a prolonged cheer.

Wallis cried out, "You're lookin' at a damn eagle, Jess!"

"If Brent gets on in three, and one-puts, you tie," said Braun. "If he two-puts, you win."

Porter nodded. "Thanks, fellas. I know."

Brent assessed his lie and pulled out his pitching wedge. By now everyone had made the same mental calculation as Braun. They knew Brent had to get the ball close to salvage a tie.

Silence reigned. Brent swung carefully, too carefully, not with his usual sure-handed looseness, and the blade took the ground too far behind the ball. As a result, the ball dribbled to the edge of the green, barely beyond the fringe. Brent turned his back on the ball and stared skyward. He now faced a thirty-two foot putt. The gallery groaned in sympathy.

Larona hugged Porter's arm and he raised a finger, cautioning quiet. Patricia stood to one side, clasping and unclasping her hands.

Brent squatted and studied the line to the cup. He walked around the green, assessing his shot from every angle. After a seemingly interminable period, he calmly addressed the ball and stroked it. The ball ran true, homing in on the cup. The gallery voices rose as one as the ball sought the target. At the last instant, it tailed left and rimmed out. Another vast groan ascended from the crowd.

Porter shook his head, stepped up to his marker, and replaced his ball. "Too bad, Morris," he said softly to his disappointed opponent, who tapped in for his final stroke.

The apparent winner now, Porter lined up his short putt. After a few seconds, an idea occurred to him, and he stepped back. The crowd murmured, but he held up his hand for quiet, then addressed the assemblage in a loud voice. "It is my understanding, folks, that all I have to do to win this match is to make this putt."

His comment surprised everyone. Several laughed. Someone yelled, "It may be longer than you think, Jesse!"

Abe Lowman said, "Even Cal Glenn could make this little pisser."

Again a few persons laughed in anticipation of they knew not what.

Porter waved again. "Folks, I'd like to remind everyone that the reason we're all out here today is to raise funds for the Harrison House and the kids it supports. That is much more important than this golf match." He turned as he spoke, projecting his voice to as much of the crowd as possible. "I think you all watched an interesting contest."

Another burst of applause punctuated his comment.

Again, he held up his hands. "Let's keep the focus on Harrison House. Those youngsters should be the winners today, not Brent Morris or Jess Porter. Therefore," he said, bending down and picking up his ball, "I'm declaring this match a draw! *Tie game! The winners are the kids!*" He walked to the astonished Brent and thrust out his hand. The two men shook hands heartily.

Several people in the gallery muttered their disagreement with Porter's decision, but most cheered his sportsmanship.

Brent said, "Thank you, Mister Port--Jess. You had me beaten. And now, this...this... What made you do that?"

"It's just a game, Morris. Just a game. Porter punched the young man on the shoulder. "It's something I learned the first day I came to Clydeston. But I didn't realize how important that is until today, I guess."

"What are you talking about, Daddy?" asked Trish.

He waved at the members of the one-o'clock gang who were crowded around. "These guys play the game for its own sake, for enjoyment. For the companionship it provides. *They don't keep score!*"

⸺⸺◦◦◦◦⸺⸺

Fans from the gallery pressed around the golfer's, some asking for autographs, all congratulating them. Porter exchanged smiles with Larona, who patiently waited for him.

"That was a wonderful show, Mister Porter," a woman said.

He looked around and was surprised to see Audine Mahon.

"Congratulations to you and Missus Starr," she added. "I mean, that proposal was even more exciting than the golf. Just so romantic!"

Porter grinned and nodded. Then suddenly he found himself facing Police Chief Still. For a second, his heart rose into his throat. He feared the officer would bring bad news after all this wonderful excitement. *Was there going to be a problem about Sanford's money? About his murder? Did the chief know all? What did he know? Had he merely been waiting for the end of the match before making an arrest?*

"Good show, Mister Porter," said the officer. Turning to Larona, he touched the bill of his cap. "I think this golfer man is a pretty solid fella, Missus Starr. I wish you two many happy years."

"Why, thank you, Richard. We appreciate your taking time out to come here today." She moved closer and gave him a hug.

The chief adjusted his cap, turned, and walked away.

"Wow!" said Porter. You know him?"

"Of course, Jess. We're old friends."

Slim Braun and the other members of the one-o'clock gang tarried nearby, basking in Porter's glory. They recounted various outstanding shots, especially the remarkable short-cut, securing them in their memories, and laying the foundation for endless future recounting.

At last, Porter and Larona walked hand-in-hand back toward the large veranda that overlooked the eighteenth green. Near the bottom steps leading up to the veranda, Doyle Dugan confronted them.

"You're a pretty lucky old fart, Porter," he declared. "That's all I've got to say."

Porter sighed tolerantly. "Somehow, Dugan, I have a feeling that is not all you have to say." Porter and Larona started up the steps with Dugan following close behind.

"Yeah, well, I want to tell you I think you would have missed that last putt if you hadn't picked it up. You were afraid you'd miss it and look like the loser you are."

"Dugan, I'll bet you a hundred dollars I can make it twenty times in a row. Right now. Put up or shut up!"

"I'm a reporter, not a gambler," Dugan replied lamely. "I still think you're a four-flusher. As a reporter for this town's newspaper, I promise I'm gonna find out more about you and let Clydeston know how you've hoodwinked Missus Starr here--"

Larona put her face close to Dugan's. "You watch what you print, Mister, or I'll have more lawyers on your case than you've got pencils!" She pressed closer until he retreated down the steps.

"Well," Dugan said. "I don't know how that will come out. But I know there's something strange about a man whose only friends are a bunch of old farts--" He gestured wildly toward the gang who had taken positions around Porter and Larona.

"Old what?" shouted Wallis.

Karns and Braun joined Wallis, advancing on the reporter. Lowman grabbed a three iron out of Porter's golf bag and poked it against Dugan's chest. The hapless young man stepped backward, tripped, and fell. Then as he scrambled to his feet, Lowman poked him again with the club, and Dugan stumbled, falling with a splash into the pool beneath the veranda.

Everyone laughed, except Dugan, who sat sputtering, waist-deep in water.

"Say, lady, you're pretty impressive when aroused," Porter said to Larona. "You know, I wonder, out there on the course, could I really have had the nerve to ask you what I think I may have asked. Did I just dream it?"

"You not only asked," she said, "you did it in front of about three hundred witnesses. "You're caught, Mister Porter."

"Um. Yeah, I guess you executive types would notice something like that," he grinned.

⸻ ❖ ⸻

Late Wednesday morning, a messenger entered Hamburger Haven on the west side of Wichita, on Highway 54, and asked to see Robert Loman, the proprietor. When Lowman identified himself, the messenger handed him a small, corrugated cardboard carton with his name and address on it. The messenger then left. Robert Lowman looked at the carton without a glimmer of understanding as to what it was. He held it up to his ear and shook it briefly. Then he opened it with great curiosity. One of the young ladies who worked the counter recognized the contents almost as soon as he did. She shrieked and he swore. The carton contained six banded stacks of currency. He read a note that lay atop the money: *This thirty thousand dollars is from a friend of your father.* Robert swore again in disbelief.

At about the same time, another messenger rang the front door of Annie Tipton, Tom's widow. When she opened the door, he asked her name. When she assured him of her identity, he handed her a plain corrugated carton container, then left. She retreated into the house, closing the front door behind her. She found a pair of scissors and cut into the top of the carton. Her shock upon seeing the contents of the carton was so great that she flung it from her as though it might explode. She fell back into a large recliner and gasped. About a dozen packs of banded currency fell out of the carton onto the floor. Then she picked up a note which had fallen amongst the packs of money: *This $150,000 represents part of the money that was swindled from Tom years ago. Now it is yours.*

A little before noon, a messenger entered the side door of the First Baptist Church in Clydeston. He skipped up one flight of steps to an open door where a sign read *Pastor's Study.* He took off his cap and walked in. Reverend Glenn looked up from his desk and smiled. "What can I do for you, young man?" The messenger asked if he were Reverend Glenn. When Glenn assured him of his identity, the young man handed over a small corrugated cardboard carton. "What's this?" Glenn asked and began to tear the package open. When he looked up, the messenger was gone. Glenn was shocked when he opened the carton to find six packs of banded currency. "Sweet Jesus!" he cried out. A note fell from the package, and he read it as his colleague, Reverend Dollenbeck, rushed in in response to the shout. *This package contains thirty thousand dollars, to be received by Pastor Calvin Glenn as a donation to the Harrison House.* "Sweet Jesus!" he cried again. "It's an absolute miracle. Actually!"

It was about twelve forty-five when Porter noticed a messenger enter the clubhouse at the municipal golf course where he sat with a beer. The messenger asked for Nancy Grimsby. When she identified herself, he handed her a plain corrugated cardboard carton. Then he left.

"What do you suppose this is?" she asked. "That guy wasn't from UPS."

"Isn't there a return address?"

"No."

"Well, open it and see what it is."

She held the carton close to her head and listened to it. "It wouldn't be some kind of gag, would it? Do you suppose a paper snake will pop out?" He laughed. "I shouldn't think so. Go ahead. Open it. You want me to do it for you?"

"No." She used a knife to cut into the carton. When she saw the contents, she shrieked. "My god! Omigod! Look!"

Porter looked at eight packs of banded currency. He pointed at a piece of paper that lay atop the money. "What does that note say?"

Nancy picked up the paper gingerly and read it aloud. *"This fifty thousand dollars is for the education of Jennifer Grimsby, best friend of Jennifer Jensen."* Tears came to Nancy's eyes. "Jennifer? This--I don't understand this. What is it, Jesse?"

He said, "Looks like an anonymous gift. To help with your daughter's education. Obviously. Doesn't it say anything else?"

Nancy tried to speak but couldn't. She handed him the note, then leaned on the counter to catch her breath, smiling foolishly, laughing, and crying, all at the same time.

"What's going on around here?" asked Jack Karns, who entered with Slim Braun close behind.

"Nancy just received--an unusual package," said Porter.

She said, "Do you think I can keep it? Is it all right? What about taxes?"

"Ask Jack. He's a CPA."

"What's going on here?" repeated Karns.

"Nancy just received a--"

"I don't mean *Nancy*," said Karns. "I mean what's going on outside here? Look out here." He pointed out the door. "Come here and look out here a minute."

Nancy held her carton of money tightly in both hands and joined Porter at the door. Then they stepped outside with Karns and Braun.

A large flatbed truck had parked outside the shop, and three men were off-loading five elegant, white, new golf carts. Emblazoned in red letters on the sides of each cart was a name: *Ray, Abe, Slim, Jack,* and *Doc.* Two men were driving the last two. The third man approached Wallis and Lowman, who had arrived a minute earlier and were staring, baffled by the scene.

In his cadillac, Doctor Jensen pulled up beside the truck and called out. "What's going on?"

Braun said, "We don't know."

The truck driver approached Wallis. "I'm lookin' for Mister Ray Wallis, Doctor Nathaiel Jensen, Mister Ford Braun, Mister August B. Lowman, and Mister John Karns." He held out a packet of papers.

Lowman elbowed Braun and laughed. "Hey, *Ford,* I thought your name was 'Slim'!"

"We're all here," Wallis said as the men gathered around him.

The driver gave Wallis the papers. "These are paid invoices and documents of ownership for these golf carts. "They're all yours now. Keys in those envelopes. Charged up and ready to roll."

Braun said, "But we didn't order these buggies."

The driver laughed. "That's tough, buddy. They're yours now and they're paid for." He and his companions climbed into the truck and slowly pulled into the gravel parking lot and road leading away from the clubhouse.

Karns studied the documents and then inspected the cart which bore his name. "I'll be damned! This looks legal to me. Some kind of anonymous gift... Beautiful!"

Braun said, "Who would do such--"

"Hello, gentlemen."

The group turned to face Larona Starr. They had been so intent on the matter of the new carts that they had failed to see her Continental pass the departing truck and silently park nearby. They spoke as one. "Oh they're from Missus Starr!"

She wore white slacks, a long-sleeved green blouse, and a white golfing visor. Her chauffeur began unloading a golf bag from the car trunk. "What's going on?" she asked.

"Hi, Sweetheart," said Porter. "I didn't know you were going to be here." He took her hands in his and kissed her upturned face. "The guys just now received these carts that you gave them."

"I don't know what you're talking about."

Abe waved his hand toward the carts. "The new buggies. We all thank you very much."

She shook her head. "I have no idea what you're talking about. I did not order any golf carts for anyone."

Nancy asked, "Then why did you come here today, Missus Starr? How did you just happen to be here at this time?"

Larona smiled. "Oh, I came to play golf with these gentlemen."

Her reply caused an outbreak of grunts and head shaking.

Wallis guffawed and declared, "We don't have women in our gang."

"I understood that anyone who showed up by one o'clock could play," she protested. It's after one. We should start."

Lowman turned to Porter. "Com'on, Jess. Tell her she's not--that we can't play golf with no women."

Porter held up his hands defensively. "Don't put me in the middle, Abe," he laughed. "I don't have anything to do with any of this!"

"It's against our rules," Wallis said.

"Where are these rules, Mister Wallis?" Larona asked. "Where is it written that a woman cannot play with the one-o'clock gang?"

The old-timers exchanged glances somewhat sheepishly and helplessly. Doctor Jensen chuckled. "Okay, Larona, you win. As usual. But I didn't know you ever played golf."

"I've been reading about it," she said happily. "Ever since I met the Tsunami Man, I knew I'd have to start playing sooner or later."

"Ever since you met *who*?"

She pointed at Porter, who looked skyward in a vain attempt to avoid the hoots and laughter.

Larona turned to her bag where her chauffeur had placed it, and pulled out a tee, a ball, and a club.

Immediately, almost simultaneously, Lowman and Wallis howled, "Those clubs have *wooden shafts!* They're old, old clubs!"

"Yes," Larona replied happily. "They belonged to Clarence Starr when he opened this course. They may be valuable antiques. This one is a mashie! Now, it's one o'clock. Let's play golf."